CAPONE'S CHICAGO

RANDY McCHARLES

Capone's Chicago

Copyright © 2014 Randy McCharles

Cover art by Jan Serne

ISBN: 1492923540
ISBN-13: 978-1492923541

DEDICATION

This work is dedicated to the Apocalyptic Four, who inspired the original material that brought Capone's Chicago to life – Eileen Bell, Ryan McFadden, and Billie Milholland.

ACKNOWLEDGMENTS

A special thanks to Jan Serne for creating the beautiful cover for this book. And much thanks to those writers and readers who provided feedback on various drafts, catching a plethora of typos and other small issues. Any errors or omissions remaining in this work are entirely my own.

CAPONE'S CHICAGO

Al Capone's vault was empty.
His bunker, not so much.

Geraldo Tries Again

Howard Russell shuffled along the snow-swept street, well off camera, as seventy-seven year old Geraldo Rivera talked and smiled and waved his hands, all in an effort to resurrect a dead career and undo the televised disaster of his failed 1986 revelation of the contents of Al Capone's vault. Even three decades later, not a single viewer had forgotten the empty, dusty chamber and Rivera's delicate apology, "Seems like we struck out."

At the time, Howard had been all of six years old and incapable of understanding the scope of what was happening or the disgrace Geraldo garnered. At forty, Howard was all too familiar with shame and would, this time, be numbered among the disgraced *we* if Geraldo once again hit dirt rather than pay dirt.

But that wasn't why Howard hid behind the other members of Geraldo's team. No, the problem was that, win or lose, a dead career of his own that he would sooner forget had already been resurrected and plastered across the newspapers and television screens of not just America, but the entire world. And compared to Howard's own ignominy, Geraldo's disgrace was little more than a modest discrediting.

"Two blocks that way—" Geraldo adjusted his headset microphone and waved until the cameraman followed his instructions "—you can see the building that now stands where Al Capone made his play to take over Chicago. You may remember the Lexington Hotel from when we were here several years ago investigating the infamous mob boss's vault that was hidden within the old freight tunnels beneath the hotel." The camera returned to Rivera's weathered face, which lit up in a smile.

Howard shook his head and tipped his hardhat down to further hide his eyes. He let out a deep breath, which frosted in the December cold. Fact was, Howard Russell had once been more of a celebrity than even the famous, now infamous, Geraldo Rivera.

In another life, Dr. Howard Russell, PhD, had been a nuclear physicist working for the University of Chicago on a high profile, high cost, high expectation, high *everything* experiment to finally solve the problem of cold fusion. Risk-free, radiation-free, unlimited nuclear energy. And his team had succeeded!

"Back then," Geraldo continued, undisturbed by Howard's inner musings, "preparations for the demolition of the Lexington led to the discovery of the underground vault, which was, unfortunately, empty. We can only assume that Al Capone emptied the vault after he was released from Alcatraz and before he retired to Florida."

So why was Dr. Howard Russell, PhD today following a has-been TV journalist into the musty ruins of Chicago's past? A small problem really, and one Howard felt sure he could have solved given the time and means. The nuclear reaction cold fusion required took more energy to create than the reaction itself released.

The University had not been impressed, and not only halted funding for the project, but fired Howard from the University staff. The nuclear physics world at large was also not impressed, and all doors were closed to him. And Howard's wife was not impressed, divorcing him and leaving him with nothing but memories of a dozen years of wedded bliss and a plain, gold ring that he refused to take off his finger.

When the dust settled, Howard had been lucky to get a job with the City as a lowly structural engineer. And now, two years later, Geraldo Rivera required the services of a structural engineer. The great City of Chicago, knowing Howard's past and the added infamy it would bring to this little televised shindig, had offered him up on Geraldo's sacrificial altar. Geraldo was not pleased, but the City said, "Howard Russell or no one." Rivera took what he could get.

"And now," continued Geraldo, "thirty-four years later, Al Capone's stomping ground is once again being excavated. And once again, evidence of Capone's underground activity has been found."

Several people in the small crowd the City had permitted to follow the camera began shouting.

"Yeah, yeah."

"Why are you calling it a bunker instead of a vault? Isn't it the same thing?"

"Another empty vault. So what?"

Howard was impressed that Rivera ignored the taunts. When the riled mobs had wanted Dr. Russell's head, Howard had been nowhere near so self-controlled. He had responded badly, and that had only made matters worse. Then again, unlike *Al Capone's Vault*, which had been broadcast live, *Al Capone's Bunker* would be cleaned up before it aired. The taunts would be edited out. Perhaps Rivera's aplomb wasn't so admirable.

"To provide some background," Geraldo said, talking

3

through the shouts, "let's hear a few words from City of Chicago engineer, Howard Russell."

Howard straightened as the camera turned toward him, and tried to adjust his metal hat so that he would look somewhat dapper. He quickly abandoned the effort as futile. Besides, civil engineers were urban outdoorsmen. They were supposed to look a little rough and tumble.

"The City of Chicago is built upon a mud plain," Howard said, not deviating from the lines he had been given and memorized. "Beneath the asphalt we are standing on, lies a layer of dirt and gravel left here by occasional floods that have occurred over recent centuries. Beneath that is a layer of blue clay averaging about nine feet in depth, deposited by glaciers that once covered the entire region from as far west as Montana, as far east as New England, and as far north as the Hudson Bay in Canada. Below that is bedrock, mostly a volcanic plain created when the earth was forming.

"In the 1860's, the city fathers had workers dig tunnels through the mud layer and install pipes to transfer water around the city, making Chicago one of the most technologically advanced cities in the world. But they did not stop there. At the turn of the century, the tunnel system was expanded to allow freight to be moved from place to place. The City of Chicago was a marvel for its time."

The camera moved back to Geraldo. "Thank you, Howard. But as we all know, the turn of the century was also when *mobs* from New York expanded into cities like Cincinnati, Detroit, and Chicago. Crime got organized and a few big fish were soon running the show, paying off politicians and bribing the police. In 1928, Al Capone moved his base of operations to the Lexington Hotel and commenced his plan to take absolute control of the city, starting by taking out Bugs Moran of the Irish mob on Valentine's Day, 1929."

Yada, yada, yada, thought Howard. He was pretty sure that Rivera was reading from the same script he had used thirty years ago. But at least the focus had been taken off him. As Howard thought about it, he did not recall hearing any snide comments from the crowd while he was saying his piece. Perhaps people had dismissed his inglorious days at Chicago University. Or maybe they just didn't equate Howard Russell, engineer, with Dr. Howard Russell, nuclear failure, despite it being all over the news. Most people just don't pay that much attention to detail.

"To my left is Dr. Maxwell Samuels, PhD," Geraldo was saying. "Head of Geology at the University of Chicago. His task is to evaluate the location and condition of the bunker, ensuring that it is a later addition to the existing tunnels, but not too much later."

This elicited several chuckles.

"To my right is Ann Smith, a graduate student also at the university, specializing in Chicago history. She is the leading expert on all things Al Capone, in the region and perhaps in the world."

The girl, a pale-skinned blonde no older than twenty-two, flushed a deep scarlet.

"Ann's task is to examine the bunker, outside and in, and substantiate its probable relationship with Mr. Capone.

"Last, but not least, is Ms. Olivia Olsen. Olivia, come over here and wave at the camera. Ms. Olsen and I have known each other for many years, though I suspect Olivia knows me much better than I know her. Ms. Olsen is a psychic."

Fraud. The word just appeared in Howard's head. Like the Tibetan personality test used by psychologists – name the first thing that comes to your mind. Howard hadn't spent more than ten minutes in the same room with Ms. Psychic Olsen. During those ten minutes, Mr. *Friend for Many Years* Rivera had completely ignored her. She was window dressing. A shill to draw attention to himself. Look at me! I have my own psychic!

"Olivia's task is to listen for any psychic resonances from the past," said Rivera. "Who knows what may have been trapped down there all these years. And speaking of *there*, here we are."

Geraldo turned so that the camera moved around one-hundred-eighty degrees, taking in Rivera's smiling face against a background of a partially dismantled storefront.

"Luigi's Bakery was a going concern in 1929, with a reputation for the best authentic Italian pastries in the district. Elliot Ness and the Untouchables even set up shop here for a while to keep Capone under surveillance. Little did Ness know at the time, that the Italian mob had built an access to the freight tunnels from the Lexington and were coming and going as they pleased. And little did we know, until just days ago, that some of this movement was right under Ness's feet. Capone must have been building his bunker while the Untouchables were just a few yards away, watching the hotel."

Rivera then waved at the crew's most important member. The camera turned and tracked a yellow, roughly man-sized and man-shaped, robot as it left Howard's side and strode toward the demolished face of the building.

"Some of you may not have seen a C-droid before," said Geraldo. "The University of Chicago has been developing construction androids for the past few years and several have been assigned to the City of Chicago to help with dangerous activities. The City has been kind enough to loan one to us to ensure that the bakery doesn't fall on our heads while we are down in the tunnels."

Howard sighed. The C-droid was the most useful member of Rivera's team, and the one Geraldo least wanted. More so even than a disgraced nuclear physicist. While media candy, like psychics, raised Rivera's profile, people with histories or non-people like a high tech robot, did the opposite. This excursion was about Rivera and nothing else. He would go in by himself with a hand-cam if the City would let him.

The C-droid was Howard's chief reason for being here. Howard was the droid operator, should anything go wrong. In the two years Howard had worked with the droid, nothing ever had gone wrong. It was state of the art artificial intelligence married to state of the art mechanical engineering. It could do many things better than any human could. And those things it could not do, it wouldn't even try. Howard had never had a better working partner.

The droid knew its stuff. Without prompting, it stepped up from the closed off section of Cremak Road onto the sidewalk, navigated past the rubble of the bakery's demolished façade, and descended the short set of wooden steps into the building's small basement. Then it stood near the access door to the freight tunnels that the City demolition crew had uncovered, waiting.

"This is it." Geraldo grinned into the camera. "We are off into the mouth of history."

Al Capone's Bunker

Off into the mouth of history? What kind of stupid sound bite was that? It was all Howard could do to resist howling with disdain. Rivera was going to bang his head against a wall when he saw the playback. Or not. Delayed broadcast. He'd edit in some ghostwriter's memorable replacement. Like "We'll soon see what Al Capone was so keen to hide." No. "Soon see" sounded all wrong. Hell, physicists are better with numbers than words, anyway.

Howard was first into the tunnels after the droid, and immediately snapped on the flashlight he carried, casting its beam in an arc across the tunnel's smooth cement walls and curved ceiling. It was colder below ground than it had been above, even without the wind. The sixty mile network of tunnels hadn't been used by the City since the 50's, and in his short career as a City engineer, Howard had rarely had cause to enter them. Still, every sojourn, including today, made him feel like a kid again, like he was crawling through some uncle's forgotten crawl space.

Behind him, Howard could hear Rivera and the cameraman fumbling down the cement steps leading from the basement down into the tunnels. He suspected the footage would include a significant amount of Howard Russell's backside. His dark, industrial green insulated coveralls provided an ample target. Never mind that it was winter, it only made sense to wear something warm and durable at a construction site. Jagged edges were everywhere, and would make short work of everyday clothing.

Howard smiled to himself. Rivera had chosen to wear soft-soled shoes, jeans, and an expensive ski jacket.

The droid waited until all of Rivera's crew joined them in the tunnel below the bakery. Additional flashlights lit up, casting the enclosed space in stark relief. Rivera faced the camera and somehow kept his teeth from chattering.

"The tunnel walls, ceiling, and floor are made of poured concrete. Through the dust and debris, you can still see the railings for the small train-trucks that carried goods throughout prohibition Chicago, including Capone's illegal beer and whiskey. Those pipes and cables along the walls once carried water, power, and telephone signals."

Howard knew the lines were dead because none of the lights spaced along the ceiling were on. Since he worked for the City, he also knew that no power had flowed through those wires for several decades. In addition to dust and debris, partly frozen rancid water and assorted trash littered the tunnel.

As a college freshman, Howard had earned a spot as a defenseman on the University of Chicago Maroons. For a time he had entertained the idea of entering the world of professional football. At six foot four and two hundred pounds of mostly muscle, his prospects seemed bright. Unfortunately, his coach did not agree; by his junior year, Howard spent more time on the bench than on the field. A friend had encouraged him to pursue a *real career* and, after what felt like an eternity of soul searching, Howard turned his back on football and sought instead to solve the secrets of the universe.

The point being that regardless of profession — athlete,

scientist, or engineer — Howard was a big man and seemed to occupy more of the tunnel than several of his companions combined. He fairly loomed in front of the others and he knew it. Fortunately, the tunnels were an almost uniform seven and a half feet tall and nearly seven feet wide, so he didn't have to stoop as he sometimes did in more modern architecture above ground, where it was often assumed that six feet was as tall as Homo sapiens ever got.

With a nod to the droid, the two of them led the way down the tunnel, following the line of shallow tracks. The others followed several yards behind. Not for safety reasons, Howard knew, but so that he wouldn't block Rivera's precious footage.

Keeping a watchful eye, Howard rotated the beam from his flashlight. Up. Right. Down. Left. Up. Right. Down. Left. The C-droid also handled a flashlight, casting its beam in the same pattern. By design, the droid outpaced Howard, moving several yards ahead of him.

Though more or less structurally sound, the freight tunnels were over one hundred and fifty years old and some damage was expected. The ceiling sagged in places, with occasional metal piping sticking down several inches. Howard had to be careful not just with his feet, but with his head as well.

Noise from behind broke the tomblike silence as Rivera, his cameraman, Samuels, the school kid, and the useless psychic, stumbled and swore a chorus behind Rivera's running description. How the reporter would make *dark*, *stinky*, and *ow* into an interesting commentary was beyond the pale.

Eventually, Howard reached an intersection. It was a perfect cross, just like a city street, only sized for dogs rather than cars or carriages. The tracks split and curved sharply, allowing oncoming freight trains a choice of three paths. How people managed to route the trains back then, without computers, and amid illegal, unscheduled shipments, Howard had no idea. He figured a computer would find it a challenge. Yet Man, somehow, always seemed to find a way to overcome any obstacle.

Following the C-droid's flashlight beam, Howard turned left, and then paused as the droid disappeared. Moving a dozen yards forward, he found an opening in the wall that was narrower than the tunnels he had been traipsing through. Dark clay, rather than crumbing cement, made up the walls, floor, and ceiling. Chunks of ancient concrete littered the tracks where the City engineers demolishing the bakery had recently discovered and torn down the false wall. Light flickered as the droid moved further in. Howard followed.

It was a tight squeeze, the floor uneven and the ceiling more so, but the cramped path eventually opened up into a fairly spacious area abutting a wide metal wall. The wall and the bolted door it contained looked to be made of steel. Not the stainless kind; the surface was dull and pitted.

Howard frowned at the bunker while the others joined him and whistled in wonder.

The cameraman had a large lamp affixed to his shoulder cam and a heavy battery pack strapped to his back. The extra lighting revealed that the steel was darker than any metal Howard had seen before.

Dr. Samuels noticed as well. "I don't recognize the material used in construction."

"Tungsten," said the droid in a crisp, mechanical voice.

"The droid talks?" asked Geraldo. He waved the cameraman to move in for a close-up.

"Of course it talks," said Howard. "But only when it has something to say." He didn't add, "Unlike television reporters."

"That's not important," muttered Samuels. He pressed a gloved hand against the metal wall near the door and rubbed away decades of dust and dirt, revealing a dull grey surface. "Tungsten is a rare metal. No one in their right mind would build a bunker out of it. I'm not even certain there was this much processed tungsten in the entire world back in 1930."

"Then you're saying," Geraldo asked, his voice empty, "that the bunker was built later than 1930?"

"What I'm saying," said Samuels, "is that this bunker should never have been built. Ever. And we don't even know how big it is yet."

"Olivia?" asked Geraldo. "Are you sensing anything?"

Several snorts echoed in the cramped space. Howard smiled. At least he wasn't alone in his assessment of Rivera's psychic.

The thirty-something woman's voice was a whisper. "Just blackness. It's a black hole. I think we should leave it alone. Just walk away."

"Well. That's not happening," said Geraldo, suddenly cheerful. "This is a mystery. If we don't solve it, others will flock here to give it a try. Walking away is not an option."

"Uhm," said the grad student. Howard saw that the blonde girl had raised her hand in the air. Everyone looked at her. "The, uhm, door isn't right. There are seven hinges and three locking mechanisms. They didn't make doors this way in the 30's. I'm not sure anyone ever made them this way."

The cameraman moved forward to get close-ups of the details of the door. Samuels reached in as best he could to brush away grit and dirt with a gloved hand.

"Can you open the door?" Howard asked the droid.

"Unknown," came the mechanical reply.

Geraldo motioned the cameraman and Samuels to give the droid room. "This is a very unusual bunker," he said to the camera in a hushed voice. "Doesn't look like we'll solve its origins here and now. Perhaps what we find inside will help." He backed away so that the camera could focus on the C-droid as it examined the locks with metal fingers.

After a few minutes the droid said, "The locks are broken."

"But you didn't do anything," said Geraldo.

The droid's voice held no emotion as it replied. "I did not say that I broke the locks. I said that they are broken.

There are indications that they were hammered with something."

"Like what?" asked Geraldo.

"Insufficient data."

"Let's assume for now that it was a steel pipe," Howard said. "Perhaps the object was left inside. Since the locks are broken, we can open the door and take a look."

Samuels reached for what looked like handgrips along the door's center seam.

Howard put out a hand to stop him. "Let the C-droid do it. That's what it's here for."

The crew backed away from the door to give the droid room.

The grips were not side-by-side, but one above the other, separated by almost two feet, with the three locks spaced one above, one below, and one between. The droid positioned itself at arm's length and clamped metal fingers around each grip. Nothing happened. The droid made no movement, standing like a statue, but Howard had worked with it long enough to know its timing. It had pulled at the door and the door hadn't moved. A second, more determined, attempt was in the making.

Dust and grit fell from the edges of the door as the dark metal groaned and then came straight out from the wall about three inches before swinging away on the seven odd hinges. Howard had never seen a door do that, and had no idea how it was done. Somehow, the designers had created a hinged door with a three inch, airtight seal. But he had to forget about the door for now and focus on what was inside. Whatever that was, hadn't tasted outside air since the last time the door had been opened, who knows how long ago.

Howard shone his flashlight past the droid and into the bunker.

He immediately knew three things. The bunker was about the size and shape of his living room; the beam of his flashlight reached each wall, the floor, and a ceiling of about seven feet. Also, the bunker was empty. No furniture. No doors to other rooms. No skeletons sitting conveniently against a wall. Not even dust. And, lastly, the bunker wasn't *quite* empty. A small pile of perhaps five dozen eggs sat in the bunker's far corner.

Actually, he knew four things, the fourth being that the mob outside had been right. There really was no difference between vault and bunker.

Without speaking, the crew squeezed in through the doorway.

"Chicken eggs?" asked the grad student. "Not what I expected."

"Not eggs," said the droid's mechanical voice. "Rhodium ingots."

"What?" asked Geraldo.

Howard laughed. "Looks like the City assigned the right engineer after all."

"What do you mean?" asked Samuels.

"Rhodium is as scarce as tungsten. And ingots like these are manmade. But couldn't have been made in 1930. Rhodium is used in catalytic converters in modern car engines."

"Incorrect," said the droid. "Rhodium-103 is used in catalytic converters. These ingots are Rhodium-105."

"That can't be right," said Howard. "Rhodium-105 is radioactive with a half-life of only thirty-five hours and—"

Howard's analysis was interrupted by the grad student's shriek of, "Radioactive!"

"Are we in trouble?" Dr. Samuels asked.

"We should leave," said the psychic.

"Perhaps," said Howard. "But look, these ingots are pristine. You can't make them out of Rhodium-105. 105 doesn't stick around long enough. And they certainly can't exist here in this vault. You need a supercollider to create Rhodium-105. Or..."

"Or what?" asked Geraldo.

Howard couldn't see the journalist's complexion properly in the glare of the flashlights, but he was pretty certain that Geraldo's tanned faced looked white as a ghost's, probably in response to the grad student's shriek.

"Or a cold fusion reactor."

"God dammit!" said Geraldo. "This is all a hoax! Who put you up to it? And turn off that camera." The aging journalist physically punched his cameraman before turning back to Howard.

Howard raised his hands defensively. "If it's a hoax, I'm not behind it. Feels more like a hoax on me than on you. I've put my past behind me. This *Al Capone's Bunker* business has done nothing but stir up bad history."

Now that he thought about it, Howard felt himself getting quite angry. If this was a trick, it was pretty elaborate. And someone would have had to reprogram the C-droid to mistake the tungsten walls and Rhodium isotope. It probably wasn't Rhodium at all. Couldn't be.

"Danger," said the droid in a passionless voice. "Do not touch."

Howard looked around and saw Dr. Samuels reaching for one of the ingots. If this really was radioactive Rhodium, being near it would be bad. Touching it would be worse than bad. Even with gloves. "Er, Doctor."

The moment Dr. Samuels' fingers touched an ingot, Howard felt something. He didn't know what. Gravity seemed to double, and his insides felt a desperate need to become his outsides. The psychic shrieked and collapsed to the bunker floor. The grad student tripped over the woman's body in an apparent attempt to run for the doorway. Geraldo and his cameraman must have been more successful. They were gone. Howard looked back toward Samuels in time to see the geologist freeze like a statue and fall toward the pile of ingots while the droid repeated, "Danger."

Then, from the corner of his eye, Howard watched the C-droid blur toward the door. He turned his head, trying to understand why a droid would flee for its life. But the droid wasn't fleeing. It grabbed handgrips on the inside of the door and slammed the door shut, trapping them all inside.

"Crap," Howard whispered.

Once the door whumped shut, the droid said, "Safe."

"We are?" Howard asked.

"Not us," said the droid. "The rest of the world. *We* are screwed."

Howard felt his body flying apart in a million different directions, but the only thought is his head was, *screwed* isn't in the C-droid's vocabulary.

The Vortex

Howard came awake to pain. Horrible pain. Excruciating pain. Pain that crawled through every fiber of his being, and then went back and crawled through it again, just in case it had missed something. Instinctively, he tensed his entire body, an almost imperceptible head to toe movement, yet sufficient to send said pain soaring to new and unbearable heights, ultimately resulting in an instant and absolute relinquishment of consciousness.

Time passed. Immeasurable. Howard woke again. More pain. Or perhaps it was the same pain as before. The discomfort, certainly, was all encompassing and defied measurement. Howard knew he must have tensed again, but this time he remained conscious as agony rolled up and down his body in angry waves. He didn't think the pain was less than before; his body was simply getting used to it.

Of necessity, Howard flicked open his eyes, even though the effort felt like flirting with razor blades. He eventually saw a ceiling that looked as savaged as he felt. The tungsten surface looked like it had been hit by a meteor shower. Pockmarks and gouges scored its surface. He wondered for a moment what could have done the damage as, except for what remained of Geraldo's team and the Rhodium ingots, the room had been empty. But there in the corner was a broken conduit, where no conduit had been before he lost consciousness. And at the opposite corner was a light fixture, weak flickering light adding to that of the few dropped flashlights.

Someone spoke. "Where am I?"

It was only as Howard's jaw and lips burned with agony that he realized the speaker was himself.

A precise, mechanical voice answered in an emotionless tone. "The Vortex."

Howard recognized the voice and therefore didn't need the words. Yes, he was still in Al Capone's bunker.

He struggled to remember what had happened to cause him to lose consciousness, but his mind refused to work. Images and thoughts flooded his awareness, things he had done earlier that day, or yesterday, or last week. They were clear and detailed, so amnesia wasn't a problem, yet they refused to arrange themselves into any sort of order.

As he fought to remember, Howard shifted his eyes to try to see more of his surroundings; he didn't move his head for fear of losing consciousness again. There was smoke in the room, possibly fire as well. He couldn't smell anything, or even hear much. He supposed his overstimulated nerves had shut down most of his other senses. Only then did Howard remember to wonder what had happened to damage the bunker and cause every nerve in his body to feel like it was drenched in acid.

Risking unconsciousness, he spoke again. "What happened?"

"A meeting of two incompatible realities is resulting in an adjustment to the participants," said the bland voice of the construction droid.

Howard thought he knew what that meant. To someone with no knowledge of quantum physics it would likely be gibberish. But that person wasn't Howard. What it meant was something impossible, but even more impossible was that the C-droid had said it. The droid was talking theoretical quantum physics. Parallel universes. Alternate realities. Paradoxes. Usually one needed a degree in quantum mechanics, an active imagination, and a lot of beer before even broaching the subject. The C-droid had none of these. Howard, in his past life as a student of nuclear physics, had dabbled in all of them. He felt he knew just enough to be on the wrong side of any debate with an actual quantum theorist. But he also knew enough to shudder at the implication of what the droid had said.

He decided to switch to a safer topic. "Where is everyone?" he asked, hoping that Dr. Samuels, Ms. Olsen, and the grad student, What's-Her-Name, were in no worse shape than he was. He almost laughed when he realized that his question was too vague for the droid's AI.

But the droid somehow deduced Howard's intent.

"Your companions are with you in the Vortex."

That was the second time the droid had referred to the bunker as *the Vortex*. Not a good sign. A vortex was the center of a storm.

Slowly, painfully, Howard turned his head and saw the yellow droid standing next to the bunker door, positioned as if to guard it. Keeping help from coming in? Or keeping trouble from getting out?

Howard turned his head the other way and saw the pile of Rhodium ingots. Only they were sitting on a wooden bench rather than the floor. Where had the bench come from? Resting on top of the ingots was a gloved hand. Just a hand. No arm. No rest of Dr. Samuels.

He turned his head further, fighting waves of pain as he did so. On the floor below the bench was an arm. And half a torso. He couldn't see the rest of Dr. Samuels. Parts were buried under refuse that had fallen from... somewhere. Other parts were... missing.

"Danger," said the droid in its impassive voice. "A meeting of two incompatible realities is resulting in an adjustment to the participants."

"Yes," muttered Howard. "You already said that."

Very carefully, and creating new agony with every movement, Howard rolled onto his side and curled his head and shoulders forward to try to get a look at himself. Given Dr. Samuels' condition — and he assumed Ms. Olsen and What's-Her-Name were no better off — he was suddenly very interested in his own state of affairs.

"Danger," the droid repeated. "A meeting of two incompatible realities is resulting in an adjustment to the participants."

But at this point, Howard was beyond caring what the droid had to say. It was all simply too much to deal with. As he plunged back into unconsciousness, his last thought was, Hades! I've got no legs!

Howard came awake to pain. But for some reason, it didn't quite feel like enough pain. Yes, it was everywhere, and yes, it was excruciating. It just didn't seem... important.

He opened his eyes and saw a familiar ravaged ceiling, and remembered. The bunker. A purely theoretical quantum event. His team dead. And... He raised his head and shoulders to peer down at his... legs. There they were. But moments ago they had been gone. He tried to move one of his feet. A foot moved, but not the one he expected.

"Danger," said the droid. "A meeting of two incompatible realities is resulting in an adjustment to the participants."

"Yes, yes, yes," Howard muttered. "So you've said."

"I have not said," the droid retorted, its voice more expressive than the droid voice of Howard's memories.

"Of course you have." Howard turned his head toward the bunker door, and froze.

"You have only just resumed consciousness," the droid said, irritably.

The construction droid was no longer yellow. Its metal surface was skin toned. And had hair. Blonde hair. And below that hair, an almost human face, one that uncannily resembled What's-Her-Name, the grad student. And below that, a naked, humanoid form that was not quite androgynous enough for Howard's comfort. He quickly lifted his eyes.

"Where is Dr. Samuels? And Ms. Olsen?"

The droid cocked a brow in an almost human gesture. "They had the good fortune of not being in the Vortex when realities collided."

"I see," said Howard, not really seeing anything except that his brain must be more addled than he thought. He was also quite sure that the foot he had just wiggled wore a shoe several sizes too small and of a style Ms. Olsen had been wearing. "Is help on the way?"

"No." The droid's posture by the door grew more rigid.

"Why not?" Howard asked, panic rising to new heights. He shifted an arm beneath him for support.

The C-droid stared at him a moment, which was uncomfortable because droids can't stare. "Opening the Vortex Gate during a collision would contaminate not one, but two realities, ultimately resulting in the annihilation of both."

Howard stared back. No amount of beer drinking had prepared him for this. "And you know this because...?"

The droid almost grinned. "A meeting of two incompatible realities is resulting in an adjustment to the participants."

"Right," said Howard. "That doesn't really answer my question."

"I will be more specific," the droid said. "Point: I am one of the participants. Point: Existence seeks to preserve itself. Point: The first adjustment was to update my database with an imperative to keep the Gate closed during collision. Do you require additional points?"

"Thank you," said Howard, finally getting a sense of what was happening, regardless of how impossible it all sounded. "So, I guess I'm doomed to die of starvation."

"Incorrect," the droid said. And this time it did grin. "There is a ninety-eight percent probability that continued adjustments will kill you before thirst or hunger does."

"But," said Howard. "What possible basis do you have for such a prediction? You've never predicted anything that didn't have hard and fast probabilities. Your most frequent answer to any question is *insufficient data*. How can you possibly make such a precise prediction of my demise?"

The droid shrugged, its mechanical skin toned arms rising slightly. "You caught me. I lied. Under the circumstances, I thought it appropriate to give you a sliver of hope."

"But droids can't lie," Howard said, raising one arm in exasperation, noticing as he did that his arm was not actually raised. His coveralls, torn at the shoulder, instead revealed a joint capped with smooth skin where his arm should be attached. He looked about and found his severed arm several feet away,

"Participants are being adjusted," said the droid, but Howard barely heard it. He was too busy fainting, the shock of the past few minutes finally taking its toll.

Howard came awake feeling... quite well, actually. He was relaxed, refreshed, and ready to get to work. Then he remembered where he was and opened his eyes. Ravaged ceiling. Check. Smoke in the air and possibly fire nearby. Check. He turned his face to the droid. Different droid. Check.

The droid stood much closer this time, and still looked like the grad student. No skin tone though. Its body was metallic yellow, still human in shape, but all shiny surfaces. It was scratched and dented from having part of the ceiling fall on it.

"Danger?" suggested Howard. "A meeting of two incompatible realities is resulting in an adjustment to the participants."

The droid turned its face toward him. "How did you know?"

"You told me," said Howard.

"How could I have?" said the droid. "I only just repaired you."

"This is the third time I— What do you mean *repaired me*?"

The droid looked pensive, which impressed Howard since a metal face shouldn't be incapable of expression.

"Unfortunately," said the droid, "This meeting of realities has been more severe than most. Much of the Vortex interior has been damaged along with its occupants. Fortunately, my self-repair systems were able to restore most of my functions."

Howard almost smiled. He was pretty certain that C-droids didn't have self-repair systems. "Any idea why the increased severity?"

"Insufficient data," said the droid. "But I can make an educated guess."

"Why not?" Howard said. "Guess away."

"Two possible scenarios. The realities that collided are so different that the core of the Vortex was more deeply penetrated than usual. Such may be expected as the shards of reality move further apart over time."

Howard tried to digest that, but couldn't. Not entirely. "The other scenario?"

"I believe this one more likely," the droid said. "A cataclysmic event occurred in one or both realities at the time of collision."

"Well," said Howard. "That sounds encouraging."

"Yes," the droid said. Then its thoughts appeared to turn inward.

While the droid pondered whatever it is droids ponder, Howard very carefully climbed to his feet. He was pleased that he had feet. They even seemed to be on the right ankles this time. But they weren't his. Given their size and shapeliness and the shoes that adorned them, he assumed that they belonged to Ms. Olsen. If Howard hadn't already just gone through Hell, this discovery would have unhinged him.

He unzipped his coveralls in order to discover just how far Ms. Olsen's legs went, and couldn't decide if he was pleased or disappointed when delicate calves met yellow droid knees, thighs, and hips.

It was about this time that he noticed that his left arm was shorter than the right. The left hand was also older. It was Dr. Samuels' arm.

The droid completed its pondering and took notice of Howard's self-examination. "You were all dead," it said. "But while repairing myself, it occurred to me that I could take undamaged parts from the three of you and create one undamaged person."

"But that can't work," Howard said, while at the same time wondering just how much of him was actually still him.

"It is impossible," the droid agreed. "However, the Vortex was still making adjustments and it helped."

"It..." Howard waved Dr. Samuels arm about the bunker, "helped?"

"It was a long shot," admitted the droid. "I should not be surprised that it failed."

Howard zipped his coveralls back up and took a few tentative steps. "I'm not sure yet how I feel about it," he said, "but it looks to me like you succeeded."

"Oh, no," said the droid. "Complete failure. Howard Russell is dead."

Howard attempted a few stretches. "Internal damage as well?"

The droid nodded. "That was the tricky part. Getting incompatible organs to accept each other."

Howard coughed involuntarily. "And yet you say you failed?"

The droid considered. "I suppose that depends upon your point of view."

"And your point of view is...?" asked Howard.

"That Howard Russell is dead."

"But I'm Howard Russell."

The droid shook its head, a slow, mechanical shake. "Within the Vortex it does not matter who or what you are." It pointed toward the closed bunker door. "Out there, it will matter a great deal." It turned its head slightly.

"Have I changed, Mr. Russell?"

Howard chose his words carefully. "The C-droid I entered this bunker with couldn't ask that question."

If a droid could look speechless...

"I think I must dismantle you," the droid said at last.

Howard took several steps back. "What? That's murder!"

"Is it?" asked the droid. "You shouldn't even exist, never mind live. There is no reality that will accept you. Or me."

A thousand thoughts ran through Howard's mind, most of them concerning how a human who has barely begun relearning how to walk can outrun a homicidal piston and steel droid. Then he remembered. "Well, I'm a dead man anyway. You said we couldn't open the door without endangering a couple of realities. I'm not about to do that."

The droid did something that Howard interpreted as a sigh. "The collision has ended and it is now safe to open the Gate. But I do not recommend it."

"I have no choice," Howard said. "I don't know if I can survive out there. But I have zero chance of survival in here."

"I can't stop you from leaving," said the droid. "Are you certain you won't let me disassemble you?"

"No, thanks. What do you mean you can't stop me from leaving?"

In answer, the droid lurched forward an inch, and Howard realized where the parts for his upper legs had come from.

"The world out there is not the one you know," warned the droid. "You may not like it. More to the point, it may not like you."

Howard sucked in a lungful of air. "I'll take my chances." He then took several slow steps toward the door that separated the bunker from the tunnels beneath Chicago.

Despite all the damage the bunker had suffered, the

door and its frame looked undisturbed. They had been built to last. Placing his mismatched hands on the two handgrips, he paused as he noticed the absence of his wedding ring. A chill ran through him as he responded more strongly to that one small loss than he had to what had happened to his physical body. For a moment, he contemplated searching the bunker for the ring, but dismissed the idea because it would require that he find his missing arm, legs, and random internal organs, never mind those of his donors. Fueled with revulsion, he pushed against the door.

Nothing happened. Crap. It had taken the C-droid everything it had to open that door the first time. Droids were much stronger than people.

"Use your legs for leverage," suggested the droid.

"You mean *your* legs," Howard quipped.

There was no place Howard could see to get leverage, so he took a stance up close to the door, grabbed the handles, locked his arms and shoulders, and pushed himself against the door with his legs. His entire body hurt like hell, and an image filled his mind's eye of a bug being squashed beneath a shoe, but he could feel, and then see, the door swinging outward.

Before leaving, he turned and looked at the droid, standing immobile on the thin beams that remained of its legs next to the wooden table with the few dozen Rhodium ingots. He couldn't see any of the body parts he had envisioned before opening the door. His hardhat and gloves had also disappeared at some point since entering the bunker. There was a flashlight on the floor near the door, which he retrieved.

"I will guard the ingots," the droid said. "Perhaps that will impede the end of yours and other realities somewhat."

"Perhaps?" Howard asked. "You don't know?"

"I only know that which the Vortex has placed in my knowledge chips."

Damn, thought Howard, looking at the droid's

humanoid features and what he interpreted as fear and uncertainty in its metallic eyes. Somewhere behind those eyes lived a part, no matter how small, of that grad student whose name he couldn't remember. Somehow, he knew that not remembering was going to haunt him for the rest of his life.

"What is your name?" he asked the droid.

The droid answered immediately. "Frankenstein."

Howard looked down at his body, pieced together with parts from three people and a droid. "I think that's *my* name."

"No," said the droid. "That is a common misconception. *I* am Dr. Frankenstein. *You* are my monster."

Howard muttered as he again squished the human parts of his body in an effort to close the door. It had to be closed; he didn't need the droid to tell him that. Leaving the door open would endanger all of existence. What in the world had he gotten himself into?

Taking one last look at Al Capone's bunker, with his creator locked inside, Howard Russell waved his flashlight in front of him and made his slow, lurching way through the ruined freight tunnels toward Chicago.

Capone's Chicago

Tony Sandoval entered Mayor Capone's office with a sense of extreme trepidation. Al Capone was not an easy man to work for under the best of circumstances. And since the Mayor's teenage daughter had gone missing two days earlier, the circumstances were anything but the best.

"Any news?" Capone rumbled before Tony had even closed the door behind him.

Tony examined the Chicago Mayor's craggy face, hoping to get a hint of the man's mood; but as usual, Capone was cold as stone. Tony assumed the man loved and was concerned for the safety of his daughter. His words indicated as much. But his face told him nothing.

"You know how it works," Tony said, having no good news to report. "We receive a dozen sightings every hour. So far, none of them have panned out. But it's only a matter of time."

"Nothing then," snapped the Mayor. "I'm replacing you."

"But sir—"

Capone waved his hands. "I have something else for you to do."

Tony released an inward breath. Most of the people the Mayor *replaced* didn't live long enough to do something else.

"Your talents are wasted on the search," Capone continued. "You're better at losing things than finding them."

That was true enough. Since his promotion within Capone's Crew last year, he had left Chicago border patrol duties to focus on special jobs for City Hall, one of which was to lose things that might become inconvenient if they were ever found. Those things often included people the Mayor *replaced*.

Capone unlocked a drawer of his desk, removed a glossy photo of a teenage girl, and handed it to him. "This is Dorothy Gale. You can find her at the Oz Club this evening. I need her to disappear."

"Of course," said Tony. He committed the girl's face to memory, and then attempted to return the photo to the Mayor.

Capone shook his head. "I need the photo to disappear as well."

Tony folded the photo and stuffed it into his pocket; he would swing by the incinerator on his way out of the building. Not even a souvenir this time. Who was this girl that the Mayor needed her gone so badly?

"Take Hudson with you," Capone said as Tony moved toward the door.

Well, that answered his question. Hudson's chief responsibility was to manage Capone's illicit assignations.

"Shall I call you when I'm done?" Tony asked. Usually the Mayor demanded immediate confirmation that his orders had been carried out.

"No," said Capone. "I'll be in and out of the office all day coddling the press about the earthquake." He frowned. "You'd think we never had one before. I still remember '86. Now that was an earthquake. There was much more damage." He sighed and shook his head. "Then I've got that damn fundraiser this evening. Just do it."

"Consider it done," Tony said, and left the office, closing the large oak door behind him.

Well, that went better than expected.

They drove mostly in silence through the streets of Chicago, Hudson obviously ill at ease to have a senior Crew officer along. Tony didn't know much about Hudson, but given that the junior Crewman was little more than a glorified chauffeur for the Mayor's *playmates*, Tony had decided to hold off on revealing the purpose of his presence. He couldn't trust Hudson not to give his mission away.

The city didn't look too bad considering only hours had passed since the quake. Most of the damage consisted of ruptured water mains, downed power lines, and the occasional collapsed lamppost blocking a street. Emergency crews were everywhere making repairs; Tony found himself taking several detours.

Traffic was unusually light and, for once, Tony was able to motor his Crew-issued Chevrolet Bel Air along the downtown streets without riding the brake. Most businesses were closed, making their own minor repairs or their owners just staying home because they knew most of their customers were. Looting after the quake had also been light, though not absent; Chicago City Police Department's *Excessive Force* policy was a good deterrent to crime.

Tony made a right turn from Michigan Blvd onto 22nd Street and saw the parking area outside the Oz Club filled with high-end Cadillacs, Buicks, and Lincolns, all vehicles he could never afford in his wildest dreams. He pulled his relative beater to the curb opposite the club entrance, and Hudson broke the silence. "Have you ever been to the Oz Club?"

"Can't afford it," Tony said. He checked the rear-view mirror to ensure they had not been followed.

"Ah, no, of course not. Who can?" said Hudson. "I meant for work. You know."

It was a rule of Capone's Crew to not mention the Crew or the Mayor when conducting a black op. At least Hudson knew to keep his mouth shut.

"Can't say that I've had the opportunity," Tony said. "Until today."

He started to open the car door, and then stopped as a figure stepped into the street from the front door of a building further down the block. He placed a restraining hand on Hudson's arm and pointed.

Hudson looked at the man, then the building. "That's a Crew building. That guy should be all right."

Tony frowned. "If it's a Crew building, then where's the Crew? Sign says it's a bakery."

"It is a bakery," Hudson said. "Bakers work there and bread gets delivered. Crew also comes and goes. There's an entrance to the underground in the basement."

"The guy doesn't look Crew. Or like a baker. He's wearing coveralls. He's a workman."

"You don't use the underground, do you?" asked Hudson. "Stupid not to wear coveralls down there. You think it's cold topside? Freeze your wazoo off down there. Guy looks familiar. I'm sure I've seen him before. Anyone using the tunnels is supposed to change into street clothes before leaving the building, though. Shall we give him some bad news?"

Tony gave Hudson's suggestion serious consideration. Sure, he knew about the underground tunnels. Never had cause to use them. And, yeah, it was probably was colder and dirtier down there than street level in December. But there was something off with this guy. He walked with a strange gait and looked up and down the street as if he'd never seen the place before.

Tony made his decision. "Better not. Our current task takes priority."

"Really?" Hudson gave him a penetrating look. "Dorothy isn't even off shift for another thirty minutes. And I've picked her up a dozen times all on my own. You still haven't told me why you're here."

Tony shrugged. "Like I said, lots of wacko things going on because of the quake. I was instructed to double up all operations and tell everyone to stay focused."

"I mean the real reason," said Hudson.

Tony gave Hudson a sober look. "For now, that is the real reason."

"Fine," said Hudson. "Let's go in and I'll show you the place. I don't think you'll ever want to leave."

They were met at the door by a midget wearing a bright blue shirt.

"ID please." The fellow's face was fifty years old, but his voice was that of an adolescent.

Hudson moved to show the midget his ID, but Tony stopped him and showed the diminutive man two Crew cards. Normally, when citizens of Chicago saw a Capone's Crew ID, they made an effort to get as far away from the card as possible, but the doorman calmly studied both cards. "Henry and Emerson," he said, reading the names on the cards. "Capone's Crew. I hope there won't be trouble tonight."

"There won't," Tony said. "Now that we're here."

"Uh-huh," said the midget. He gave Tony a cold stare and Hudson an even colder one, then moved aside to let them pass into a short hallway of blue carpet, blue wallpaper, and a number of landscape paintings that featured the color blue.

"What's with the bogus IDs?" Hudson asked when they

were out of earshot. "I've been here a dozen times in the past few months. That guy knows I'm not called Emerson."

"Tonight, Emerson is your name," Tony said. "Hudson was never here."

"I think you'd better tell me what's going on."

"Not yet," said Tony. "After we leave. What's this room up ahead?"

The bright blues of the hallway gave way to even brighter greens as the Crewmen entered a noisy room filled with affluent citizens dressed more gaudily than even Tony's imagination could come up with. The apparel was bright, certainly, and made an attempt at protecting modesty, but seemed only passably functional as one person after another tugged at lapels, sleeves, and hats to bring errant garments back in line.

The members of the club were mostly men, though there were several women dressed in long, flowing gowns with stylish hair garnished with glittering crowns, and waving sparkling wands. They flitted among the men and engaged them in conversation, sometimes brief and sometimes long and intimate.

Tony was starting to form an opinion of what kind of club this was and concluded that the fairylike witches *worked* here.

"Have you noticed the monkeys?" Hudson asked.

Tony followed Hudson's gaze upward and saw acrobats. They leapt across the ceiling from perch to perch, sometimes using a hanging rope for longer leaps, sometimes climbing to a higher perch and leaping a short distance toward a lower one. There were about a dozen of them. Smallish, teenage girls or petite women, dressed in form-fitting monkey costumes that had nonfunctioning wings attached to their backs.

"I wonder if they ever fall?" Tony said.

"Not that I've seen," said Hudson. "The bar is this way."

Tony waved off any of the witches who approached and followed Hudson through the garish throng to a high counter that lined the far wall. There were three bartenders, one dressed as a lion, one as a scarecrow, and the one closest to them wearing a suit of tin, including a tin helmet.

"Two beers," Hudson told him.

"Doesn't it get hot in there?" Tony asked as the Tin Man pushed foaming pint glasses in front of them.

"No," came the reply in a curt, emotionless voice.

Hudson smiled. "The bartenders are droids. They tried using people when the place first opened, but the costumes did get too hot. Also, the actors had difficulty staying in character."

"Pretty menial job for a droid," Tony said. "A waste of good money."

"This place can afford it," Hudson said. "Dorothy should be on any minute. Let's get closer to the stage."

Should have expected this, Tony told himself. Capone is one sick bastard.

The stage was smaller than others Tony had seen. Just a raised platform a few feet wide and deep, with a small curtain that fluttered like someone was behind it beating the cloth with a broom. A dwarf dressed in blue, even smaller than the midget at the door, marched back and forth across the short stage waving a sign that said *Pay no attention to the man behind the curtain.* Tony now noticed discordant organ notes coming from behind the curtain as well as flashing lights.

"Not much of an act," he said to Hudson.

"They just do this between acts," the junior Crewman said. "Filler."

A few moments later, a trumpet sounded and a man stepped out from behind the curtain. He wore what appeared to Tony like a court jester costume that looked all the more ridiculous because the man was well over six feet tall and filled out like a football player. Flashing lights sparkled along silver strips that ran the length of the costume's arms and legs. The remainder of the suit was a bright, blood red. Tony then realized, given the theme of the club, that it must be a wizard costume and that this was the Great Wizard of Oz.

"Isn't that the spaz we saw outside when we arrived?" he whispered to Hudson. "The one you said was a Crewman who forgot to change into street clothes?"

Hudson puckered his lips in thought. "That's the MC and club manager. Some people think he owns the place as well. But now that you mention it, he does look a lot like the guy we saw outside. You think he might be Crew?"

"But we just arrived a couple minutes ago," Tony said. "How could he have followed us in, changed his clothes, and gotten behind that stage without us seeing him?"

"Back door?" Hudson suggested.

"My friends!" called the man. "Welcome to the wonderful land of Oz!"

The room applauded.

Not a Crewman, Tony decided. No Crewman grins like that or waves his hands so expansively. This man was a professional showman, and seemed good at it.

"It is time for the spectacle you have all been waiting for," the Wizard continued. "Without further ado, Dorothy and her Magic Slippers!"

The Wizard then slipped back behind the curtain, where there was a flash of light and a puff of smoke that billowed out to fill the stage. When the smoke cleared, a little black dog stood in front of the curtain. Specifically, a Cairn Terrier.

Tony frowned. "If the dog breaks into song, I will be forced to shoot something."

The people standing around them laughed and the Wizard stepped back out from behind the curtain, grinning like a maniac. He picked up the dog.

"Let's try that again," he said, and took the dog with him back behind the curtain.

A second flash of light and billow of smoke, and this time a young woman stood before the curtain. She was dressed in a white and blue schoolgirl outfit with braided black hair and shiny red slippers. Despite looking older than her photo, this was undoubtedly Dorothy Gale, the girl Capone had sent him for. Part of Tony was relieved to discover that she looked closer to twenty than sixteen, but it didn't make his job any easier.

Dorothy gazed out at the room with big wide eyes and trembling lips. The crowd grew hushed and the lights dimmed, while a spotlight took the stage where Dorothy stood. Nervous fingers found their way to the top of her shirt and she undid a button.

Tony expected the crowd to cheer, but instead they grew even more hushed.

Then Dorothy opened her mouth, and Tony understood.

Tony had never seen the film from which the club drew its theme, but supposed there wasn't a soul in Chicago who wasn't familiar with the song. *Somewhere Over the Rainbow.* He himself had heard it performed by several artists with varying degrees of success, but he had never heard it sung like this. Dorothy Gale was the voice of Heaven itself. It didn't matter what the words were. It didn't matter that she was slowly removing her clothing as she sang. Just the rise and fall of her voice, hitting each note and filling it with emotion, was so enthralling, so unimaginable, it was like evidence of the existence of God.

Perhaps this is what had attracted Capone to her. Though as pious as the Pope in public, the Mayor had kept a pool of mistresses for at least as long as Tony had worked for him. In the last year, Tony had personally *dismissed* two of them. Capone could have any willing woman or girl in Chicago, and for the most part, he did. But this one was special. Tony could see why Capone would want her. What he couldn't see is why Capone now wanted her gone.

All too soon, the song ended and Tony's glimpse of the sublime receded until it was just a pretty, young woman standing on a stage wearing only her underwear and a pair of shiny red slippers. Dorothy smiled, bowed, and then fled behind the curtain. Two dwarfs in blue jumped onto the stage, collected her clothes, and then jumped back down and disappeared. The spotlight vanished and the room lights came up. The flicker of lights resumed behind the fluttering curtain.

Tony turned to Hudson. "That's it?"

Hudson grinned. "You want more? Sorry to disappoint you, but Dorothy isn't like the witches. You can't pay her for additional services."

"No," Tony said. "Is that all she's going to sing? Is she coming back on stage?"

Hudson winked. "Right. No, Dorothy is done for the night. The girls from here on out get increasingly more risqué and Dorothy isn't into that scene. She's a good kid. Really. She'll come out in a minute when she's dressed and we can go."

"I need another drink," Tony said, and they returned to the bar.

This time they received an overpriced beer from the scarecrow, who appeared jittery and nervous and kept looking around. All part of the droid programming, Tony decided.

Sitting at the bar was a man who appeared almost as nervous. There were four empty lowball glasses in front of him and he was chugging a fifth. If it wasn't for the torn and battered dark green coveralls, Tony would guess it was the Wizard of Oz.

"Isn't that the same goof from outside?" asked Hudson.

The drinking man must have overheard; he turned to face them and gave them a hasty once-over. Then he moved further down the bar and ordered another whiskey.

"Maybe that's what the Wizard wears when he's not on stage," Tony suggested.

"The look doesn't inspire confidence," said Hudson.

Moments later, Dorothy appeared wearing an oversized mohair sweater, slacks, and an elegant, fur-trimmed hat. She carried a matching fur lined coat and white gloves and scarf over one arm. "Hey Hudsy!" she said in a cheerful speaking tone that sounded almost as wonderful as her singing voice. "Who's your friend?"

"Co-worker," Hudson said. "People have gone a bit kooky after the earthquake, so none of us are working alone right now."

Tony did his best not to stare. "I'm Tony."

Dorothy took his proffered hand in both of hers and squeezed. Her skin was very warm.

"Pleased to meet you," she said. "If you're half as nice as Hudsy, we'll get along famously."

Tony smiled. *Nice* was not an adjective he used to describe himself.

"Let's get going," said Hudson. "If Dorothy stays in one place too long she gets mobbed by her fans."

Dorothy gave a coy smile and looked at Tony. "That never happens. Hudsy's my biggest fan."

"Then I am your newest fan," Tony said, and he meant it.

The sun had set while they were inside. Enough of the streetlights had survived the quake or been repaired throughout the afternoon to make driving more or less safe. The streets themselves were relatively quiet.

Tony looked up and down the street and sidewalks while Hudson escorted Dorothy to the Bel Air and helped her into the back seat. Then Tony and Hudson climbed into the front and they pulled out into light traffic.

Since the first moments of Dorothy's song, Tony's mind had been spinning. First about how amazing her voice was, and then in search of a way to preserve that voice. It was a one of a kind talent. Throwing it away would be a crime. Unfortunately, so was crossing the Mayor.

"Where are you from, Dorothy?" Tony asked.

"Dorothy's not my real name, of course," said Dorothy, "but I am from Kansas. Really."

Tony had no idea why either statement was significant. "And where did you learn to sing?"

Dorothy giggled. "Born this way. I was a child prodigy."

I've always been able to sing. I came to Chicago looking to make the big time."

"At the Oz Club?" asked Tony.

Dorothy laughed. "Only until something better comes along. You have to get discovered somewhere."

"The Oz Club is that," Tony said.

"Is what?" said Hudson.

"Somewhere to leave for something better," Tony said.

"This isn't the way," Hudson said suddenly.

"C isn't there," said Tony. "His plans have taken him to Hegewisch."

"I should have been told," Hudson said.

Tony sighed. "I am telling you."

They continued in silence, passing museums, banks, nightclubs, and shopping malls. Even though it was now dark, several men were still repairing an array of road traffic spikes in a Taco Bell drive-through where part of the cement wall had collapsed.

When they reached the Pullman district at Chicago's far north, Tony stayed on the main roads, which appeared to set Hudson at ease. That changed when Tony pulled into the tiny Pullman Bus Terminal parking lot and parked the car in a disused area near the back.

"This can't be right," said Hudson.

Tony turned off the ignition and spoke as he very slowly reached beneath his trench coat to his chest holster. "Miss Gale has a bus to catch."

"Serious?" Dorothy said, doing a very good imitation of a sixteen year old.

Tony had his Jericho 941F out, but was disadvantaged in that he was in the driver seat and was right handed. He turned to face Hudson and Hudson already had his giant Desert Eagle trained on him. Apparently, Tony wasn't the only one willing to make difficult choices over Dorothy Gale.

"You are going to tell me what is going on," Hudson said through gritted teeth, "and you are going to tell me now."

Tony kept his finger poised on the trigger. "We are putting Dorothy on a bus back to Kansas."

"Not bloody likely!" Dorothy shouted.

Hudson's Desert Eagle remained in an undesirable position. "Why?"

"Because C has ordered her disappeared."

"What?" This time Dorothy's shriek was startlingly loud, and Tony almost jerked the trigger of his handgun.

"He wouldn't..." Hudson began, but then he slowly lowered his gun. "No, I suppose he would."

"That bastard!" Dorothy shouted.

Tony turned to look at her, as he couldn't imagine that word coming from such innocent lips.

Dorothy's eyes widened, a seeming instinctive response to having gotten his attention; they held a coldness Tony hadn't seen before. Dorothy, the innocent nymphet was gone. And what replaced her didn't look sixteen or twenty, but something as timeless as evil itself.

"I spent four months bonking that bastard. He hasn't given me anything yet. Well, not anything worth anything. And he's already dumping me! I've never been so insulted in my life."

Tony didn't know how to react to these words coming from someone who only moments before he couldn't imagine speaking them. "Better insulted than dead," he said, then flinched as Hudson raised his gun again. Hudson understood his meaning even if Dorothy didn't. "Instead, I'm sending you back home. Don't come back and our good Mayor" — there, he had said it — "will never know the difference."

To Tony's surprise, Dorothy laughed, a deep-throated bray that sounded more animal than human. "Go home! You can't be serious. Everyone I knew back there, I killed. I can't go back."

"Killed?" said Hudson. His jaw sagged like he had just been jilted by a lover.

Dorothy gave him a dirty look. "Bashed their brains in, you moron. All they wanted to do was take, take, take. So I gave it to them. More than they wanted."

"Your parents?" Tony asked.

"They were the worst," Dorothy growled, a sound the cowardly lion droid would be wise to imitate. "Wanted to pimp me out for my voice. No one pimps me out. Anyone wants something from me, they're going to pay big time. And believe me, my folks paid."

Hudson looked like a man who had just lost everything he believed in. "Why are you telling us this?"

Dorothy sneered. "Because you're going to pay, too."

And then she screamed.

If Tony thought her earlier shriek was loud, this was a jet engine taking off. It was as though Dorothy had taken her singing voice and raised and amplified the pitch. The windows began to vibrate and pressure built in his ears. Tony dropped his gun into his lap so he could cover his ears with his hands, but it was no help at all. He barely noticed through the pain as Dorothy's gloved hand dipped over the seat and grabbed his gun. Then she stopped screaming, pointed the gun at Hudson, and fired.

Hudson fell back against the dashboard, a bullet-sized hole squarely in the middle of his forehead.

Tony stared at the dead, younger Crewman in amazement as he pulled his hands away from his ears. Then he twisted around toward Dorothy in the back seat.

The girl had a big smile on her face. "I've never killed anyone with a gun before."

"Why did you do that?" Tony said. "We're just trying to help you."

Dorothy took her rapt gaze away from Hudson and stared at him. What he saw in her eyes and in the twist of her mouth could only be described as madness.

Her wide smile shrank into a frown. "That's what your Mayor said. He wanted to help me. Help my career. Then he sent the two of you to kill me."

"But we were going to let you go."

"I can't go. I have to do something first."

"What's that?"

"Kill the Mayor."

"What?"

"No one crosses me. No one. Now, where is he?"

"I don't know." But Tony did know. Capone was at the fundraiser, or shortly would be. From the corner of his eye, he could see Hudson's Desert Eagle lying on the seat next to the Crewman's cooling body. He inched his hand towards it.

"The Mayor's not your friend," Dorothy said in a singsong voice. "Someday he'll order someone to disappear you."

"Probably," Tony said. He tried to look confused, stalling for time as he reached for Hudson's gun. "Actually, I do think I know where he might be." Capone may not be Tony's friend, but neither was Dorothy, and Tony knew how this was going to end if he didn't do something to stop her.

Dorothy's expression didn't change as Tony heard the sound of his gun firing. At some point Dorothy had moved it lower behind the seat. Now he knew exactly where.

The bullet tore through the seat, entered his side just below the rib cage, burning like a hot poker, came flying out of his lower back, then embedded itself in the dashboard.

"Guns are fun," said Dorothy. "Are you going to tell me where the Mayor is?"

Tony gave no answer. Instead, he sat with his guts leaking out of two coin-sized holes left by his own gun, thinking that of all the ways he thought he might die, this was never one of them. His fingers were still seeking Hudson's Desert Eagle when he felt the heated barrel of his Jericho 941F pressed against his right temple.

"Any last words?" Dorothy asked.

Tony found that he did have something to say. "Before I die. Sing for me. One last time."

"You really are a fan," Dorothy said.

Tony felt the pressure change against his skull as Dorothy Gale pulled the trigger. And then he felt nothing at all.

Frankenstein's Monster

Howard knew he'd had too much to drink. He wasn't really a drinking man. But he also knew that he had no better option.

His walk through the tunnels beneath Chicago had given him time to think. And the more he thought, the more he realized how screwed he was. First of all, Ms. Olivia Olsen's feet and shoes had never been designed to carry someone of his weight. And the metal hips and thighs only increased that weight. In no time at all, Howard's feet were killing him. He could barely walk.

Then it occurred to him to wonder what the power source for the tiny motors in his droid parts was. At any moment would his hips just stop, leaving him with no more mobility than a statue?

The intelligent thing would be to get to a hospital. Immediately. Intelligent, yes; easy, no.

According to the Dr. Frankenstein C-droid, Howard was now in an alternate reality where anything in the world he had known may have changed, including the laws of physics. Even so, he had still clung to the hope that, upon leaving the bunker, he would find a distraught Geraldo Rivera and an EMS vehicle waiting to race him to the nearest hospital.

But long before he reached the surface of Chicago, he knew that he was not in Kansas anymore. The reality he had returned to was not the one he had left. It was the one *his reality* had collided with.

His first clue was that the concrete wall separating the freight tunnels from the crevasse that led to the bunker was partly intact and insufficiently large enough for a person his size to squeeze through. Howard would have been dead, trapped inside, if the cement hadn't been brittle enough for him to chip away at with his bare hands.

Twenty minutes of cursing, scraped fingers, and bruised elbows allowed him to finally force his way through and into the freight tunnels, where the damage and litter was noticeably unlike the damage and litter he had encountered on the way into the bunker. And the skinny tracks in the floor were well oiled. They had been used recently, not abandoned for decades.

His second clue was that the overhead lights were lit, casting a weak, yellow haze along the shadowed tunnel.

At the top of the stairway leading up into the bakery, instead of a winter sky greeting him, Howard found a door. It was locked. The doorframe, however, looked a bit off. With some effort, he was able to force the door open, taking part of the frame with it. On the other side, he found sweet bakery smells and a man in a three-piece suit pointing a gun at him.

"Who are you?" asked the armed man.

Howard let out a deep breath of air. "Please, I need help."

The suit cocked the gun. "I didn't ask if you needed help. I asked who you are. It's more of a demand, really."

"Howard," Howard croaked, stumbling toward him. "Howard Russell."

"Well, Howard Howard Russell, this looks like one of those times when it may be better to shoot first and ask questions later."

"You're kidding me?" said Howard.

The suit chuckled. "I've given you ample opportunity to explain why you're here. You haven't. You really shouldn't be here."

Before Howard knew what had happened, the suit's gun was flying across the room and the man was screaming. Howard watched his leg straighten and his foot return to the cement of the basement floor. Somehow, faster than Howard's eye could track, he had kicked the gun out of the man's hand. Instinct had kicked in and Howard's mechanical hip had kicked out. His foot hurt like he had broken it, but the man's hand was undeniably broken.

To Howard's surprise, the suit twisted his body and picked up a wooden chair with his remaining good hand.

"You've got to be kidding!" Howard said, and flung himself across the floor, conveniently in the direction of the fallen gun. Grabbing it with both hands, he scrabbled with the unfamiliar weapon until it was pointed in the suit's direction.

The suit ignored the gun and continued swinging the chair toward Howard's head.

Howard had no choice but to pull the trigger, repeatedly. Loud explosions rang in his ears, until only quiet clicks came from the gun. Then he stopped pulling the trigger.

Howard didn't remember closing his eyes or opening them again. But neither did he remember watching the suit fall to the floor, the chair tumbling off to one side.

I've killed a man, Howard told himself. He'd had no choice, but that wouldn't change anything. He didn't even know what the penalty for murder was in this place. If he wasn't a dead man thirty seconds ago, he certainly was now.

He tossed the gun into a growing pool of blood, but only after wiping it down with a sleeve of his coveralls. Who knows? Maybe by some dumb luck they wouldn't trace the murder to him. He laughed aloud knowing that would never happen.

The rest of the bakery was empty. At least, no one appeared as he made his way to the street-side door, which was also locked, but Howard had buried the revulsion of what he had done and searched the suit's pockets to come up with a key, some peculiar looking cash, and an ID card of a kind Howard had never seen before. Since, unlike his driver's license, there was no photo on it, he thought it come in useful.

Howard stood on the sidewalk outside the bakery feeling like a stranger in a strange land as well as in a strange body. He knew he wasn't thinking clearly. Autopilot, that's what it was. Kicking out at the suit, diving for the gun, shooting the man before he could smash Howard's skull with the chair, then searching the body. None of it had been a conscious decision. Howard began to sweat as he wiped the key against his coat and then tossed it into a sewer drain. Getting rid of evidence. Surely, that had been a conscious decision. Or did he only think so after he had already done it?

The weather outside the bakery was the same cold December Howard had left behind, but that was where similarity ended. Cermak Road was no longer a boulevard. The center median was gone and there were antique cars parked along its length on both sides. Howard watched in amazement as a mint condition Chevrolet Corvette two-seater cruised past him. It was like watching a movie from the 50's.

Then it occurred to him that perhaps it was the 50's. Could Capone's bunker, the Vortex according to Dr. Frankenstein, have dropped him off in a different decade rather than a different reality?

Howard pulled the collar of his coveralls tighter. The wind was stiffer than it had been earlier, or seventy years later if he was indeed living in the past. But as he looked out across an unfamiliar skyline, he realized that evening was approaching and that could explain the increased cold and wind.

He took a few moments to look up and down the street. Some of the shops looked similar to the ones he had briefly seen earlier that afternoon, their shapes if not their names. They all appeared to be closed. Wooden poles the color and texture of railway ties and strung with power lines touched the sky at regular intervals along the opposite side of the street. One of the lines had detached and was dancing on cracked cement, sparks flying. There were no antique cars parked near it.

Up the street, an old, mint condition Chevrolet Bel Air sat parked. It was pastel blue with fins and a white hard top. Two people were inside. The driver looked like he had started to get out and then stopped. Howard watched them for a moment, but they remained in the car. Nothing to do with me, he told himself.

He looked up at the bakery sign on the building he had just exited. It said *Luigi's*, just like the bakery he had entered; only this sign was freshly painted and the building it belonged to was anything but demolished. The windows were clean. As were the floor and counters inside. There had been bread smells. The building was closed now, but bread had been baked there recently. This was a working bakery.

Across the street from the Bel Air stood the Beachwood Bed and Breakfast. The TV studio producing *Al Capone's Bunker* had booked the entire place to house Geraldo Rivera and his team, including those who actually lived in Chicago, because it literally stood just yards away from the film site. Howard figured they got a good price because half of the block across the street was being demolished. Regardless, it was a comfortable establishment and Howard had enjoyed the few days' vacation from his tiny apartment in Wicker Park.

The Beachwood B & B Howard saw now was beyond recognition. Though roughly the same shape, the façade was different and a neighboring building was gone, making room for an extended parking lot currently jammed with mint condition, antique cars. A giant neon sign near the entrance flashed *The Oz Club*.

Doctor Frankenstein hadn't been wrong. This most definitely was not the Chicago he knew.

He heard a car door slam followed by another and looked up the street to where the blue Bel Air was parked. The two men had gotten out. They were dressed in A-line trench coats and fedora hats. Both coats and hats were the gaudiest shade of yellow Howard had ever seen. The shoes and trouser cuffs beneath their coats were black or charcoal grey. In addition to being dead ugly, the coats looked inadequate to keep out the winter chill.

Both men gave Howard a careful look, and for a moment he was afraid they were going to come toward him, or perhaps shoot him. Instead, they glanced at each other and then crossed the street and entered the Oz Club.

With no better plan presenting itself, Howard limped his way up the street and followed the two men inside.

He knew the dwarf at the door was trouble, and watched the little man give his coveralls the once over before moving his eyes up to Howard's face. The eyes were not friendly. But then the little man's face twisted in what looked like near panic.

"Mr. Russell!" the dwarf said. "What are you doing out here? They'll need you inside!"

The dwarf was dressed in a bright blue shirt, and when he stepped out from behind the counter, Howard saw he wore yellow pants with turned up cuffs.

"A Munchkin!" Howard tried to control his laughter. Given the business sign outside, there could be no mistake.

"You been drinkin', Mr. Russell?" the Munchkin asked, apparently shocked by the idea.

"Not yet," Howard said. "But that sounds like a plan."

The dwarf nodded. "After the show, of course." He waved a beckoning hand. "Come on, come on. They'll all be expecting the Wizard to make his appearance."

"Of course they will," Howard said, lurching past the Munchkin and into the land of Oz. Damn but his foot hurt where he had kicked the suit's gun hand.

The residents of Oz gave Howard a poorer reception than did the dwarf. People stared and moved aside, making him feel like the monster the droid Frankenstein had told him he was. One man whispered "nice threads" before beating a hasty retreat. Howard walked through the crowd throwing his arms, one longer than the other, ahead of him to give him momentum and dragging his injured foot. He felt like shouting *Nnggh!* at them, but was afraid that might result in torches and pitchforks.

To create this obscene re-visioning of Oz, the builders had gutted the place. The walls separating the living room, parlor, games room, and kitchen had all been torn down, creating one giant common room. The bedrooms at the back looked to be intact and Howard could only imagine that they still contained beds, though he doubted that much sleeping happened in them. Flying monkeys commanded the area near the high ceiling, while the floor was commanded by monkeys of another sort, 50's Chicago's proud and haughty, by the look of them, all dressed in outrageous period style.

As Howard neared the expected bar area, the lights dimmed and the onlookers turned their attention to another part of the room. Apparently, Howard wasn't the biggest spectacle the place had to offer.

"What'll ya have?" asked a bartender dressed as a lion.

Howard didn't answer. A man had appeared on a small stage and was shouting, "Welcome to the wonderful land of Oz!"

It wasn't the words that surprised Howard; it was the man shouting them. He turned to the lion. "Whiskey. Make it a double."

The lion smiled at him. "Why, I can whip that up with one paw tied behind my back. Ruff!"

The girl could sing. No denying that. Her voice almost succeeded in distracting Howard from the trauma of the past... how many hours? But that man. That man who had introduced her. It was Howard Russell. Himself! A Howard Russell who somehow lived in 1950 Chicago and worked as a burlesque pimp. Could he be a relative? Some great-uncle his parents had been too ashamed to mention? But that was impossible. The man was Howard's identical twin.

There could only be one answer. This was not the 1950's and he had not gone back in time. This was exactly what the C-droid Dr. Frankenstein had said it was. An alternate reality. One where automobiles had evolved at a slower pace and, apparently, fashion in clothing as well.

And the man behind the curtain was none other than himself, the Howard Russell he would have become had he been born and raised in this reality.

The longer Howard observed this other version of himself, the Wizard of Oz Howard, the less he liked him. After that first girl who could sing took off her clothes, Howard was merely annoyed with himself. How could he introduce such an act! Well, not him, but the other him. Surely they were the same person, merely exposed to different circumstances.

Howard downed the last mouthful of whiskey and signaled for another.

"Aw shucks," said the lion. "Are you sure you can pay for all that?"

Howard dumped onto the counter all the funny money he had taken from suit he had murdered.

The lion plucked a handful of bills from the pile and set down another glass.

Each act that followed was more perverse than the one before, and with each act Howard, the Wizard Howard, gloated more and more while Howard, not the Wizard Howard, clenched his fists and swallowed more whiskey. And also with each act, Howard the murdering, monster, engineer, ex-scientist slowly transformed himself into Howard the drunken, murdering, monster, engineer, ex-scientist while Howard the Wizard of Oz slowly transformed himself into Howard the King of Sleaze.

At some point, Howard stared into his empty glass and decided that this could not stand. Enough drink. He needed his wits, not whiskey. His chance would come to do something about this travesty. His one chance. He did not want to miss it.

And, eventually, it came.

Howard looked up as the crowd cheered one final time. The evening's entertainment, if you called it that, was over. The Wizard of Oz bowed and waved as he descended from the stage and made his way to the bar. Of course the Wizard would have a drink. He'd had a long, hard night leering at naked women. Who wouldn't be thirsty after that?

Howard's luck turned for once as Howard, the other Howard, came up to the bar just two stools down and ordered a whisky from the Cowardly Lion. If the lion noticed any resemblance between the two Howards, he gave no indication.

The Wizard of Oz received his drink and lifted it to his lips, but his hand froze as Howard yelled, "Howard! You bastard! You could have been somebody!"

Howard could see the Wizard's ears perk up. Perhaps no one besides the doorman called him by that name in this place, or perhaps he recognized his own voice. Whatever the reason, Howard slowly turned his head toward Howard.

But Howard had not been slow. After shouting his epitaph, he had lurched from his stool, wincing as he put weight on his damaged foot, and made two quick strides toward the Man Behind the Curtain.

"Who—?" the Wizard began, but that was as far as he got before Howard smashed his whiskey glass into his alter ego's teeth.

The room filled with shouts and screams as Howard slammed his lowball glass into the Wizard's face over and over again. At one point, several men tried to pull him off, but Howard hip-checked them with his droid hips and they went flying. He got in several more smashes before being pulled away by forces he could not repel.

As the adrenalin faded, Howard saw three things: Dr. Maxwell Samuels' hand smashed to a pulp, white bones still clutching a shattered whiskey glass; the Wizard of Oz on the floor, his caved-in face surrounded by a pool of brains and blood; and the Tin Man, the Scarecrow, and the Cowardly Lion holding his arms in a death grip.

Dr. Howard Russell, PhD, let out a deep breath, and then hung his head and cried.

He said nothing as they waited for the Police. Neither did he try to fight Dorothy's companions from the Land of

Oz. When the Police finally did arrive and surveyed the scene, they made a cursory examination of Howard's clothes and state of health and eventually discovered his smashed hand, broken foot, and droid hips and thighs. They then called for something called Capone's Crew and the wait continued. By this time, Howard had figured out that the bartenders were droids, an unimaginable waste of money in the Chicago he came from. Maybe this Chicago was *that* different, different enough that the Howard Russell who grew up here would eschew science and become a glorified pimp instead. But it didn't matter. The Frankenstein droid had called Howard its monster, but to him the real *Howard Russell monster* lay on the floor with his head caved in.

Capone's Crew arrived, looking a lot like the suit he had killed in the bakery and the two trench coats he had watched escort one of the singers away earlier. The suits had chains instead of handcuffs and locked Howard's wrists behind his back, hardly blinking at his ruined hand. Then they chained together his ankles, barely allowing him to walk.

The suit in charge looked at the Wizard and then at Howard. "Looks like we got us a murder."

Howard spoke for the first time. "Suicide."

The suit raised a brow.

"And it goes downhill from there," Howard said.

Mitigating Circumstances

They must have drugged the coffee.

Howard remembered being escorted in chains out of the Oz Club and into an old style police van, the shape and durability of the milk wagons he had known as a child. It was windowless and empty except for a bench along the three walls where six suits cloaked in trench coats sat with guns unholstered and trained on him. Howard couldn't help but wonder what would happen if they hit a bump in the road.

After they had traveled for several minutes and Howard failed to start something, the suits seemed to relax and one of them passed around a coffee thermos and some plastic cups. The last suit's eyes shot Howard an unspoken question, to which Howard nodded, and in short order a cup of lukewarm coffee was pressed to his lips. Howard had never much cared for coffee, but he was feeling the whiskey he had drunk all evening and decided that caffeine wouldn't hurt even if it didn't help. Since he'd passed out after the first swallow, Howard decided that he still didn't much care for coffee.

It was dark when he'd been dragged away from Oz, and wherever he was now he could see light filtering in through curtained windows, so at least one night had passed. The curtains prevented him from getting any sense of the time of day, but the checkerboard grid of lines behind the white curtains did give him the sense that the window was barred. He was lying in a bed, no longer chained, which was a good sign, and could taste antiseptic in the air. A hospital then, a secured floor, or perhaps a medical ward of Cook County Jail.

A hospital was not the worst place he could wake up in. In fact, it was exactly what he needed given what had happened to him in Capone's bunker. The problem was that, even if he knew what exactly *had* happened to him, how could he even attempt to explain it to anyone?

"Ah," murmured a deep, baritone voice. "I see our patient is awake."

Howard's gaze moved toward the sound. A tall, dark-skinned man with graying hair, wearing doctor's whites and Buddy Holly glasses, and pressing a clipboard against his chest, strode through the door from the corridor outside. Howard caught a glimpse of a rifle barrel as a guard shifted to allow him entry.

The doctor smiled as his gaze ran from one end of Howard's bed to the other. "How is your hand this morning?"

"My hand?" Howard said.

The doctor's smile broadened. "The hand you damaged in — what was it? — a bar fight?"

A memory of white bones dripping skin and blood clutching a smashed whiskey glass flashed through Howard's mind, and a shudder ran through his body. He looked quickly at his hands, both of which rested on his stomach above the hospital blanket. Both looked fine. It took him a moment to remember which hand was his and which belonged to the arm he had inherited from Dr. Samuels during his adjustments in the bunker. Gingerly, he lifted both hands into the air and flexed his fingers.

"This is *some* hospital," he said.

"Wesley Memorial. Best in the city. And I am Dr. Montgomery."

Howard looked at the doctor. Damage like he had done to his hand didn't heal overnight, no matter how much medicine you threw at it. He was surprised they could do anything at all. That they *would* do anything. After all, he had been arrested for murder. Two murders if they tied him to the suit in the bakery. Then another thought. If they could fix his hand, maybe they could fix his Frankenstein body. This was not the Chicago he knew. Perhaps, just as the evolution of automobiles had been stunted, medicine had progressed at an escalated pace.

"How long have I been here?" Howard asked.

Dr. Montgomery looked at his clipboard, then back at Howard. "Twelve hours."

If the doctor was waiting to see Howard's expression at this news, he wasn't disappointed.

Howard coughed and looked again at his hands. "But that's—"

"—Impossible?" Dr. Montgomery grinned and nodded his head. "So you see my problem. What am I going to do with you?"

To that, Howard had no answer.

The doctor hemmed and hawed as he took Howard's pulse, flashed a penlight in his eyes, and consulted his clipboard. "Well," he said. "You appear to be in perfect health."

Howard cast him his best open stare.

The doctor moved his eyes across the blanket. "Excepting, of course, for some... modifications that I don't understand."

"Is there anything you can do about that?" Howard wouldn't even have asked had it not been for the miraculous restoration of his ruined hand. Nothing short of amputation should have been possible.

"I've called in an expert," Dr. Montgomery said, not exactly answering the question. His pager buzzed and he looked at it. "Ah. She has arrived. I'll be back shortly and we'll see what we shall see."

Howard watched the doctor leave, and counted two guards in the corridor outside his room as Montgomery shuffled past them. Once again on his own, he took the opportunity to further explore his environs.

He decided to perform this exploration without the benefit of leaving his bed; the look one of the guards had given him when Dr. Montgomery left reminded him of the *shoot first ask questions later* comment he'd received from the suit in the bakery. He settled for lifting up his sheet and blanket to verify that nothing had changed. Sadly, he still had Dr. Samuels' arm, Ms. Olsen's feet and calves, and mechanical hips and thighs, all acquired in some mad Frankenstein operation performed by a construction droid that had mutated in appearance and capabilities while they were both trapped inside what the C-droid called the Vortex. He did notice that, like his borrowed hand, the borrowed foot he had injured also seemed good as new.

So, not just a bad dream. Somehow the impossible had really happened and, apparently, continued to happen, whatever *it* actually was. None of this boded well, but for the first time Howard felt that at least he wasn't alone. Dr. Montgomery seemed like a good sort.

Having finished his self-inspection, Howard looked

around the room and discovered that he was not alone literally, as well. On a second bed lay a man connected to a fluid bag and some kind of monitoring equipment. He couldn't see the display from where he sat up in bed, not that he would know how to read it. Howard held his Doctorate in Physics, not Medicine. The side of the man's head was bandaged. Still, he looked vaguely familiar.

Noise at the room's single door drew Howard's attention and he turned to watch Dr. Montgomery and a middle-aged woman enter. The woman had reddish brown hair with severe curls and reminded him of a bitter Lucille Ball.

"This is Dr. Moreau," said Montgomery. "Dr. Moreau will be helping us."

Howard nodded. "Exactly what type of help are we talking about?"

Dr. Moreau glanced at Dr. Montgomery, but said nothing.

"Let's start with your name," Dr. Montgomery said.

So that's how they were going to play it. Well, what did he expect? Of course, he could play games, too. "Dr. Howard Russell."

Montgomery frowned and looked at his clipboard. Moreau had her own clipboard and looked at it as well.

"Dr.?" said Dr. Montgomery.

"PhD. Physics."

"What school?" Dr. Moreau asked, speaking for the first time.

"Chicago University. I'm home grown."

"I am intrigued," said Dr. Montgomery. He flipped a page on his clipboard. "Because of how you were brought to us—" He gave a half nod toward the guards outside the door. "—the Crew requested a priority DNA test."

"And?" Howard asked.

Dr. Montgomery shook his head. "And we had to run the test three times because we thought there must be a mistake."

"Because it told you that I am, in fact, the man I killed

last night?" Howard was surprised that he could speak these words so calmly.

"Well," said Dr. Montgomery. "Yes. And no."

Dr. Moreau slammed her clipboard against her other hand and glared at Dr. Montgomery. "This is taking too long." She turned her fierce gaze on Howard and said, "The tests show that you do indeed have Howard Russell's DNA. Also, the DNA of two others. Dr. Maxwell Samuels, who has not been seen since the earthquake yesterday and who, by the way, is a PhD, and Mrs. Olivia Nelson, a homemaker."

"Don't you mean Olivia Olsen?" Howard said. "Geraldo Rivera's psychic friend?"

Dr. Moreau flipped through the pages of her clipboard and showed a page to Dr. Montgomery, who clucked his tongue. "Apparently *Olsen* is Mrs. Nelson's maiden name."

"Who is the Harold person you mentioned?" asked Montgomery.

"You wouldn't believe me if I told you," said Howard.

Dr. Moreau tapped a part of the page with her finger and then snarled at Dr. Montgomery. "We need to talk!"

Howard listened as best he could to the two doctors hissing at each other from where they stood at the far side of the room behind the bed with the bandaged man. There was only so much toying with your fingernails a person could do to look like he wasn't paying attention, but the two doctors were so engrossed in their conversation or argument — Howard couldn't tell which — that they seemed to have forgotten he was in the room.

The name *Capone* came up a lot, not in any particularly endearing way, and for a moment Howard wondered if perhaps they did know something about the bunker and what had happened to him. But then they seemed to be referring to the bandaged man and Howard began to wonder which patient it was they were discussing.

The huddle ended when Dr. Moreau stormed out of the room. Dr. Montgomery returned to Howard's bedside and several telltale signs, such as a pinched and sweaty brow and fidgeting fingers, suggested that he had not been the victor.

"I take it that didn't go well," Howard said.

"Mr. Russell," Dr. Montgomery said in a low whisper, likely for the benefit of the guards in the corridor. "In some strange way I do believe that you are who you say you are, even though I examined your corpse not one hour ago downstairs in our morgue. Regardless, at this juncture I have no idea what *going well* is or isn't. But I will tell you what I do know. And that is that this hospital has done nothing to treat your damaged hand."

Howard could think of nothing to say to that, so the doctor continued. "You appear to have repaired your own hand, probably by the same means that allows you to be an amalgam of three people and, well, a machine."

"So," Howard whispered back, at last finding some words. "Then there is nothing you can do to... make me less of a freak?"

Dr. Montgomery's worry seemed to turn to agitation. "My plan was to study you, to try to understand you. Eventually I might learn enough to... reduce the negative aspects of your condition."

"Was?" said Howard.

"Dr. Moreau disagrees with me. She seems to think you might be of interest to the Mayor's Office. She wishes to call them in."

"The Mayor's Office? Why would they be interested in me?"

Dr. Montgomery frowned. "Why, Olivia Nelson, of course. I don't know who this Harold person is you mentioned, but Mrs. Nelson is a close friend of the Mayor. His personal psychic, in fact. That you seem to have her DNA flowing through your veins is something that must be brought to the Mayor's attention. And then there is the matter of the Capone's Crew ID card."

Howard gave him a blank look.

"It was found in your coveralls when you were admitted. Unfortunately, it belongs to a Crewman who was found dead less than a block from where you were arrested."

"I can explain that," Howard said. "Well, mostly."

Dr. Montgomery shook his head and reached into the pocket of his hospital coat. "That is not important to me, though whoever comes from the Mayor's Office may be interested in your explanation. We have very little time."

"Time for what?" Howard asked as Dr. Montgomery removed two small metal rods from one of his coat's large pockets.

"I am going to draw some blood. I'll use it for tests to try and discover what has happened to you." He pressed the end of one of the rods against Howard's forearm. The extraction was cold but painless. When Montgomery pulled the rod away, Howard could see a small hole in his skin that vanished even as he watched.

"Is that normal?"

"No," said Dr. Montgomery, and repeated the action with the second rod.

Howard watched as Montgomery put one rod back into his coat pocket. The other the doctor fitted it into a syringe that must also have been in his coat. Then he looked at Howard.

"What I am going to do next, you did not see. Even though this man is in a permanent coma, it breaks every moral code ever written to do what I am about to do. And yet, doing so may tell us more about you than any other test I could devise. There really is no other way."

The doctor turned and stepped over to the other bed, and injected Howard's blood directly into the man lying there.

Howard thought back to every medical movie, television show, and book he had ever seen or read, and tried to recall what fiction said would happen if you injected one person's blood into another. He remembered something about blood types having to match, but had no real idea what would happen if they didn't. Having three different sets of DNA, Howard didn't know if his blood type was a match for anyone.

He watched Dr. Montgomery walk around the bed to the far side and stand against the wall, the doctor's nervous gaze passing back and forth between the man on the bed and the monitor display.

Howard didn't know if the doctor was fearful because he had just committed a crime that could cost him his license, or because he was afraid of what the result of that crime might be.

Seconds turned to minutes and nothing happened. Dr. Montgomery frowned and he adjusted some controls on the monitor. Then he looked suddenly toward the door, and Howard heard heavy footsteps as Montgomery quietly left the other bed and came to stand next to his.

Three people entered the room: Dr. Moreau, a heavyset man in a dark grey, three-piece suit, and a man so nondescript that he must be Capone's Crew, whatever that was. The Crewman's gaze swept the room and he was first to speak, pointing at the other bed.

"Isn't that Tony Sandoval?"

The heavyset bigwig glanced over. "Shot twice. Once in the gut. Once in the head. Damn shame he lived. Better to die on the job than live as a vegetable in a hospital."

"But why is he in this room?" asked the Crewman.

Howard decided that this was a very good question.

"The bed was available," Dr. Montgomery said. "Since the earthquake, we've had a bed shortage. A severe coma case was the safest choice to put in with a murderer."

A good answer, Howard agreed, even though he didn't appreciate the suggestion that he was a danger to other patients.

Bigwig returned his heavy gaze to Howard. "Let me get this straight. This clown claims to be the man he murdered?"

"Yes," said Dr. Moreau.

"And we are certain he is the murderer?"

It was the Crewman who answered. "Dozens of witnesses. My own unit brought him in."

"And who did he kill?"

Again the Crewman. "Howard Russell."

Bigwig frowned and glanced at the Crewman. "The Wizard of Oz?"

"Um, yes sir."

Bigwig turned his gaze to Howard's face and looked him up and down. "There is a resemblance. Must be a relative."

Dr. Montgomery spoke up. "The DNA—"

Bigwig cut him off. "I've read the test results. DNA similar to, but not a direct match for the Wizard."

Dr. Montgomery tried again. "It's more comp—"

Bigwig cut him off again, this time with a look. "I also read the forensics report for the murder of Joe Cardinal. Killer's DNA matched this man's."

"Who?" Howard asked, speaking for the first time.

"Friend of mine you murdered in the bakery," growled the Crewman. "Capone's Crew."

"If you tell me what Capone's Crew means," Howard said, "I'll explain what happened with this Cardinal character."

Bigwig waved a meaty hand. "Not necessary. Penalty for killing a Crewman is immediate termination."

"But—"

Bigwig's lips twisted in a tight smile. "There are no buts. No mitigating circumstances." He turned to his companion. "Crewman, do your duty."

"Gladly," said the Crewman. "He drew a gun from his holster and aimed it at Howard's forehead."

"You can't do that here!" cried Dr. Montgomery. "This is a hospital."

Bigwig raised a thick eyebrow. "Perhaps you need to look up the meaning of the word *immediate*."

By this time the guards in the corridor had entered the room, probably having overhead that the murderer they had been guarding was about to be executed and eager to see justice served. It was getting a bit crowded. Howard was surprised he even noticed, as he was busy staring down the barrel of a gun. He knew his metal hips were fast when he needed them to be, but would they be fast enough to dodge a bullet while struggling to climb out of the confines of the hospital bed's sheets and blanket?

And then the question became moot as Howard's head exploded in pain. Had the gun fired without him noticing? In addition to the agony in his head, he could hear screaming. He assumed it was the beckoning call of Hell. But then he somehow worked through the pain and noticed that his eyes were still open, the gun was still aimed at him, unfired, and the scream was coming from Dr. Moreau. Everyone in the room was facing away from him, looking at the other bed.

Despite the gun still directed at him, Howard also looked, and discovered the cause of Dr. Moreau's scream. The comatose man in the other bed had sat up and was looking at him.

The screaming stopped and was replaced with words. "S-sorry," stammered Dr. Moreau. "But that m-man is as good as dead. He can't sit up like that."

"Neither can he climb out of bed," suggested Bigwig. "But Crewman Sandoval appears to be doing just that. Are you certain that his injuries are as severe as reported?"

"He lost almost a third of his cerebral cortex," said Dr. Montgomery.

"That means nothing to me," said Bigwig.

"Then, yes," said Dr. Montgomery. "His injuries are that severe."

Howard watched as the bandaged man — Tony Sandoval — walked towards him. His head still ached, but he could think clearly now and saw that the man's face held no expression and his eyes seemed very cold. Tony stopped next to Howard's bed and looked directly at him, and Howard suddenly knew why he seemed familiar. He had been at the bar in the Oz Club, sitting with a second

Crewman. Howard was certain they were the same two men in the Bel Air outside Oz. He had been afraid that they were watching him, but they had simply been waiting for the girl who could sing and had left with her early in the evening. Howard couldn't help but wonder what had happened that resulted in this one being shot and almost killed a short time later.

Howard's musings were cut short when Tony abruptly turned to the other Crewman and punched him hard in the gut. The gun fired and Howard blinked, but the bullet missed him and entered the wall. Faster than Howard could see, Tony grabbed the Crewman's gun hand and twisted it until he cried out and the gun was suddenly in Tony's grip.

Movement near the door caught Howard's eye. The two guards had thrown down their rifles, something Howard thought odd until they drew handguns of their own. He guessed that the room was too crowded to use the rifles. Two shots fired and the two guards dropped to the floor. Tony reached down and retrieved both handguns, which he carried in his left hand while still brandishing the surviving Crewman's gun in his right.

And then Tony left the room, walking at a steady pace.

Howard was still trying to figure out if Tony Sandoval was escaping somewhere he had no need to escape from, or if this was all some bizarre stratagem to rescue a murderer he didn't even know, when Bigwig's Crewman picked up one of the rifles and stepped into the corridor. There was a single shot and the Crewman crumpled to the floor.

That left Howard in a hospital room with two doctors and a Bigwig who wished Howard immediately terminated. If Tony Sandoval's actions really were an elaborate ploy to affect Howard's escape, then this was Howard's cue. All three of Howard's companions stood stunned and indecisive, even Dr. Montgomery, who Howard suspected was less surprised by Tony's recovery than the others, but perhaps equally stunned by Tony's actions. Howard, however, had already been through Hell several times in the past twenty-four hours and found himself surprisingly capable of taking such things in stride.

Whipping off the bed's blanket, as much as anyone could whip off the tightly tucked blanket of a hospital bed, Howard swung what currently functioned as his legs to the side and stepped onto the floor. His hospital gown did a poor job of covering bright yellow metal thighs, and he couldn't help but smile as Dr. Moreau repeated her screams from earlier and Bigwig's eyes bulged in their sockets.

Calmly, he picked up the remaining rifle and pointed it at Bigwig. "If there was no such thing as mitigating circumstances," he said to the bulky man, "I would pull this trigger and it would be you suffering immediate termination, not I. Since there is, however, I will not do that, but will instead ask you listen to what Dr. Montgomery has to say. I am an innocent man and people will want to hear my story. But that story will never be heard as long as bullheaded buffoons like you make snap decisions. Good day."

Bigwig just stared at him.

Howard gave a brief nod to both doctors, the now sobbing Dr. Moreau and the white-faced Dr. Montgomery, and stepped into the corridor, hopeful that Tony was far enough ahead of him that he would not, like the Crewman lying at his feet, receive a bullet from the escaping patient's gun.

This apparently was the case. Even better, the corridor was deserted, its occupants having fled. Gunfire had that effect on people.

First matter of business was to find some clothes that would hide who, and what, he was. He'd worry about finding a second matter of business later.

Dead Men Walking

Tony Sandoval knew he was walking along a sidewalk, but not because he could see his surroundings. The pain in his head was so excruciating that it left him virtually blind; eyes open or closed, all he saw was an endless bouquet of fireworks throwing off rapid-fire rainbows of colored lights. He could, however, sense cold, hard cement beneath his feet and feel the gusts of freezing air from passing cars. He was a bat, sensing his surroundings without the benefit of eyes.

What Tony didn't know was how he had come to be walking blind and in agony along a nameless street. There was a gunfight. He was pretty sure of that. He felt around in his coat pockets and found guns. Guns? Three of them. Had he been shot? Was that why his head hurt and he couldn't see?

He realized that his coat wasn't his coat. It didn't fit right. It was too small. Had he taken it from someone? Someone he had shot? Before or after he shot them? Was he on the run? Was someone chasing him? The answer to any of those questions might be essential.

Tony walked a little faster, and then stopped as he heard the click-click warning of a *Don't Walk* pedestrian alarm. He was at a downtown intersection. He tried to turn his head, seeking which way was safe to go. He didn't care where he was going. He just had to get away. How did blind people manage this with just a little click-clicking sound? Agony screamed at the attempted movement, so he turned his body instead, keeping his neck rigid. Two steps and he seemed to be going in the right direction. He stepped off the sidewalk and tensed against the possibility of being hit by a car. His feet kept moving and nothing hit him except the sound of an angry horn.

Two more steps and he heard a tweeting sound, an audible warning that the light was about to change. Tony finished crossing and felt the short rise in altitude as his feet stepped from asphalt up onto cement again. He kept going straight, hoping that he wouldn't walk into the side of a building.

Tony could hear other pedestrians, and this helped keep him on the straight and narrow, straying neither into the side of a building nor off the sidewalk. No one spoke to him, and Tony imagined them making efforts to not get too close. There must be blood. He resisted the urge to explore his head with his hands. He couldn't get distracted. Had to stay focused on putting one foot in front of the other, on seeing the ground with his feet, on hearing the clues around him that told him where to go.

A church bell pealed nearby and Tony almost stopped dead in his tracks. First United? Tony could only assume that most church bells sounded the same, but he swore this was the same bell that he heard every fifteen minutes when he was in his office at City Hall. He continued to listen. The bell pealed one more time, and then stopped. Two o'clock. Given the sunlight he was sure he felt on his face and that there were more than a few pedestrians, two in the afternoon. And he couldn't be more than a few blocks from City Hall.

Tony knew he could manage a few more blocks. He may not even have to; someone he knew may be on the street and see him. He'd get whatever damage he had received fixed up. And then, if he hadn't already killed whoever had done this to him, he'd find that person and finish the job.

Howard found a small room off the corridor that contained a closet filled with hospital whites. He had never understood why doctors and orderlies didn't take their work uniforms home at night like most other professions, but right now he was glad they didn't. He quickly found some loose fitting pants, a large shirt, and pull-on shoes. A second closet held a variety of thin coats made of felt and other materials he didn't recognize. None of them looked as warm as his coveralls, but searching for his own clothes didn't seem like a good idea. He grabbed a coat that looked like grey felt for the simple expedient that it was the largest.

Then he stared at the rifle, still not quite believing that he had actually threatened people with it, but smiling at the expression on Bigwig's face when he had. Briefly, he contemplated wrapping it in a towel and taking it with him, just in case. He shook his head and stashed it in the closet. The cops in this version of Chicago were too quick to shoot, and a gunfight was the last thing he wanted to participate in.

Walking out of the hospital was easy. Apparently, a half-dressed patient toting three handguns was distraction enough that less dangerous looking people, such as himself, weren't given a second glance by the hospital staff or the swarm of police that burst through the front entrance. Howard walked right through them, suddenly glad he had left the rifle behind. The police, dressed in crisp blue uniforms, were looking for armed killers, not an orderly trying to get out of the way.

Once outside, Howard faced the grim reality that he didn't have a second order of business. He had avoided *immediate termination*, but what was he to do now? He was wanted by the police for murder in an alternate reality of Chicago. The hospital, which is where he needed to be, had already told him they could do nothing. The University? Perhaps he could speak to someone in the Physics Department. Then he laughed. If he hadn't been disgraced by his failed cold fusion project, he'd be teaching at the University himself. What would *he* say if someone came to him with this story? He suspected he'd call the police. Or the loony bin.

He started walking, if for no other reason than to put some distance between himself and the police inside. Wesley Memorial Hospital stood out in big letters above the broad front entrance. He didn't recognize the name, but he knew the building. Looking north across Huron Street he saw the sprawling campus of Northwestern

University, only in this reality the signs said Chicago University — North Campus. The proximity of familiar ground almost convinced him to try speaking to someone there anyway. But then he watched two policemen halt traffic to cross from the hospital to the University, and he continued walking away.

By the time he reached Michigan Avenue, Howard was shivering inside his stolen coat. He turned south, walking with the wind at his back for seven blocks to the Chicago River. Many of the buildings were unfamiliar, and there were more bars and nightclubs than he remembered, but the Chicago Tribune building looked exactly how he remembered it. Most of the establishments were open for business, though a few had locked doors with handwritten signs. *Closed due to earthquake.*

He passed a street vendor willing to brave December in Chicago and took in the aroma of steaming hot dogs and hot mustard. Howard's stomach growled, but he had no money, or ID, or anything else for that matter. He pulled the collar of his coat tighter and kept walking.

The Michigan Ave Bridge had just been let down after allowing the passage of a cargo ship. Howard frowned. The bridge he knew was raised only a couple of times a year, for show and to keep the wheels greased. Large cargo ships had stopped coming in off the Great Lakes almost before he was born. The pedestrian path on the lower level was familiar enough, however, and Howard stepped lively making his way to the south bank. Midway across he looked down into the cold, dark water and frowned a second time. The river was flowing the wrong direction, pouring water into Lake Michigan instead of pulling it out and sending it to the Mississippi River. He sighed and kept walking. By now, nothing could surprise him.

On the south bank, he found the familiar McCormick Bridgehouse, but there was no sign of the River Museum. The building that should have been a museum was unmarked and, frankly, uninviting. Howard suspected that if he tried to enter it, the only souvenir he would find was a bullet. If there was one thing he had learned about this version of Chicago, it was that life here was cheap.

Howard continued south for three blocks, passing a field full of railway tracks in place of what he knew as University Park. Cargo trains carrying coal chugged past at a snail's pace, sending columns of black smoke into the winter sky along with the stench of burnt coal and diesel fuel.

At the corner of Randolph Street stood a small park with a sign that said *Grant*. Howard remembered that there once had been a Grant Park, named for President Grant.

He turned west and kept walking until he stopped to watch a Ferris wheel for cars. He didn't know what else to call it. It was rectangular rather than round, and occupied the entire narrow end of a twenty-story building. As Howard watched, a parking attendant drove a boxy Chevrolet Corvair into a stall at the bottom of the wheel. Then he hung the keys on a rack in a phone booth sized office before working a gear that caused the wheel to rotate, lifting the new arrival into the air and moving an empty stall down to pavement level. Howard figured the device might hold forty cars. He shook his head and continued walking, and saw a similar device on the next block.

Further south, the bells of First United Methodist rang once, then twice. Two o'clock. In the grey cold of December, its tone was mournful, echoing Howard's mood, but somehow not his physical condition. It was only then that he realized he had been walking for at least twenty minutes and his feet weren't killing him. In fact, he felt great. Invigorated. Whatever adjustments had been made to him appeared to have reached some kind of truce, with all his parts, old and new, working together.

He reached Clark Street after a few minutes and Howard arrived at a second realization. Since leaving Wesley Memorial, he'd had a destination all along. City Hall. He wasn't surprised. That had been his destination every workday for the past two years. What did surprise him was that he didn't recognize City Hall at all.

The City Hall Howard knew was a single building occupying an entire city block and towering twelve stories, cramped in among buildings that towered even higher. This City Hall was still surrounded by skyscrapers, but was only about five stories itself, had its own car park — the normal kind rather than the Ferris wheel kind — and had a paved walk space and even some grass and trees. To Howard it was what a City Hall should look like.

And now that he had arrived, Howard had no idea what he would do. Report to his office? His office didn't even exist in this building. His department? What would be the point? The Mayor? Well, that was something. If he could explain himself to the Mayor, maybe he could at least get the police off his back. Yes, he had killed two men. But there had been extenuating circumstances. Surely, the Mayor would understand that. And maybe reduce his crimes to a misdemeanor? Doubtful. But he couldn't just stand outside in the cold.

The main entrance to Howard's City Hall was on the west side. He assumed that was still true and continued on to LaSalle Blvd.

Howard shivered, wishing once again that he had found warmer clothes at the hospital. Few people on the street seemed to acknowledge the chill weather, except perhaps that they walked a bit more briskly than folks at home. Howard quickened his pace and soon felt a bit warmer.

It struck him how the people in this Chicago were so fashionably out of date. The men dressed in dark two or three-piece suits made of heavy wool against the winter cold. Almost all of them wore crisp fedora hats. Some wore pea coats or trench coats over their suit jackets. The women wore ankle-length dresses, also of thick material, adorned with stoles that Howard assumed were real animal fur rather than the mandated artificial materials in his reality. Hair worn long and thick was invariably curled or permed or both. Most women wore hats of some kind, no two of which looked alike. There wasn't a child or teenager in sight, however, except the occasional boy wearing nothing but jeans and a cardigan, shivering and selling newspapers. Howard would have bought one if he had a dime.

No one had ear buds, though he did see the occasional cellular flip phone that looked twenty years out of date. He didn't see any bizarre punk hairstyles or artificial colors. No piercings, though some of the younger adults did sport tattoos.

All that and the antique cars gave this Chicago a Dick Tracy 50's flavor. Technology must have moved at a much slower pace. Perhaps he could use that to his advantage; maybe verify his story by inventing a few nifty gadgets that were common knowledge back home, but lacking here. Would be too much to ask for this Chicago to have never encountered a toaster?

But what about the robot bartenders at the Oz Club? They had seemed pretty advanced. More advanced than the C-droids back home. And less expensive to construct? No one in his Chicago would spend a fortune on droids and then dress them up as refugees from the Land of Oz to tend bar. It didn't matter how much money you had to throw around. Could droids in this Chicago be an everyday commodity? Like personal computers back home?

Howard let out a deep breath. He needed answers and all he had were questions.

After turning south on LaSalle Blvd he saw that the open space in front of City Hall's main entrance was filled with reporters and Chicago citizens who apparently had nothing better to do than idle away the afternoon. Howard slipped in among the onlookers and asked what was going on.

A woman wrapped in furs turned to him and said that the Mayor's daughter had been found, but that was all she knew. Everyone was waiting for the Mayor's Office to make a statement.

Howard tried to remember if Mayor Gonzales in his

reality had a daughter. If such a daughter had been missing, he was sure he would have heard about it. Another difference? On the bright side, the recovery of a beloved daughter should put Gonzales in a good mood, perhaps good enough to pardon a murderer for an hour while he listened to an impossible story. Howard shook his head. There was just no way he could see a good outcome to his problems.

Still, he tried. In his mind, Howard envisioned Gonzales coming out onto the front steps and speaking to the crowd. Afterward, when he asked for questions, Howard would raise his hand and say just the right thing for the Mayor to hustle him inside where he could tell his story to a room full of reasonable people and receive the help he needed. But in that same vision, any words that he attempted resulted in him being either *immediately terminated* or hustled away and then *immediately terminated.*

The sad truth was, in the City Hall Howard knew, he could count the number of reasonable bureaucrats on the fingers of one hand. It would be difficult to get anyone to listen. No. He had to focus on the Mayor and the Mayor only. As difficult as it would be to get Gonzales to listen to him, the more people in the room, the harder the sales job would be.

And on top of his other problems, the headache that had hit him out of nowhere in the hospital was starting to come back.

Howard looked for somewhere he might sit down for a moment and wait for the headache to pass as it had when he left the hospital, but anywhere that was even remotely sittable was already sat on. He began walking toward a service entrance he had passed at the northwest end of the building, his headache rising, and barely made it to a shaded alcove near the service door where he could sit on a concrete stoop.

The sound of voices at the main entrance rose and Howard deduced that the Mayor or someone speaking for him had made an appearance, but he was in no shape to go back out there, and he still had no idea what he would try to say to whoever was there if he did.

The more he thought about it, the more he realized that it was a bad idea anyway. He would have a better chance of success if he just went inside after the statement and sneaked his way through the building's poor excuse for security. Having worked there for two years, he knew all the flaws in the system... provided it was the same system. Worst case, someone would stop him and tell him to bugger off. He didn't think anyone would shoot him just for asking. Of course, he would have to give a different name. Until he told his story, his real name could get him killed, and he didn't think Tony Sandoval would walk up and rescue him. Again.

At that moment, a man dressed in a long coat and hospital slippers walked up to the service door, placed his hand against a palm reader, and entered the building. It was Tony Sandoval.

Tony's vision began to return as he neared City Hall. It was mostly just shapes and shadows, but it was enough that he was able to tell that he was at the back end of the building. He wasn't sure if that was a good thing or bad. If anyone was following him, being thrown off himself could have helped throw off his pursuer. He could also hear a commotion from the direction of the front entrance, like there was a crowd of people there. Again, help or hindrance, he didn't know.

What he did know was that there was a secluded side entrance near the car park that City employees used when they felt a need to come and go while keeping a low profile. Tony didn't think his profile had ever been lower. He heard the chirp-chirp of the walk signal and made his way across Randolph Street, letting out a sigh when he felt hard cement once again beneath his feet. He wasn't sad that his precarious journey was almost over.

He walked twenty paces along the sidewalk, and then turned where a metal handrail led along a narrower sidewalk toward the building. Tony could see well enough that he didn't need to grasp the handrail. It hovered at the edge of his vision, a long, black shadow.

His vision had not recovered enough to see the door framed by the wall. The entire side of the building was one massive blob. But he knew that the handrail led to it. When the railing ended, Tony took two more steps and reached his hand out to where the palm reader should be. He missed only by an inch or two and slid his hand across its surface until the sensors locked onto his palm print. The reader found his print on file and the door unlocked. A pump let out two small jets of air and the door swung outward.

Before him stood a black cave. Tony walked inside and heard the air pump shoot again. This time, a larger blast to push the door all the way closed. Normally Tony waited to make sure the door closed, which it always did. But this time he didn't wait. In the lesser light he was blind again, and this depressed him. He had to find someone who could summon a doctor to look at him. Tell him how bad it was. But before he did that, he wanted to see for himself. And he thought he knew where to do that. After walking through the open door, he kept on walking, this time running his hand along the wall to tell him where he was. Behind him, the air pump slowly pushed the door shut.

As the service door swung shut, Howard stuck out Ms. Olsen's foot and prevented it from closing. The door was probably on a timer and an alarm would go off if he didn't allow it to close in the next several seconds. Which side of the door to be on when it did close was not an easy decision. If he was caught entering City Hall by any means other than the main door it would look highly suspicious.

If someone questioned him, reasonable answers would be much harder to find. That he was dressed in a hospital uniform was in his favor. He could say to whoever stopped him that someone at City Hall was in need of medical aid, and that he had gotten lost. Hmm. That plan had potential.

Moments later, Howard was inside City Hall with the service door closed behind him. It was only then that he wondered if Tony might be waiting inside, ready to shoot him. But Tony was nowhere in sight.

The air pump moving the door was a surprise. As was the palm reader. In Howard's Chicago, there was usually a simple RFID reader and you had to manually move the doors before they either relocked or an alarm went off. Security here seemed several degrees higher than the building he worked in, and his plan to sneak around the building was beginning to look a lot less viable. What other changes might he run into?

Howard needed a place to hide and think this through. And in a downtown office building, there was only one place to hide.

Howard looked for the nearest stairwell and headed down.

Tony descended the stairs by gripping the railing with both hands and feeling the steps with his feet. By the time he reached the bottom, he realized that the cave wasn't as dark as it had first been. He could now see the glow of ceiling lights, and as he turned down the corridor, he could make out the walls and darker blotches of various doorways. He even decided that his headache had become almost bearable.

He walked down the corridor using his eyes more than his other senses and pushed open the Men's Room door.

The lights above the counter were brighter than in the corridor. Tony could even see the shapes of the lanterns with the brighter bulbs inside. He moved his gaze to the mirrors below the lights and saw a stranger.

He didn't recognize the coat. Then he moved closer to the mirror and stared at the face, which came into focus even as he watched. His face. No blood. Not on his face. Not on the coat. Not on the bandages that wrapped his head.

Bandages? How would he get bandaged up while fleeing a gunfight? And it was a professional job, too. Could he have been bandaged up *after* the fight?

And then he remembered. Dorothy. Dorothy had shot him in the head with his own gun. At least that explained his headache. It didn't explain the three guns in his pocket. Or how he found himself wandering the streets of downtown Chicago.

Carefully, Tony worked off the bandages to see how bad the damage was. But there was no damage. So why the bandages? He remembered being shot. In the head. And in the gut. He ran his hand along his back and then his lower ribcage. Nothing. No injury. No pain. His headache was almost gone now as well.

Running some water onto his hands, Tony slicked back his hair. He could deal with being dressed like a street person, but he took pride in his hair.

The door from the corridor creaked and Tony spun to watch it creep slowly open. A face appeared and Tony recognized it. "The Wizard of Oz?"

The Wizard stared at Tony for a moment. Then said, "You aren't going to shoot me, are you?"

Tony was about to reply, "Of course not", but then it struck him what an odd question it was. Instead he said, "Why do you ask?"

The Wizard pursed his lips as though considering his reply. "Because you shot the last three people I saw you with."

Immediate Termination

Howard spilled his guts. Well, not all of them, but he told Tony Sandoval the tale of a comatose Crewman waking up in the hospital and shooting a second Crewman and two policemen in front of an audience that included a City Hall Bigwig, and then walking away with the handguns belonging to the victims.

"That explains the guns in my coat," Tony said, not once appearing to disbelieve Howard's story. "And the hospital slippers on my feet and the gown beneath this coat. Do you know the Crewman's name?"

Howard shook his head.

"I hope it wasn't someone I liked," said Tony. "You don't know the City Official's name either?"

Again Howard shook his head, and then added. "I'm pretty sure you don't like him; he's a jackass."

"Requirement for the job," Tony said, though his thoughts appeared to be elsewhere. "So what you're telling me is that I miraculously awoke from a coma only to kill three cops, which means that as soon as they find me I'll be summarily executed."

"Won't they make an exception—" Howard began.

Tony laughed. "You mean mitigating circumstances? No such thing. If you kill a cop, you get killed in return. It's the Mayor's law. It's better than other jurisdictions, with cop killers biding their time and sometimes even going free while lawyers bankrupt the economy."

Howard had no comment. Before a couple of days ago, his life as an anonymous civil engineer had kept him pretty much apart from Chicago's legal system, which is why his execution order in the hospital had come as such a surprise. He was pretty sure that his Chicago still behaved like other jurisdictions and that this was another aberration. But who knew? When his cold fusion project had been shut down and his disgrace became a top media story, he had stopped watching the news.

"So what are you going to do?" Howard asked.

Tony replied without hesitation. "I'm going to turn myself in. After I take care of some unfinished business."

"Uh," said Howard. "I wonder if before you do that, you could do me a small favor. I don't know anyone here and I really need to speak with the Mayor. It's life or death."

Tony chuckled grimly. "Meetings with the Mayor usually are. Since you're inside City Hall, I assume that you somehow managed to make an appointment."

"Uh," Howard repeated. "I didn't exactly come in the front door."

A frown filled Tony's face.

"I considered trying to speak with the Mayor during his press conference out front, but — where are you going?"

"To save the Mayor!" Tony shouted as he roughly brushed past him.

Howard was suddenly alone in the Men's Room.

Tony had never heard a more outlandish story in his life — and, as a cop and then as a member of Capone's Crew, he had heard them all. Even the part where the MC of Oz needed to have a life or death chat with the Mayor. People don't just wake up from comas twelve hours after being shot, only to find no evidence of the gunshots. But he had to believe the Wizard's story because anything else would be even more outrageous.

He had no doubts that Dorothy Gale had shot him in the gut and the head, and now, mere hours later, there was no sign of either wound. Whatever miracle had been worked upon him in the hospital had given him the chance to find Dorothy and stop her before she could kill Capone.

Tony had run, not walked, from the Men's Room, and his first stop was an unused office down the corridor that he knew had a working phone. He punched in the number for the Crew's private emergency line and entered the pass code for his old partner, Simon Sanderson. Entering his own code would send the entire force chasing him, rather than Dorothy.

"Priority One," he shouted into the phone. "The Mayor's life is in danger. Suspect is Dorothy Gale, a singer from the Oz Club. Looks twenty. Five foot two. Long black hair. Armed and dangerous. She has already killed two Crewmen." Two because Tony had watched as Dorothy shot Rory Hudson and because he considered himself as good as dead. He remembered something Dorothy had told him. "Originally from Kansas, where she also committed murder, including her parents. Dorothy Gale is a stage name." That should help them identify her.

He slammed the phone down and headed for the side entrance where he had entered the building. He'd have to go outside and search for Dorothy in the crowd. Even having made the call, no one stood a better chance of stopping Dorothy than he did.

A place to hide hadn't been the only reason Howard had sought refuge in the Men's Room. Relieving himself with his modified anatomy was an experience he decided not to share with anyone. Some things were simply need-to-know and this was one of them.

He washed his hands and smoothed his hair, and then pondered whether he should follow Tony or try to sneak into the Mayor's office while everyone was distracted with the news conference. It could very well be his best chance to talk to the Mayor. Following Tony was madness for all sorts of reasons, and yet, a few minutes later he found himself exiting the service door; no palm required to exit.

How he even knew that Tony had gone outside that way was a question Howard could not answer. If he closed his eyes he could almost see Tony walking among the crowd, listening to the Mayor speak, looking for someone.

There seemed to be an affinity between them. That would explain the headache that had hit him when Tony woke from his coma and again when they both arrived at

City Hall; Howard had felt the other man's head wound. Somehow. It could also explain Tony's actions after waking. With no awareness of his own, Tony Sandoval had been a puppet on Howard's strings, turning Howard's desire to avoid *immediate termination* into a violent escape. And now Howard seemed to feel whatever was driving Tony, and it was driving him, too. Perhaps that is how they had both arrived at City Hall at almost the same time, and then again in the same Men's Room.

Reaching this conclusion, Howard almost began to cry; his condition was even worse than he had thought. He had already lost parts of his physical body. Now his mind wasn't even his own. The only explanation for it was his Frankenstein blood that Dr. Montgomery had injected into Tony's comatose body. What would happen if even more people were injected with his blood? Dr. Montgomery still had a vial. And an endless quantity of blood could be produced from Howard's own body.

An image ran through his mind of sitting in a padded cell, a raving lunatic, as his blood was harvested and sold to Chicago's elite for its healing properties. Of course, the affinity probably worked both ways, making his blood almost worthless. "We can inject you with this serum and it will save your life. Side-effects include being assimilated into an insane hive mind."

Howard shook himself. This was a problem to worry about later. Right now he should find Tony and stick with him until he could save the Mayor. Perhaps Gonzalez would be grateful enough for being saved that he would listen to Howard for more than five seconds.

The man speaking wasn't Gonzalez, but he was the Mayor. You could tell by the authority with which he spoke. The words bordered on audacious and Howard suspected that in this Chicago, the job of Mayor didn't rely on anything as fickle as popularity. The Mayor spoke with the confidence of a man without fear of ever losing his job. Perhaps anyone who opposed him met with *immediate termination*. Howard was familiar with nations that operated on that principle. He didn't see how it was possible that a city in the good old US of A could.

But was this the good old US of A? Or was it a completely different USA, with perhaps a little extra old and a little less good, just as Chicago seemed to have?

Cold shivers run down Howard's back, but he cast those fears aside. He had bigger problems.

Whoever this Mayor was, his daughter was not with him and he was no longer speaking regarding what had happened to her, if he had at all, or her recovery. He spoke instead about replacing the Alderman for Armour Square, which made no sense. Armour Square was a community, not a ward. If every community had an Alderman, Chicago would have eighty aldermen instead of fifty, and equal representation would be out the window. As he listened, he deduced that the current Alderman had been killed, though by villains or by the Mayor's Office itself, he couldn't tell. Several men and one woman had thrown their hat in the ring to take the vacant position. It sounded like the Mayor would choose the winner in a few days and wanted to include what the people of Chicago thought as part of his decision-making process. That was the only part of the entire spiel that Howard found reasonable. The onlookers listened with rapt attention.

Despite the weirdness of it all, Howard eventually shut out the speech and focused on seeking out Tony in the crowd, which had grown since he had seen it earlier.

People glowered and gave him dirty looks as he forced his way through the front ranks looking for anyone else who was doing the same. And soon enough he did find someone pushing their way forward, but it wasn't Tony.

The girl, or perhaps she was a young woman, fought her way through taller and heavier bystanders with a fierce determination. Her face would be pretty if it wasn't for the scowl. Howard realized that he recognized her — the girl from the Oz Club who had sung so beautifully before leaving with Tony and the other Crewman.

Howard also realized, through the blood affinity he had

pondered earlier, that Dorothy of Wizard of Oz fame was the threat Tony was looking for.

Almost without thought, Howard made his way toward her, pushing through complaining people with a greater haste than he had felt just moments before. The girl had stopped near the front of the crowd and Howard began feeling desperate. Using his mechanical hips and thighs to push himself past otherwise unyielding onlookers, he grabbed hold of her left arm. Just as Tony grabbed her right.

Her face swung toward Tony's, and Howard heard Dorothy gasp. "Didn't I kill you?" Then she swung toward Howard and gasped again. "Howard?" She looked down at where he clutched her arm. "I'll kill you next."

Wordlessly, Howard and Tony began pulling Dorothy back through an accommodating crowd and toward the service entrance. Dorothy shouted obscenities at them the entire way. Howard couldn't remember ever hearing a fouler mouth.

"I've never killed anyone twice," she shouted at Tony. "I think I'll enjoy it."

Tony responded by twisting her arm behind her back and letting go with his right hand, which he used to search her and retrieve a handgun.

"Thanks for your help, Wiz" he said to Howard. "I can take it from here."

"What are you going to do with her?" Howard asked. He had a feeling he knew.

"Immediate termination," Tony said. "She killed two Crewmen. One of them was me. Step back so that you don't get hurt."

Howard almost let go of Dorothy's arm just because Tony wished it. But he fought the urge. "She's just a girl. A foul-mouthed one, admittedly. But you can't just kill her in cold blood."

In response, Tony hit Dorothy in the jaw with the barrel of his gun. Hard. Dorothy yipped and blood began pouring from a torn lip.

"Why did you do that?" Howard shouted.

"She was about to scream," said Tony.

Howard gave him a blank stare.

"Her scream is... disarming," Tony said. "Last time she screamed, she got my gun and killed Rory Hudson and then me with it."

Howard could see in Tony's face, and perhaps through the affinity between them, that this was true. He let go of the girl's arm and stepped back.

Before he could even register what had happened, Dorothy had a second gun in her hand and shot Tony in the gut.

Howard's own gut felt as if someone had just kicked it. The gun fired again and Howard had a heart attack. Literally. But only for a moment. Then the pain lessened until it merely felt like his chest was in a vice. Somehow, Howard remained standing. Tony, on the other hand, hit the pavement.

"I took Rory's gun too," Dorothy said, laughing at Tony's corpse. "I bet you never considered that."

She glanced over to the front of the building where the gunfire would have been heard by the crowd and the security people protecting the Mayor. Then she looked at Howard. "Looks like I won't have time to kill you slowly, which is something you deserve for making me sleep with you to get that crappy job."

"I didn't—" Howard refuted.

Dorothy gave him no time to speak. "And for helping this prick, who should've been dead already."

"But—" said Howard.

Dorothy glanced again to the front of the building. "Time's up. Say goodbye, Howard."

"I—"

Dorothy aimed the gun at his head and pulled the trigger. The gun went *click*.

"Damn," said Dorothy. "Should have just used one bullet on the prick."

Howard stood watching her as the pain from Tony's

inflictions subsided, wondering if he should wait for the security people from the Mayor's speech to put her down, or if he should throttle her first. Then he wondered how such thoughts could cross his mind; he was not a violent person at heart. And finally, he realized where the thoughts had come from. He smiled at Dorothy.

Dorothy glared at his smile. "No need to get cocky." She reached down and picked up the gun Tony had dropped. "I can still kill you before taking it on the lam." She pointed this gun and fired. *Click.*

The security people were almost on them now. Howard suspected they would shoot her the moment she tried to run.

"It's over," he said.

Dorothy screamed.

Howard put his hands over his ears, but it didn't help. Fortunately, being outside in the open dispersed the sound somewhat; he'd hate to think how it would be in an enclosed space. He forced himself to lower his hands and repeat, "It's over."

She couldn't have heard him over her scream, but she got the idea; the scream wasn't buying her anything. She stopped and shouted, "You're still a goner. I bet the prick picked up another gun before coming after me."

"You'd be right," Tony said. "Just to be sure, I picked up three."

Dorothy spun on her red slippers just in time for Tony Sandoval to shoot her dead center in the forehead.

Howard watched the back of her head explode, spraying him with blood and brains.

"Sorry about that," Tony said as he dropped the gun to the pavement and rose to his feet. The front of his borrowed coat had two bloodstained holes in it from where Dorothy had shot him.

"I've had better days," Howard said.

It was at this point that the security people from the Mayor's speech arrived. The one in charge looked at Dorothy. "This would be the suspect that was called in."

He looked at Tony. "Tony Sandoval. I was sorry to hear about your coma."

"Thanks Freddie," Tony said.

"Seems I have a warrant for your immediate termination. Sorry about that, too."

"No fault of yours," said Tony. "Now that the Mayor is safe, I'm ready."

Freddie nodded, and then turned to face Howard. "Howard Russell. I have a warrant for your immediate termination as well."

Tony cast him a questioning look.

"I can explain," Howard said.

Freddie shook his head, pulled a gun from his holster, and shot Tony through the heart. Then he turned the gun on Howard and fired.

The Ghost of Olivia Olsen

Howard and Tony revived at about the same time. Howard glanced about to collect his bearings and saw that he and Tony were both sitting upright in side-by-side armchairs, solid oak if he was not mistaken, in a large, ornate office. In front of them stood a large desk, also oak, its surface relatively uncluttered. Mounted on the wall behind the desk was a glass case containing, of all things, a baseball bat. Howard could see no description tag on the case or signature on the bat, but the length of well-used wood seemed to sport several dark stains. Behind the desk, filling a wide leather chair and smoking a putrid cigar, was the man who had given the speech.

The stocky, fortyish-looking man placed his palms on the desk, leaned towards them, and spoke around his cigar. "Well now, it appears we have us a case of mitigating circumstances."

While this version of Chicago paralleled his own closely, Howard had never seen this man before. With thin black hair, thick brows, and the bedside manner of a used car salesman, Howard was not impressed.

As much as he disliked Mayor Gonzalez for all sorts of reasons, not the least of which being his complete disregard for his underlings, Howard already knew that he would like this Mayor even less. From the bits of his speech Howard had listened to and the wolfish sneer on his face right now, this Mayor struck him as an arrogant, sell-his-own grandmother for a buck kind of politician who viewed the city of Chicago as his own personal fiefdom where he could do as he pleased and damn anyone who got in his way.

"You should know," the Mayor continued, leaning back and removing the cigar from between thick, pouty lips, "that despite the fact that you are sitting in my office, both of you are officially dead."

"Does this mean that we won't be terminated again?" Tony asked. The officially deceased Crewman's voice was uncomfortably calm.

The Mayor grunted. "What would be the point in that?"

"Then what are we to do?" asked Tony. "Leave town?"

The Mayor's expression changed from domineering to near apoplectic. He actually sputtered before repeating, only more emphatically, "What would be the point in that?"

He stood up suddenly and walked around in front of his desk. "You two are an opportunity. Don't you see?" He lifted up a file folder, but didn't open it. "My scientists tell me that both of you are virtually indestructible. You can be maimed or even killed and come back fighting."

"Indestructible?" Howard blurted.

The Mayor looked at him. "*Virtually*. I suspect that if you get blown to bits that the bits will stay bits." He rubbed his chin. "Though the bits may go on living. That would be interesting to see." He looked at Howard and shrugged. "If the opportunity arises. As things stand, you are more useful to me as a functioning man than as a tank full of living goo."

Howard spent a moment pondering how first

impressions are always correct.

Tony spoke up. "I'm guessing that you have a job for me?"

The Mayor nodded. "For both of you. This is a task of the utmost importance, and one that is particularly suited to Mr. Russell here."

"PhD," Howard added. "I need to speak with you and these scientists you mentioned about what happened to me."

The Mayor glared at him. "I know all about you, Dr. Howard Russell, PhD." He waved the file folder. "Everything is in here. My scientists haven't been idle since you were taken to Wesley Memorial. From the minute you were arrested last night we've been collecting information on you. Most of the questions have been answered, and the few that remain will be solved soon enough. Don't ever mistake myself or my staff as incompetent."

"So," said Howard, "then you intended for that clown in the suit and his gun slinging Crewman to terminate me in the hospital?"

The Mayor frowned and took a puff from his cigar. "Sub-director Johnston no longer works here." Then he brightened. "Not that it would have mattered. Based on the miraculous healing of your smashed hand and broken foot we had already surmised that you would likely survive a more serious wound."

"Like a bullet in the heart?" asked Tony.

"After receiving this man's blood your brain repaired itself in just a few minutes. I felt confident signing your termination orders."

"Right," said Tony. "So what is this utmost important task you have for us?"

The Mayor grinned. "That's what I like about you, Sandoval. Straight to the point. No distractions."

The Mayor placed the folder back on the desk and picked up a different one. From it, he withdrew a glossy photograph of Ms. Olivia Olsen.

"Mrs. Olivia Nelson has been missing since the earthquake. I need you to find her and bring her to me. By midnight at the latest."

Tony looked like he was going to say something, but held his tongue. Howard had no such self-restraint.

"You want us to find your psychic? This is your utmost urgent task that you need virtually indestructible agents for?"

The Mayor glowered at him. "Mr. Russell, I am confident that after you spend a few hours with Mr. Sandoval that you will learn when to keep your thoughts to yourself. Do you know why I am confident?"

Howard said nothing, correctly assuming that no answer was expected.

"Because," continued the Mayor, "if you do not, then I will be encouraged to try that *blown to bits* experiment I mentioned earlier. Do you understand me?"

Howard had never appreciated being threatened and he didn't appreciate it now, but he had no doubt that this man would not blink at pushing the button personally. And now that he had made the threat, he would be obliged to follow through. It was a twisted sense of honor, but it suited this particular Mayor to a tee. How Howard had ever thought this man would help him...

"I understand perfectly," Howard said, "but I do have one problem. I don't work for you. Why would I willingly become your errand boy?"

The Mayor sat on the edge of his desk and clucked his tongue. "I could compel you. In a hundred different ways. But I am a reasonable man. You don't get to be Mayor without doing a lot of horse-trading. Here's the deal. You become my *errand boy*. Permanently. And I will give you your body back."

Howard nearly swallowed his tongue. "And how will you do that?"

"It's really quite simple," the Mayor said. He paused to flick cigar ashes onto the floor. "I have your body sitting on ice at the Wesley Memorial Hospital morgue."

"What was that all about?" Tony asked after he and Howard had left the Mayor's office and were alone in an elevator on its way to the basement.

"Which part?" Howard asked.

"Good question," said Tony.

The Crewman led Howard a short distance down a corridor and palmed a door. Inside were two walls of wardrobe and a third wall of glass cases containing guns, ammunition, listening equipment, and a host of other devices used for surveillance and undercover work.

"Pick some clothes that fit," Tony said. "Do you know how to fire a gun?"

"Um, no," said Howard.

Tony palmed open one the gun cases. "Take one anyway. I suspect Capone will send us on missions that result in people shooting at us. It will go better for us if you can shoot back."

"Capone?" Howard stared at Tony. The term *Capone's Crew* he had been hearing since he had arrived finally made sense. "You call your Mayor, Capone? Like a title of some kind?"

"A title? Don't be ridiculous. It's his name. Mayor Al Capone."

"Al Capone?" Howard echoed. "You're kidding. Is he some kind of relative?"

"Relative?" asked Tony, joining the *repeat back the question* game. "Relative of who?"

Howard pressed his hands against his temples. "The other Al Capone. The famous one."

"Mayor Capone is famous. He's been mayor for ninety years. You don't get more famous than that."

Howard leaned against a bench. "Ninety years? He's not a day over fifty. Start making sense here."

"You really don't know?" asked Tony. "How can anyone live in Chicago and not know?"

"Humor me."

"There's not much to tell," Tony said. "Back in 1930 when everyone was feeling the crappy national economy, Al Capone was a brilliant entrepreneur who got Chicago back on its feet. In 1932 he was elected Mayor and in 1935 he declared Chicago a city state."

"He what?" cried Howard.

"Have you been hiding under a rock? Lots of cities were forced to go independent. New York. Detroit. Cincinnati. The national government was in shambles and those cities that didn't take a stand were caught up in at least one of the civil wars of the Lost Decade."

"Lost Decade?" Howard asked.

"1935-1945," Tony said wearily. "World War Two forced the country to stop fighting internally and join together to face an outside enemy, but there was never a good reason for the city states to rejoin the union. So are you finished pulling my leg now? Every school kid knows this stuff."

Howard took a deep breath. "Before my head explodes, just one more question. You still haven't told me how Al Capone hasn't aged in ninety years."

"Right," said Tony. "The Feds in Washington sent a crew to take Capone down. Called themselves the Untouchables. Anyway, The Untouchables had Capone holed up in the Lexington Hotel and eventually twigged to the fact that he was using the freight tunnels to come and go. So they followed him down there and ended up in some kind of underground shootout. Long story short, Capone surfaced victorious while the Untouchables were never seen again. But something weird happened. It was two full days before Capone resurfaced, even with his entire crew searching for him, and he had suffered a blow to the head. He had trouble remembering some things and he seemed to know other things that some people thought he shouldn't."

"I'm not surprised," Howard said. "But do go on."

Tony squinted at him. "Anyway, Capone's victory over the Untouchables, as well as some revolutionary ideas he had, fast-tracked him to the Mayor's office where he was re-elected time and time again. And as the years went by, people noticed that he wasn't getting any older."

Howard held up one hand. "Ageless since his two day disappearance after fighting the Untouchables in the freight tunnels."

"Looks that way," said Tony. "Sounds like you know something about it."

"Theories. I'll need more information."

"Don't ask the Mayor for it," Tony said. "He doesn't talk about those days. Doesn't appreciate people pointing out that he's almost 150 years old either. Safest to speak with the Mayor as little as possible, if you know what I mean. He's quick to anger and keeps what he knows close to his vest anyway. Now, why don't you tell me what the Mayor meant by holding your body in the morgue?"

"It's not technically my body," Howard said, unbuttoning the white technician's shirt he had borrowed from the hospital. It belongs to the Wizard of Oz. I, uh, killed him last night."

"But I thought you were the Wiz. You look like him."

"It's hard to explain," said Howard. "No, I can't explain it. The man I killed is me. We are both Howard Russell."

"Right," said Tony. "Let's skip that for now. Next question. Why would you want your other you's body?"

In answer, Howard dropped his pants.

Howard was impressed that Tony had merely turned green in the face, rather than throw up. The more time he spent with the officially dead Capone's Crewman, the more he liked him. Being made his partner in — What? Crime prevention? — wasn't the worst thing that could have happened after Al Capone — *the Al Capone* — had ordered them both shot. Howard only hoped that he could contribute something to the partnership.

But for now, Howard wasn't looking that far ahead.

Capone had promised that if they found Ms. Olivia Olsen, or Mrs. Olivia Nelson, before midnight, that he would have an operation tomorrow to replace his borrowed arm and lower body with corresponding parts from the corpse of the Wizard of Oz.

He would still have a mishmash of internal organs, but Howard felt he could live with that. The important thing was that he feel, and look, like a normal person again.

"Where to, boss?" Tony asked, the first words he had spoken since they left City Hall in a Capone's Crew ghost car, the same vintage Chevrolet Bel Air Howard had seen last night. The last time he had sat in one of these was in an antique road show. Apparently, in Al Capone's Chicago, they were state of the art. As were the dark grey, three-piece mohair suit, repp tie, polished black shoes, and yellow fedora he had picked out to compliment the Browning 9 mm he now carried in a paddle holster slipped into the left side of his pants.

"Hey," said Howard. "I'm the junior partner in this outfit, even if I am a decade older than you. I've had exactly zero hours of training for this job. Got some electrons you want to collide? Or a building to demolish? I'm your man. Anything else, I follow your lead."

"Fair enough," said Tony. He paused. "The Mayor said you were particularly suited to this assignment. Why?"

Howard grimaced. "Ms. Olsen — I mean, Mrs. Nelson, and I have the same shoe size."

"Wha? — Oh. Any suggestions on where to start?"

"None," said Howard.

"Then we talk to the husband."

The drive through Chicago was uneventful. No one shot at them. Al Capone may be a bastard of a Mayor, but his city felt no less safe or clean than Chicago back home. Though of course back home, Howard hadn't had to carry a gun. He shifted the holster that was digging into his side.

Signs proclaiming candidates for Alderman of Armour Square were everywhere, with more being put up as Howard watched. It was becoming an eyesore.

"Why the big interest in ward elections?" Howard asked. "It's not as if any of these people can vote. From what I gathered from Capone's speech, not even the people of Armour Square will get to vote."

Tony glanced at him, and then returned his attention to the road. "You really must be from another universe. If the Mayor loses the confidence of the people, it won't matter how big his crew is. His kingdom will crumble. Listening to the people is the best thing he can do to ensure their support."

"So," said Howard, "Capone will install whomever the population prefers?"

Tony snorted. "Of course not. He'll put in whomever he pleases. But the people will know they've been heard, and many will agree with his choice."

Howard shrugged and continued looking out the window. He had a lot to learn in this new reality. He *had* refrained from asking Tony about the bloodstained seat and the bullet hole in the dash of his car, so perhaps he had already begun to learn prudence.

After a while, Howard lost too many familiar landmarks to know where exactly in Chicago they were. The houses had gotten ritzier and the yards larger, with giant, leafless trees that he imagined would look spectacular in summer. The cars parked in driveways resembled yachts: Cadillacs, Oldsmobiles, and a dozen big-as-a-boat cars he couldn't identify. There were even some real yachts, sitting on trailers that could be pulled to one of the many lakes and rivers in the area. These were homes whose residents could afford to be patrons of places such as the Oz Club.

Tony stopped the car in front of what some people, including Howard, would call a mansion.

"Are you sure this is the right place?" Howard asked. "The Olivia I met seemed pretty tight with a dollar, if you know what I mean."

Tony looked at him. "Olivia Nelson is the personal psychic to Chicago's rich and famous. She charges more by the hour than I make in a week. Capone alone must pay her a fortune just to be on his speed dial."

Howard harrumphed. "My Olivia was a con artist who got paid for telling people what they wanted to hear. I doubt she could predict what she'd have for breakfast five minutes before she ordered it."

Tony continued to look at him. "Doesn't sound like much of a psychic."

"Exactly," said Howard.

The door was answered by a distinguished gentleman of indeterminate middle age who Howard assumed was a butler. Tony flashed him his Capone Crew card. As they were escorted inside, Howard made mental note to ask for one. If he was going to work for Capone, he'd need to be able to wield some clout.

The butler brought them to a splendidly appointed sitting room, and then surprised Howard when he sat with them and asked, "Any news?"

"I am afraid not," Tony said. "The Mayor has pulled additional staff from other areas to assist with the search."

The man barked a laugh. "What you're saying is that, now that his daughter has resurfaced, he can finally start looking for my wife."

"The reappearance of Ms. Capone did free up additional resources. Mr. Nelson, what can you tell us of how Olivia went missing?"

"I've already told this to the police." Olivia's husband failed to hide a frown.

"And now you can tell it to us. We may hear something important that the other officers missed."

Mr. Nelson let out a deep sigh. Howard couldn't tell if it was heartfelt or feigned for effect.

"It feels like forever now, but was only thirty hours ago," said Mr. Nelson. "Yesterday morning Olivia woke with a premonition of impending disaster. She knew an earthquake was coming. She called the Mayor and told him, and especially mentioned that the South Loop district could be in trouble."

Howard had heard people mention an earthquake non-stop since he had left the Vortex, but this was the first time his thoughts were clear enough for the implications to set in. "There was an earthquake?"

Mr. Nelson cast him a look of utter bewilderment. "What did you do? Sleep though it?"

"Please continue," Tony said, and then passed Howard a *shut up and stay shut up* glare.

"Anyway, after hanging up the phone, Olivia said that the Mayor wasn't going to listen. *What should we do?* I asked her. She just said to *batten down the hatches.* We spent the morning wrapping up breakables and putting them into drawers or boxes. And then the earthquake struck at midday.

"After the shockwaves were over, Olivia got on the phone to call clients and friends, most of whom she had warned earlier, to ask how they had fared. The phone system was a mess so this was taking a while.

"I went into the kitchen to cook us an early supper, and when I came back out Olivia was gone."

"Could she have left on her own?" Tony asked. "Perhaps someone she called needed her help."

"Not a chance," said Nelson. "She wouldn't have left without telling me. Also, the phone was lying on the floor and some furniture had been disturbed."

Ignoring Tony's admonition to keep quiet, Howard said, "It's kind of gutsy to kidnap a psychic. She may have foreseen they were coming."

This time both Tony *and* Mr. Nelson glared at him.

"It doesn't work that way," Mr. Nelson said with the air of someone who had explained this more than once. "Olivia is attuned to the world to a degree greater than most of us. She gets feelings. Take the earthquake. Olivia sensed that something would happen that day. She didn't know what. She just felt that something would happen."

"Like animals seem able to sense an earthquake shortly before it happens," said Tony.

Mr. Nelson nodded.

"But," said Howard, "Olivia predicted that something

would happen hours before the earthquake struck. You said that she also mentioned the South Loop in particular."

Nelson raised his chin. "Olivia is more attuned than any mere animal. She is the greatest psychic of our time." Then he added, "But you are right about the South Loop. That amount of detail is unusual." He looked at Tony. "Did anyplace in that district suffer any particular or unusual damage?"

"Not that I'm aware of," Tony said.

"The Lexington Hotel is in the South Loop," Howard said.

Nelson nodded. "Did something happen to the hotel?"

"No," said Tony, who then brought the discussion back to Olivia's disappearance. "Is it possible that your wife felt she was in danger prior to her kidnapping?"

Mr. Nelson seemed to think about that. "It's possible. If she felt it before the quake, it would have been masked by the pending quake itself. If she felt it, or still felt it, after the quake, that could be why she was so adamant about phoning her friends. Since we came through unscathed, she may have interpreted that feeling as one of them being injured."

"There has been no ransom call?" Tony asked.

Nelson shook his head.

Howard sensed that Tony had run out of questions and that they hadn't learned anything that would give them avenues to pursue. Their search had hit a dead end.

Then the front door slammed and an older woman came running into the sitting room shouting, "Olivia! Olivia's back!"

The woman's face faded from one of ecstatic exuberance to one of sheerest confusion as she noted each person in the sitting room and then looked about in search of anyone she had missed.

"I—I—I was certain," she said. "My premonition said that Olivia had returned home."

"Mr. Sandoval, Mr. Russell, meet Ontalia Olsen,

Olivia's mother. I'm sorry Ontalia, but these Crewmen have no new information."

"But Olivia is here! She has to be." The older woman continued to gaze about the room, and then, slowly, her gaze settled on Howard and her lips and forehead pinched with exasperation.

Feeling uncomfortable beneath the woman's stare, Howard said, "I take it that you, like your daughter, are a psychic?"

Ontalia Olsen let out a heavy sigh and then dropped her lean frame into a hard-backed chair.

"I have some skill in the art. Nothing like Olivia's."

Tony spoke up. "And yet you felt certain of your premonition." He glanced quickly at Howard. "Have you had any other premonitions?"

The older woman laughed. "Usually my premonitions raise more questions than answers, and haven't been much use. Olivia now, Olivia gets stronger thoughts, more certainty, more... feeling. She predicted that earthquake. I felt nothing about it coming."

"Anything you may have felt or sensed could be helpful," Tony said.

"Like what I'm feeling right now, that Olivia is in this room? A lot of help that is."

"Please, Mrs. Olsen," Tony said. "Anything at all."

"Well," said the older woman. "I feel strongly that Olivia is still alive, if that is any help. If she were dead, I would know."

She looked at Tony's face, then Howard's, and then Mr. Nelson's. "If there was more, I would tell you. If only I had Olivia's skill, just for a moment."

It was odd saying goodbye to Olivia's family. In the few hours Howard had worked with her, the con artist Olivia rather than the real thing, he could never have imaged a husband or even a mother loving her as much as Mr.

Nelson and Ontalia Olsen appeared to.

Of course, Howard had been ill-disposed towards her from the beginning; the Olivia he knew had nothing to contribute to Geraldo's TV special. This one however, a real psychic as Olivia Nelson appeared to be, may have been useful. For one, she had warned against an earthquake. If Capone had actually listened to her, fewer people may have been hurt. Which raised the question, why hadn't he listened to her? Or perhaps he had. The mass hysteria resulting from making such a warning public would have probably caused more damage than simply keeping quiet. Or perhaps, being forewarned, Capone had simply played up being the lone calm voice in the aftermath. Yeah, self-serving is exactly how the Mayor would have played it.

"Done daydreaming?" Tony asked.

Howard came out of his thoughts and found himself standing beside the passenger door of the Bel Air. Tony stood beside the open driver's door.

"It's just hard to get used to the idea that Olivia is a real psychic. The one I met was a fraud. I didn't even know there were real psychics."

Tony laughed. "Welcome to Chicago. The psychic capitol of the world. And even here, most psychics are pretenders."

Then his face turned serious. "We should continue this discussion in the car."

Once they were inside, Tony said, "Did you hear anything in the house that can help us?"

Howard shook his head. "Only that we're looking for a living person and not a corpse. How about you?"

Tony grinned. "Oh yes. I think we've found the key that will allow us to deliver Olivia to the Mayor."

Howard stared at Tony Sandoval, wondering what the Crewman had heard that he had not. Apparently, years of police work did improve one's detection skills.

"Okay," Howard said, "impress me."

"You heard Ontalia Olsen. Olivia was in the room with

us."

"What? She's hiding in the house?"

"No," said Tony. "Olivia is hiding in you."

"Huh?"

"Your DNA," said Tony. "You told me yourself that you have Olivia's shoe size. You have more than that. You have her feet, her calves, and most important, her DNA."

"I don't see where you are going with this."

"Olivia is a psychic. You have Olivia's DNA. You are also a psychic."

"That," said Howard, "is a pretty big stretch. Besides, my Olivia was a fake psychic."

Tony shook his head. "It's less of a stretch than you think. You said that when the hospital tested your blood they found Olivia Nelson's DNA, psychic Olivia's DNA."

"Yes, but—"

"Olivia's mother is a psychic. That means that the talent is passed down. DNA."

"I'm no doctor," said Howard, "but—"

"You are not a doctor," Tony said. "But you are a psychic, and for no better reason than that if you are not a psychic, then we have no clues. None. Which is the same as our chances of finding Olivia and you getting your surgery tomorrow."

Silence filled the car.

"Look," said Howard. "That is the most stupid argument I've ever heard."

"Then you don't get out much," said Tony. "I've heard far stupider arguments. But you have to admit that there is a chance, however small, that whatever happened to you to give you part of Olivia's body could also have given you her psychic ability."

Howard said nothing because Tony was right. Both of them were living, breathing impossibilities. Acquiring Olivia's psychic ability was no more impossible, so why not?

"You can at least give it a try," Tony said.

"Try?" Howard echoed. "I don't know how to try. From

what we heard in the house, it just kind of happens."

"Maybe it already has," said Tony. "What do *you* feel happened to Olivia?"

Howard didn't think he felt anything, but then again, he had never stopped to ask himself. He closed his eyes, leaned back against the seat of the car, and focused on Olivia.

Immediately, he saw in his mind what he had seen when he had first woken up in Al Capone's bunker – destruction everywhere and Dr. Samuels' detached hand. The droid telling him that the rest of Geraldo's crew, presumably including Olivia Olsen, was in the bunker, dead.

Howard mentally wiped that image away and tried again.

Once again he had awoken, only this time the C-droid was saying that none of Geraldo's crew were in the bunker when the destruction happened. Both of those events couldn't be right. And the droid had no knowledge of the first time Howard had awoken. Alternate possibilities?

Trying again, Howard saw the third time he had woken in the bunker. Olivia's feet and calves were attached to metal knees and the Dr. Frankenstein droid was doing things that droids shouldn't be able to do, such as lie and guess and build a living man out of spare parts. Howard's existence was an impossibility, but for the first time he considered that the same was true about the droid. The Vortex, or the universe, or perhaps it was the mass of Rhodium-105, whatever was responding to a collision of realities, had reached out and changed the laws of physics, possibly repeatedly, and the end result was two beings that should not be able to exist.

The droid had stayed in the bunker, where Howard assumed it would continue to change whenever additional realities decided to collide. Perhaps that had happened already and Howard wouldn't even recognize the droid if he returned.

Howard had left the bunker, and now roamed an

alternate city of Chicago where his very existence defied the laws of physics. He had a dark feeling that there would be a reckoning at some point. Was that a psychic prediction?

The Mayor — Al Capone, no less — had pompously waved Howard's file and claimed that he knew everything there was to know about Howard Russell. A claim he might make if Capone himself had survived a collision of realities while inside the bunker. And what further explanation did Howard need to look for to explain the mob boss's longevity. Al Capone was no less adjusted than Howard himself was. But were they the same adjustments? Was Al Capone also virtually indestructible? Was Howard also a man who had ceased to age?

But that was something to consider later. For now, he had a job to do, and none of these recollections were helping him find Olivia Nelson. He strongly suspected they were merely the result of his own thinking, and nothing to do with any supposed psychic ability.

He was about to give up and say as much to Tony, when an image of the election signs they had passed on the way to the house flashed through his thoughts, and what had happened to Olivia became obvious.

"Tony," he said, "I've just had my first psychic premonition."

Psychics and Politics

Tony Sandoval knocked on the door of the house and it swung open instantly to reveal Mr. Nelson and Ontalia Olsen.

"We noticed that you hadn't driven away," said Mr. Nelson.

"I had a feeling you'd be back," Ontalia added.

"I have one more question," Tony said. "This election in Armour Square. Which candidate does Olivia support?"

Mr. Nelson frowned. "Alderman Caruso was murdered

after Olivia went missing. Is this important?"

Before Tony could speak, Olivia's mother said, "Yes, it is! I can feel it."

"I think," said Mr. Nelson, "that I can safely say that Olivia would favor Peggy McArthur."

"Yes," agreed Ontalia. "Peggy McArthur as the new Alderman would bring some much needed stability to Mayor Capone's crew bosses."

"And," said Tony, "Peggy McArthur's only serious challenger is Caruso's right hand man, Lenny Alfonso. Correct?"

"So says the scuttlebutt," agreed Mr. Nelson.

"Lenny Alfonso has some shady history," said Ontalia. "Cutting deals behind Caruso's back. Some extortion on the side. Setting up his own personal crew. His supporters claim that, if true, this will help him in office."

"But you don't believe this?" asked Tony.

"No," said Ontalia. "It just means that Alfonso will pull the same crap on Capone. And when Capone takes *him* out, it will be messier than Caruso's removal."

Sandoval cocked an eye at the older woman.

Ontalia held firm. "Look sonny, I don't care how your boss gets his job done. But I'm not going to speak *politically correct* if it might impede you doing *your* job."

"That's all I need to know," Tony said. "Thank you for your time. I'll keep you apprised of any developments."

Tony climbed into the car and nodded at Howard, "You were right. Alfonso's campaign benefits from Olivia's disappearance. But if Alfonso took her, that has more serious implications."

"Such as?" Howard asked.

Tony shook his head. "First, he must have foreknowledge of Caruso's murder. Either Alfonso set Caruso up or he has a spy in City Hall. And second, since Alfonso didn't kill Olivia outright, he must want her for something."

"I can keep this up all night," said the man wearing the Mayor Capone rubber mask.

"Like you did all last night?" whispered Olivia. She stood with her hands bound above her head and tied to a pipe attached to the ceiling. Her feet touched the floor just enough to shift her weight between her wrists and her toes.

"And like we did all day," said the other man. He also wore a Capone mask, but Olivia had long since sorted out who was who based on their voices and body language. The first man she thought of as *Capone*, the second as *the Mayor*.

Olivia sighed. "I told you, I can't help you. My ability doesn't work that way."

Capone dipped the leather flail into the bucket of water. "Can you predict where I will whip you next?"

"I told you," whispered Olivia. "My ability doesn't work that way."

The whip came at her, striking across her stomach and leaving furrows of ripped cloth and raw flesh behind. Olivia gritted her teeth and numbed herself to the pain.

She had tried everything she could think of to end or delay the torture, but soon learned that these men enjoyed their work too much. She had tried the silent treatment, refusing to cooperate, pretending to cooperate, even feigning unconsciousness. Currently she was trying honesty. Nothing worked. They would whip her to unconsciousness, throw water in her face to revive her, and then whip her again.

Every nerve ending in Olivia's body vibrated with agony. At first, each touch of the whip had felt like knives slicing through her flesh. Eventually, her whole body felt as if it was on fire. Now, she almost welcomed the whip. Its touch let her know she was still alive.

"If you can't help us," said the Mayor, "then we may have to end this fun. Putting you out of action achieves half our goal."

"I thought you wanted to know who the Mayor will choose as his new Alderman?" Olivia said.

The whip came again, this time striking her across the knees.

"The next Alderman of Armour Square," said Capone, "will be of our choosing. It would just please us to hear a little confirmation from you."

Maybe I should just give them a name, Olivia thought. I could even give them the right name. But then they would just kill me.

The door opened and two more Capones entered dragging a struggling woman between them.

"Olivia Nelson," said one of the new Capones. "We'd like you to meet Ms. Kimberly Charron." He chuckled through his mask. "I bet you didn't see this coming."

The two of them tied the young woman to the ceiling about ten feet in front of Olivia so that they were facing each other.

"You can't do this!" shouted Kimberly. "I have rights. My family will sue."

"If you don't care about your own safety," one of the new Capones said to Olivia, "perhaps you'll be more concerned for someone else's."

Kimberly kicked and shrieked from where she hung from the ceiling, just as Olivia had done when she first arrived.

Olivia knew there was nothing she could do or say to help this woman. Speaking a name, any name, would just get them both killed. She shook her head. "I told you. My ability doesn't work that way. Hurting her won't make any difference."

The new Capone dipped a flail into the water bucket and thrashed it across Kimberly's face. Kimberly shrieked louder than she had earlier.

"We'll be less careful with this one," said the Capone. If she doesn't last until you tell us what we want to know, we can always get another."

He whipped her again. Then the other three Capones joined in, four wet flails thrashing at Kimberly from all sides. The woman screamed and moaned as the flails shredded her clothing and tore her skin.

Olivia closed her eyes. She could tell them. With her attention so brutally focused on the appointment during the last twenty-four hours of torture, she had received a solid premonition of who *should* be appointed as well as who *would* be appointed, if the future remained on course. But she also had a third, even stronger premonition that she would escape from her captors. Not rescued; she would save herself. That couldn't happen if she was dead. And within minutes of giving them what they wanted, both she and this other woman would be dead. Rubber masks or no rubber masks, they had no intention of letting anyone leave this room alive. Olivia had been waiting for an opportunity to escape. It hadn't come yet, but it would.

The whipping stopped and Olivia opened her eyes. It was looking into a mirror.

Kimberly Charron hung from the ceiling like a side of flayed beef, her ravaged flesh so bloody Olivia couldn't tell torn clothing from torn skin. She could see that Kimberly was still breathing, but had lost the energy to scream.

Just like me, Olivia told herself. Human beings reduced to hamburger. If she'd had any food or water in her stomach, she would have thrown up.

One of the Capones, she couldn't tell which now that there were four of them, came and stood in front of Olivia. "Tell us what we want to know and we'll call EMS and leave."

That was a lie.

"Don't tell us, and we'll finish this one off and go find another. Perhaps this time we'll pick someone you know."

That was not a lie. Olivia closed her eyes and said nothing. Escape. I'm going to escape. I know this as much as I know anything.

Somehow, Kimberly found the energy to scream as the Capones resumed their business.

Howard sat in the passenger seat of the Bel Air watching election signs fly past as Tony drove through the streets of Chicago. Most of the signs displayed just a candidate's name, though some included a grinning head shot. Several neon building signs had also been appropriated and showed blue or yellow candidate caricatures smiling and waving.

"We can't just drive over to Alfonso's office and accuse him of kidnapping," Tony said. "As interim Alderman he can make things difficult in Armour Square, even for Capone Crewmen. As defacto Alderman, he could make things more than difficult. And if Alfonso is guilty, chances are we won't walk out his office alive."

Howard looked at him.

"Not immediately, anyway."

"If I was going to kidnap someone," said Howard, "I wouldn't take them to my office. And if anyone came to ask me about it, my office, my home, my car — you get the idea — these would be the last places they would find any evidence."

Tony nodded. "Alfonso has a hidey-hole off the radar. But where?"

"I used to work at City Hall," Howard said. "Records of property ownership were pretty thorough."

"They are here as well," said Tony. He paused. "Thorough doesn't always mean simple."

"Still worth checking, though."

They pulled to the side of the busy street and Howard watched the sun set over the city skyline while Tony chatted with somebody downtown over his flip phone. Howard had scarcely been on the job two hours and already he was amazed at how much police work consisted of driving, waiting and speaking on a phone.

It killed Howard to see a sunset so similar to those he had watched all his life. The colors, the shadows, the feel of the day winding down and night moving in, were indistinguishable from any he had experienced in the past. Yet this was a whole new world. Antique cars driving past fifty-story skyscrapers. Cell phones tucked into felt pockets. Howard had yet to see a single personal computer, and was afraid to even ask about it. Building signs were all print board or neon. No digital displays. Al Capone was the freaking mayor. And Howard Russell carried a gun holstered to his waist. Howard felt lost and didn't know how he would adjust to any of it.

Tony hung up his phone and tucked it into his coat pocket. "Nothing unusual tied to Alfonso. We're looking for a needle in a haystack."

"Where would you hide a kidnap victim?" Howard asked.

"Somewhere quiet," Tony said. "With as few people around as possible. An acreage. Outside the city if I could get past border security. Armour Square is nowhere near the border. Doesn't mean Alfonso doesn't have connections."

Howard nodded. "You're thinking like a cop. Try thinking like a politician. Alfonso's working his way to the top. He'd want someplace he could access while maintaining a tight schedule, but with deniability should he be found out."

Tony looked at him. "So it has to be outside Armour Square. But close enough to access without drawing attention to himself. And ownership can't be traced back to him."

"How about something in the South Loop?" Howard said. "Olivia's earthquake prediction specified that district for no apparent reason. Perhaps that was a different prediction entirely."

"Something that overlapped the earthquake? Like Olivia getting herself kidnapped in the aftermath? You mentioned the Lexington Hotel when Ontalia told us about South Loop."

"I did," said Howard. "But I was thinking about the freight tunnels beneath the Lexington. And the context I had in mind was the earthquake."

"Oh," said Tony, disappointed.

"Doesn't mean I was right," said Howard. "Are the freight tunnels used much these days?"

"No reason to," said Tony. "The Mayor keeps some of the lights on and has a few Crewmen keep watch. Mostly near the Lexington, now that I think about it. I always figured the Mayor kept on eye on the tunnels so that his aldermen wouldn't get any bright ideas about doing business behind his back."

"Such as the deal-cutting Alfonso is suspected of?"

Tony shook his head. "No. Too dangerous. If Alfonso is using the tunnels, he'll get caught. Get spotted down there and there's no place to hide. Capone learned that the hard way when the Untouchables found him in the tunnels. Since then, Capone's been the one doing the spotting. Alfonso would be a fool to be on the other side of that equation.

"I still get the feeling that we're looking in the right place. Where in the South Loop could Alfonso go without attracting a second look?"

Tony laughed. "Any one of a hundred bars, restaurants, or brothels. And a dozen other more-or-less public places."

"And which of those could hide a kidnap victim with zero risk?"

Tony stopped laughing. "We'd want to start with the brothels."

"Who owns the brothels?"

"All sorts of people. Nothing illegal about owning a brothel." Tony frowned.

"What?" Howard asked.

"Last night we were at the Oz Club."

"A brothel in the South Loop," Howard agreed.

"A high-end brothel," amended Tony. "City officials wouldn't be caught dead in a low-class house." He paused. "And Rory said something. He said that no one knew who owned your club."

"Let me guess," said Howard. "You've got a feeling?"

Tony nodded.

"Me too'" said Howard. "Looks like we're both psychics. By the way, it was never *my* club."

The sky darkened as they sped across town. Howard gazed at the passing city lights and wondered at the easy transition he had made from ex-physicist to detective. It was all about discovery wasn't it? Looking for clues, drawing conclusions, solving mysteries.

He felt the gun holster dig into his side again and remembered that scientists rarely got shot at. Howard had been shot at four times today. One had missed. The next two, the guns had been out of bullets. The forth had taken him in the heart. And that was before Capone made him into a cop. Now they were about to face kidnappers. No doubt bullets would fly again. Maybe the transition wasn't so easy.

"Looks closed," Tony said as he pulled the Bel Air into the empty Oz Club parking lot.

Howard peered through the windshield at the Beachwood Bed and Breakfast or, in this version of Chicago, the Oz Club. "I understand the MC was murdered last night. They probably haven't found a replacement yet."

Tony ignored the sarcasm. "I don't think they'd let a little thing like a murdered MC stop them from staying open. The prestige of a recent murder would bring running the kind of customers who frequent this place."

They got out of the car and walked toward the building entrance.

Howard felt uneasy and decided it was from the sight of the darkened Oz Club sign. There was something desolate about a dead neon sign. He saw that Tony also looked nervous, his eyes darting across the windows of buildings along the empty street. Howard glanced at the bakery that was an entrance to the freight tunnels and Capone's bunker. It, too, was closed, though doubtless one or more Crewmen kept watch inside.

Howard pulled his handgun out of his holster and shoved it into a coat pocket. The fingers of his hand found and unlatched the safety. Better unsafe than sorry.

As expected, the entrance door failed to open when they approached.

"Are we going to have to break in?" Howard asked.

Tony pulled out his Capone Crew card and pressed it against the palm reader. The entrance slid open. "It's breaking in when civilians do it. When we do it, it's called *doing our job.*"

"I guess this means they know we are here," Howard said as he followed Tony into a darkened vestibule where last evening a dwarf dressed as a Munchkin had mistaken him for the MC.

Tony didn't slow his pace, but continued walking into the short corridor that led to the main room. In the faint light that seeped out from the interior of the building, Howard could see that Tony now held his gun out ahead of him. Grudgingly, Howard did the same.

The large room was empty. No monkeys flying among the rafters. No witches offering their charms for money. No obscenely rich residents of Chicago looking for thrills and chills. No dancing dogs or singing strippers on the small stage. The bar, too, was dark and silent. Then Howard corrected himself. Not quite empty. There at a table near the center of the room, three figures sat playing cards in the near darkness. One of them stood as Tony and Howard entered, the sight of two guns trained on him of no seeming consequence.

"We are closed," said the scarecrow. "I haven't got a brain, and even I know that."

"We're Capone's Crew." Tony flashed his ID card. Howard assumed that the droid bartenders could see the card across the room just as they could see the playing cards on the table in the low light.

"We're still closed. No food. No drink. No

entertainment. No reason to be here."

The other two droids now stood. Howard had the unmistakable feeling that Oz's bartenders were also Oz's bouncers.

"Our reason to be here," Tony said, "is Crew business."

The Cowardly Lion raised his fists like a boxer. "Your guns and your ID cards don't scare me. Put 'em up. Put 'em up."

Howard felt the time had come to be useful. He lowered his gun and took a step forward. "It's okay boys. The narc is with me."

The Lion stared at Howard and then slowly lowered his fists. "It's the Wizard."

"The Wizard's dead," said the Tin Man.

"I saw it," said the Scarecrow. "The Wizard killed him."

"Nonsense," said Howard. "I'm right here. What you saw was part of the show."

The three droids made no sound or movement as they processed this. Finally, the Lion said. "The customers did seem entertained."

"Bar sales went up twelve per cent," added the Tin Man.

"Patronage went up eight percent," said the Scarecrow. "Until we closed."

"Why did you close?" Tony asked, also lowering his gun.

The three droids looked at each other, and then spoke in unison. "Special event in the basement."

"Technically," said the Lion, "the special event started before we closed."

The Scarecrow added, "They saw the murder last night as an opportunity to shut down until they were done."

"Made no sense to me," said the Tin Man. "Business is business."

"Where's the ba—" Tony began.

Howard waved. "It's over there." He turned back to the droids. "Please resume... whatever it is you were doing. We'll go see if this *special event* needs me."

The droids took their seats, picked up their cards, and

the Scarecrow threw down one card and said, "Hit me."

Howard watched, almost expecting one of the other droids to literally hit him, Three Stooges style, but the Tin Man merely tossed the Scarecrow the top card off the deck.

As they walked toward where Howard remembered the stairs to the basement being when he had stayed at the Beachwood Bed & Breakfast two nights ago, he whispered to Tony. "Are droids supposed to—?"

"No," said Tony. "Droids are like toasters. They should be sitting idle when not in use."

"That's what I thought. I've got a feeling there's trouble brewing."

"A psychic feeling?" Tony said. "Me too."

The whipping stopped and this time Olivia knew that Kimberly Charron was dead. In a way, Olivia envied her. She knew exactly the pain the woman had endured and knew as well that for her, it was over. It was not over for herself. She watched silently as the four Capones caught their breath. In her imagination, she could see the cruel smiles beneath their masks. They enjoyed their game.

"Time to go shopping," one of them said. It was one of the more recent voices. One of the pair who had brought that poor stranger. "Who shall our next guest be? One of our friend's cherished customers? Her husband, perhaps?"

Olivia made every effort not to react to the man's words. The supreme poker face. If she reacted, she would be choosing their next victim. She refused to do that.

"Too bad she has no children," suggested one of the others. "How about her mother?"

Olivia continued to take slow, shallow breaths. In her mind she was counting, blocking out the voices.

Nine. Ten. Eleven.

"I know. We'll make it a surprise." And suddenly two of the Capones were leaving.

Twelve. Thirteen. Fourteen.

The remaining villains, Capone and The Mayor, dipped their whips into the bucket of water. "Recess is over. Before we begin, perhaps you'd care to mention who you feel the Mayor will appoint?"

Olivia said nothing. I'm going to free myself. It's only a matter of time.

Fifteen. Sixteen. Seventeen.

She grunted when wet leather struck her. To help distract herself from the pain she kept her eyes focused on the dangling corpse of Kimberly Charron.

Eighteen. Nineteen. Twenty.

Then the whipping stopped.

"What was that?" said the Mayor.

"Maybe the others forgot something," suggested Capone.

"Sounded like gunfire," the Mayor said.

Olivia looked past Kimberly's body to the stairs door, which burst open revealing two armed men not wearing rubber masks.

"No," she croaked. "This isn't right. They can't rescue me."

Olivia knew. She knew, like she knew the sun rises in the morning, that she would rescue herself. These clowns couldn't rescue her. Then she felt a cold pinch in her lower back followed by a jarring pain. If she thought the wet whips caused pain she was fooling herself. This pain caused her lungs to stop breathing. The pain grew in an arc across her lower left side and she assumed it was a knife.

"Sorry the party's been cut short," the Mayor whispered in her ear.

From the stairwell someone shouted, "Freeze! Capone's Crew!"

Olivia's head began spinning, but through the pain she heard movement to her right and then a gunshot. A body tumbled to the floor in front of her and she assumed it was Capone because the Mayor was still behind her, whispering something in her ear.

"We'd rather take you alive," said the voice from the stairwell. "But we don't mind doing the paperwork if you end up like your friends."

The Mayor ceased whispering and raised his voice. "If you don't kill me, my employer will."

"And who would that be?" demanded the Crewman.

Olivia felt a new stab of pain, higher up, where she assumed her heart was. As darkness took her, she was sure she heard another gunshot. Her last thought was a question. Was the gunshot the Mayor shooting her in the heart through her back? Or had he used his knife again, and the shot was one of the cops shooting the Mayor, albeit too late?

"Damn," said Tony. "I didn't expect a Hamlet ending."

"Hamlet?" Howard couldn't take his eyes off the two whip-ravaged women hanging from the ceiling.

Tony sighed. "Where everybody dies."

"*We* didn't die," said Howard. "None of them even got a shot off."

"They aren't shootists," said Tony. "I doubt they're even kidnappers. They're torturers."

"Chicago has professional torturers?"

Tony grunted in response, and then pulled the mask off the third man he had shot. Like the two on the stairs, he didn't recognize him. He peeled the mask off the fourth with the same result.

"When Chicago CSI identifies these men we'll learn they are known criminals. Probably thugs for hire."

Howard couldn't help but chuckle. "Al Capone is going to flip when he hears the bad guys wore his face."

"He's going to flip even more when we come back with Olivia Nelson's corpse. I'm pretty sure he wanted a living psychic, not a dead one."

Howard flicked his gaze at the two whip-ravaged

women, a sight he had been studiously avoiding. Never in his life had he even imagined anything so gruesome; he was glad the four men responsible were dead. With effort, he looked again at the one Tony had indicated was Olivia. He wasn't going to examine them closely enough to determine who was who. "Maybe we can fix that."

"She's already dead," said Tony.

"You don't know until you try," Howard said.

Mechanically, he picked up the bloody knife from the floor and began sawing on the rope that secured Olivia's wrists to the ceiling. Tony helped catch her body when the weakened rope snapped.

Tony grunted. "She weighs a ton."

"Scientific fact that dead people weigh more than live ones," Howard said. He knew he was babbling to distract himself from what they were doing. At this point, their piss yellow trench coats were covered with Olivia's blood.

"What about the other one?" Tony pointed at the unknown dead woman with his chin.

"We can't save everyone," Howard said. "If this works, we'll have two Olivias in our head instead of one. I'm hoping that, because they are the same person, it won't make much difference."

Howard was out of breath by the time they carried Olivia up the stairs and into the main room. Three droid heads looked over at them from the poker table.

"I told you the two women they brought in weren't hookers," said the Scarecrow.

"What can I say?" said the Tin Man. "Once every year or six you get it right."

"Were those gunshots we heard?" asked the Lion. "I know I heard gunshots."

"If you knew something was going on, why didn't you interfere?" asked Tony.

"Orders," the three droids said in unison.

"Whose orders?" asked Howard.

"Our owner's orders," said the droids.

"Who would that be?" asked Tony.

The droids said nothing.

Howard tried. "Who would that be?"

The droids answered in unison. "You."

"Oh," said Howard. "Um, when did I give you these orders?"

"Just after the earthquake," said the Tin Man, "when you instructed us about the special event downstairs."

"Great," said Howard. "Here are some new instructions. Carry this body for us."

The Tin Man got up from his chair and took Olivia's corpse from them as if she weighed nothing, and carried her out to the Bel Air.

"Better put her in the trunk," said Tony.

"Sure," said Howard. "Though I don't think anyone around here would make much noise if they saw a bloody corpse in our car."

Just as they were closing the trunk, a milk truck-shaped van pulled up and six Crewmen jumped out.

Howard spoke to the Tin Man. "The basement is a crime scene. Help these policemen investigate."

The Tin Man saluted. "Yes sir. This way men."

The Crewmen gave Howard a strange look and followed the droid into the Oz Club.

"You're getting good at this," Tony suggested. "Are you sure you're a scientist?"

"If you think that, why did *you* shoot all the bad guys? I never fired my gun once."

Tony laughed. "I said you're *getting* good. I didn't say you were there yet. Let's get going. Our corpse is getting cold."

Wesley Memorial Morgue

Howard felt a bit nervous returning to Wesley Memorial Hospital. But knowing that he wasn't under an execution order this time helped. As did knowing that he wasn't under arrest for murder. He didn't *think* they would try to do medical experiments on him, but that fear continued to grow in the back of his mind.

Dr. Montgomery met them at the emergency entrance with a gurney and two burly assistants. Howard could see two hospital security people watching from inside the door, and was reminded that both he and Tony had left this building just this afternoon under less than cordial circumstances.

It had begun to snow, but no one paid the weather any attention as white-smocked assistants lifted Olivia out of the trunk and onto the gurney.

Dr. Montgomery glanced briefly at the flayed and bloody woman being handled by his staff, and then peered long and hard at Howard. "So, you're a cop now? When just this morning you were a..."

"Criminal?" Howard finished. "It's complicated."

"And your partner killed three cops this morning."

"Like I said. It's complicated. Did you bring what I asked?"

Montgomery patted his pocket. "Though there's no reason you couldn't—"

"Yes," said Howard. "There is. I'll tell you about it after we get this done."

The assistants were now rolling the gurney into the hospital. Before following them inside, Tony flipped his keys to a hospital valet to park the Bel Air and clean the blood off the front seats and trunk.

Dr. Montgomery seemed ill at ease. "Are you sure you want to do this in the morgue instead of—"

"Yes." Howard suddenly realized that he was cutting Montgomery off on every sentence, and tried to decide whether it was from nerves at returning to the hospital or if adrenalin was still running from the Oz Club. He decided it didn't matter.

Once they were in the morgue, located unsurprisingly in the hospital basement, Montgomery asked the assistants to leave. He then asked the morgue staff to leave, which they did reluctantly.

"Let's do it," said Howard.

Montgomery pulled a metal rod from his pocket and fed it into a syringe from one of the cupboards.

"How long has she been dead?" he asked.

"Twenty minutes," Tony said. "Perhaps a bit longer."

Montgomery shook his head. "No one has ever been revived after that length of time."

"We're not talking revival," said Tony. "Besides being dead she has major organ damage including a punctured heart, but Howard thinks this could work. If it does, it won't be revival; it will be something else entirely."

Montgomery plunged the needle between Olivia's ribs and into her ruined heart. "Now we wait."

The three men sat silently watching the corpse, still dressed in shredded rags, as nothing happened. Howard sat on the end of an unused mortician's slab, knowing that he would need it if this worked. He also knew that he would feel evidence that something was happening before any of them saw it.

And then it happened. Howard flung himself backward onto the slab as explosions of agony erupted in his chest and lower back. He heard screaming. Some of it was his, but he was sure some also belonged to Tony. He writhed and shook as the pain slowly subsided, not going away, but reduced to where it was manageable. As he sat up, he realized that his skin itched, head to toe. He looked over and saw that Olivia's eyes were open.

She looked nothing like the Olivia he remembered, the fake psychic fawning after an aging TV personality and reading tarot cards and tea leaves over breakfast. The cuts on her face from the torturers' work made her look hard. Strong. The Olivia he knew had never looked strong.

Olivia coughed and her lips moved. "Did I rescue myself?"

Howard thought about this. "Actually, yes, you did."

A smile creased Olivia's face and she closed her eyes.

Howard slid off the slab and walked about the morgue. Tony joined him and they shared a knowing look. They could measure Olivia's progress by measuring their own.

"This is marvelous!" said Dr. Montgomery. "I don't understand your reactions to her recovery, but Mrs. Nelson's return from the grave is the greatest medical miracle of our time!"

"And you can't tell anyone," Howard said.

Montgomery drew his lips tight. "No. No. Of course not. Just as everyone who witnessed your and Detective Sandoval's recovery have been sworn to silence. But I saw it. And that's what counts. What I don't understand is what happened to you and the detective before Mrs. Nelson revived."

"It's why my blood can't be used again," said Howard. "There are drawbacks and that's the least of them. I'll tell you all about it tomorrow. After my surgery."

Insurance. Howard could see in Montgomery's eyes that he understood. If anything untoward happened during the surgery, Montgomery would never learn more about his miracle. And Montgomery wanted to know more. Whoever said *knowledge is power* knew what he was talking about.

"I want to see him," Howard said.

Montgomery nodded. "That's why you wanted to bring Mrs. Nelson to the morgue."

"One of the reasons. The fact that she was dead also counts."

The doctor walked over to a wall filled with square metal doors and opened one. He pulled out a sliding slab and on it lay Howard Russell, minus half his face.

Howard glared at the corpse. "You bastard! Not only are you an abusive pervert and a rapist, but you're somehow involved in Olivia Nelson's kidnapping and torture."

"He was?"

Howard looked up and saw Olivia standing on the other side of the slab. Tony was holding her arm to steady her. Already the cuts on her face were shallower. The rest of her was covered by a borrowed lab smock.

116

"He provided the location where you were held."

"Probably just a hired thug," Tony said. "Like your kidnappers. He's not the one who ordered it."

"Oh, I know who ordered it," said Olivia.

When she didn't continue, Tony asked, "Who?"

"Lenny Alfonso," said Olivia. "I need to speak to the Mayor."

Tony pulled out his flip phone and hit speed dial.

Olivia looked closer at the ruined face on the slab. Then up at Howard. "Isn't this you? And how am I walking around. I thought I was dead?"

Howard offered a lopsided grin. "Mitigating circumstances."

Al Capone hung up the phone and leaned back in his chair, pleasantly surprised. They had done it. Somehow, Sandoval and that wild card scientist had not only found his needle in the haystack, but had returned it unharmed. And Olivia already had the information he needed. He hadn't even had to tell her what he wanted. After being betrayed by one of his lieutenants and his own daughter, he thought today would be a total write off, but he was wrong. Things couldn't be going better.

The phone rang again. Capone listened for thirty seconds then hung up, frowning.

He walked over to a portrait of himself and touched the frame in four places. The portrait opened away from the wall, revealing itself as a metal door covering a second metal door. Capone entered a code in the pad, pressed his palm against the reader, and positioned his eye for a scan. He then entered a second code into the pad.

The inner metal door swung open, revealing three shelves. The middle shelf contained papers and a handgun. The top shelf held stacks of currency and some gold, silver, and platinum coins. The lower shelf contained a box that hummed.

Capone removed the box and opened it. Inside were a self-contained refrigeration unit and three metal rods.

"Drawbacks," Capone said aloud.

The Saint

"Har! Har! Har! Merry Christmas!"

The fellow shouting this worn-out phrase wore red. Red Shorts. Red T-shirt. Red beret. Black shoes. And a thick black belt, not that the shorts needed a thick belt; it was just part of the costume.

"Aw dude!" groaned Chris. "It's not Christmas again, is it?"

Ed took a long sip of his candy-cola before answering his witless sidekick. "It's December twenty-fourth, dude. Tonight's the big night."

"I hate Christmas," Chris growled.

"I thought you ignored Christmas. That's what I do." Ed lifted his waxed brows as Chris stared at him. The move was usually condescending enough for Chris to drop his *complaint du moment.*

"Yeah," Chris said finally. "Got that right. But look, dude. Christmas is easy to ignore. This guy though — The Saint — he's in your face all the time. Ringing his bloody bells. Shouting Har! Har! Har! And browbeating you into buying crap that nobody needs."

"Suppose," said Ed. "If he told us to buy beer I bet you'd stop your complaining."

"Har! Har! Har!" Chris snarled.

"Not so loud, dude" Ed said. "You want to attract his attention?"

Chris rose from his seat at the food court table they were sharing and climbed up to stand on it. "Har! Har! Har!" he shouted. "Har! Har! Har! Have a crappy Christmas!"

Everyone else in the food court stopped their conversation and stared.

"Oh crap," Ed muttered.

Chris climbed down, flopped into his seat, and folded his arms across his chest, a wide, stupid grin on his face. "See. I could be The Saint. Any clown could do his job."

"Suppose," Ed said, his voice still low as those around him resumed their conversations. "But you're not just any clown. You're the king of clowns."

"That he is," agreed a deep, resonant voice.

Ed looked up to see The Saint standing next to their table, his large, blue eyes burning, and his square jaw jutted forward. Somehow, the Harbinger of Christmas had advanced on their table without either of them seeing him coming. Perhaps he was magic after all, as the tales Ed had heard growing up suggested.

"Hey!" said Chris. "I don't have to take that from you! You're supposed to be jolly, and reward all the good little boys with milk and cookies."

"That's not—" Ed began, but The Saint cut him off by reaching out and clutching Chris's throat in a thick-fingered fist.

Ed had never seen The Saint from this close before. Well, perhaps he had as a child when his parents had turned him over to The Saint's green-clad Elves to bully for an hour while they shopped the mall. But like other childhood trauma, Ed had erased those experiences from his memory. Now that he was old and wise, having turned eighteen just a few weeks ago, he could read The Saint like a book. And as a book, The Saint was trash.

Standing at six foot two and probably three hundred pounds, The Saint was all muscle. He was maybe fifty years old, with short brown hair turning white at the edges, his short beard and moustache mostly white. Ed bet he used to be a wrestler, and was now a has-been put to pasture, hawking toasters and bullying kids for a living. A royal bastard.

"Argle," Chris croaked, staring at Ed with bulging *Help Me!* eyes.

"Hey!" said Ed. "Do I have to call Mall Security? You

can't strangle my friend. Only I get to do that."

The Saint snorted. "Cut the gas! I'm not going to kill the spaz. Just gonna leave him something to remember me by."

"Argle," Chris repeated, waving his arms.

"His parents will sue," Ed said.

The Saint laughed a hearty, "Har! This thing has parents? Anyway, it doesn't matter. You can't sue The Saint. I'm an icon."

Someone else at the food court must have called security; two armor-clad Mall Cops came driving up in a diesel-powered jeep and jumped out moments before crashing into their table."

"Down boy," said one of the cops to The Saint. He wore a name badge that said Gary. "We don't want an incident here."

Ed said, "Hey! This is already an incident."

"No," said the other cop, "it isn't." His name badge said Bart, and he spoke like a Bart, his lips curling in a half-sneer, and his eyes focusing and unfocusing like he had been hit on the head too many times.

Cop Gary tapped The Saint's extended arm with his baton and the Christmas *icon* slowly relaxed his fingers.

"Gagh!" Chris rasped. "I think he crushed my windpipe."

"No," said cop Bart, "He hasn't. If you insist that he has then we'll have to take you to the Mall infirmary."

"You don't want to go to the infirmary," said cop Gary. "If you get my meaning."

Ed had no idea what cop Gary's meaning was, but he didn't get a chance to ask as the Mall cops wasted no time jumping back into their tiny jeep and racing away. The Saint also raced away, walking back to his pot of gold, or whatever the black cauldron he rang his bells over was.

"Har! Har! Har!" The Saint shouted. "Get your family a Red Ryder BB Gun this Christmas."

"Gagh!" Chris repeated. "I think I should go to a hospital."

"You don't need a hospital," Ed said. "This guy knows how to hurt without leaving permanent damage. Drink your cola, dude."

"But—" Chris began.

Ed waved a hand. "This isn't over. I'm still thinking."

Chris slurped on his drink. He may be a clown but he knew not to interrupt while Ed was thinking. When Ed finished, he asked Chris what time it was.

"Four O'clock," Chris said in a voice that didn't sound like it came from a crushed windpipe.

"Okay," Ed told him. "We got an hour before the Mall closes for Christmas Eve. Let's go gear up."

Chris's face expanded into a stupid grin. "Dude! Now you're cookin'!"

"Har! Har! Har! Five minutes to finish your Christmas shopping! Don't forget to check out all the fabulous *last chance* deals at your checkout counter. Har! Har! Har!"

"So that's the plan?" Chris whispered from where they sat on one of the wooden benches perhaps thirty yards from where The Saint stood ringing his bells. Ed's plans were usually pretty smart. This didn't sound like one of them.

"Simple plans are always the best," said Ed.

"But dude, what if someone sees us following him?"

"Doesn't matter," said Ed. "Walking in the same direction as someone who later takes a bruising isn't a crime."

"But—"

"*Sneaking* after someone who later takes a bruising *can* be construed as a crime. Just relax and don't look suspicious. Hey! He's putting his bells away."

The Saint had abruptly stopped hawking the Mall's wares and was stowing his bells inside the black cauldron. He then folded up the tripod legs that held the cauldron and tucked them inside as well before carrying the cauldron by its handle and walking at a fast clip toward the inner maze of the Mall's shops.

"He's going the wrong way," Chris whispered.

Ed stood up and began walking after The Saint. Chris sat for a moment, wondering what to do, then raced after his friend. When he caught up, Ed said, "The plan is to follow him, so we follow."

"But we're supposed to be leaving the Mall!"

Ed let out a big sigh. "Dude, just act like you know what you're doing and no one will question you."

"But—"

"Hey, you guys are going the wrong way!" It was the two Mall cops from earlier. They spun toward them on their tiny diesel jeep. "Closing time, boys," said cop Gary.

Chris stopped walking, but Ed kept going. "Gotta get my mom," Ed said. "She works here."

The cops looked at each other. Then cop Bart shrugged and they drove away.

"That was unreal!" Chris said when he caught up to Ed.

"I told you, dude. Just act like you know what you're doing and people will think you do."

"Groovy!"

Chris picked up his pace as The Saint outdistanced them, walking at an insanely fast clip toward the center of the Mall.

"Where's this guy going?" Ed asked.

"Maybe his mom works here too," Chris said, panting to keep up.

Ed gave him *the look*, and Chris shut up.

At last The Saint slowed and walked through a door that said STAFF ONLY.

Chris shook his head as Ed halted outside the door. "That's it then," he said hopefully, puffing for breath.

In response, Ed pushed the door open three inches and peered inside. "A corridor," he whispered, then pushed the door far enough to slip past it.

Chris took a quick look around, saw no one, and followed.

The corridor was narrow and poorly lit. The first room they encountered was a janitor's closet. No sign of the janitor or The Saint.

"Should we be here?" Chris whispered.

"Don't be a wet rag," Ed whispered back. "Now shsssh."

The second room was larger and looked like storage. Old chairs and folded tables. Boxes with unlabeled contents. There was no light inside and they didn't look for a switch.

The corridor ended at a left turn. Chris hung back as Ed took a peek and then slipped around the corner. Chris followed only to discover that the hallway ended after three feet at a third and final room. Ed stood looking inside. Chris looked over his shoulder.

It was a large room, filled with benches and more junk. This time the lights were on and Chris could see all sorts of crap, most of it holiday displays. The Thanksgiving paraphernalia that had been crowding the Mall a few weeks ago. Halloween skeletons and zombies. Easter bunny signs and flying eggs. Al Capone Day silhouettes. Summer crap. It was twelve months of mall all crammed into one room.

Chris could also see The Saint. He stood at one of the benches, fortunately with his back toward the door, his attention focused on the bench in front of him. The Saint's shoulders and arms moved as he worked at something, but the rest of him was statue still.

Directly in front of him, Chris could almost feel the confidence ooze off Ed, and he had to agree that the circumstances couldn't be better. The Saint. Alone. Oblivious that they were there. No witnesses. Chris watched as Ed pulled the pipe from where he had concealed it inside his pant leg, held in place by his sock. His friend's knuckles were white where they clenched the pipe. Carefully and quietly, Chris reached down and retrieved his own length of pipe.

Chris's throat still hurt from where The Saint had nearly strangled him. The *Christmas Icon* deserved everything he was about to get. Chris knew that he would feel no remorse afterward.

As an omen that right was on their side, The Saint switched on some equipment. A hair dryer? No, it was too loud for a hair dryer. Some kind of industrial dryer. Was he making toys? Toys to deliver on Christmas Eve? Not that it mattered.

Ed stepped forward, obviously confident that The Saint couldn't hear him over the equipment noise, and Chris moved up beside him. They both raised their metal pipes.

Chris felt an adrenalin rush, or what he assumed was an adrenalin rush. He felt his pulse quicken and his temperature rise, and he knew he was grinning in that way that annoyed Ed so much. So what. He was going to enjoy this. He deserved the right to grin.

Ed's pipe began to swing down, so Chris followed suit. He could see that Ed was going to smack The Saint directly on the back of the head, and suddenly wondered if the *Christmas icon*'s skull would smash, spewing brains and blood across the room. Chris didn't want to get in the way of Ed's blow, so he swung to the side, aiming for the right ear. Another omen of righteousness, both blows struck at the same time.

There was a loud CLANG, followed by two terrific cries of pain, one of them Chris's, followed moments later by multiple clangs as both pipes bounced on the floor and rolled under the bench. Chris was certain he had just broken his hand, his wrist, and possibly his arm. By reflex, he held his damaged hand in his good one, the pain of caressing broken bones somehow more bearable than not caressing broken bones.

Chris was about to glance at Ed to confirm what he already knew, that they were both in the same boat, when The Saint spun around and caught his gaze with those burning blue eyes of his. Somehow, Chris pulled his gaze away to the focus on the dent on the right side of The Saint's head.

"You two!" shouted The Saint. And then "Har! Har!

Har! Congratulations. You've moved from my naughty list to my shit list."

"Holy crap," Ed sputtered from where he stood beside Chris. "You're a droid! How can you be a droid?"

"And you two," shouted The Saint, "are probably the only two clowns in Chicago who didn't know that Santa is a droid."

"Santa?" Chris said. "Who the heck is Santa?"

"Dude, The Saint is Santa," mumbled Ed.

"Har! Har! Har!" yelled The Saint. "And before that I was Nick. And once upon a time I shouted Ha! Ha! Ha! Instead of Har! Har! Har!"

"What's going on here?" said a new voice.

Chris turned and saw the two Mall cops standing in the doorway. Both were frowning. Cop Gary looked at Chris's hand.

"Jeez. It's the infirmary for you." He glanced at Ed. "And you. I warned you."

Cop Bart was looking at The Saint's head. "And you damaged the merchandise. Maybe the Mall should sue you instead of bandaging you up."

"I can fix myself," boomed The Saint.

Cop Bart chuckled. "Too bad for you boys. You'd prefer the lawsuit to the infirmary."

Chris turned and saw what the droid had been working with at the table and now held in its hands. It was a head. The head of an old, old man.

"Father Time," shouted the droid. "That's who I'll be next week. Har! Har! Har!"

Cop Gary placed a firm grip on Chris' shoulder. "Speaking of Time, it's time to come with us."

As they were marched out of The Saint's lair, Ed said, "I want to call my parents."

"And tell them what?" asked cop Bart. "That you tried to brain a Mall employee."

"It's just a droid," Chris said. "No law against braining a droid." He heard Ed grunt and knew he shouldn't have spoken.

Cop Bart laughed, and then cop Gary said, "Actually, it is against the law to *brain* a droid. If you had done any serious damage I doubt your folks could afford it."

"You didn't know it was a droid until after you tried to kill it," said cop Bart.

"You can't know that," said Ed.

Then Chris heard Ed's voice say, "Holy crap. You're a droid!" followed by a click. A recording.

"How did you think we knew you were back there?" said cop Gary.

They continued in silence, and a few minutes later were escorted into a cinderblock crypt deep in the basement of the Mall complex.

"Your infirmary is down here?" Ed asked.

"I did tell you that you didn't want to come here," said cop Gary.

The crypt ended in a dark space with dust covered boxes sitting on skids. There was a single door with a coded security pad. When the door opened, the Bride of Frankenstein stood on the other side. She was tall. Maybe six foot one. Her coiled midnight hair stood an additional foot taller. She wore a white nurse's coat that covered her from collar to ankles and she held a clipboard in her hands.

"Patients?" said the Bride, smiling. "It's been days since I've had patients."

"A Christmas present," said cop Bart.

"It's another droid, isn't it?" said Ed.

Chris stared at her, and knew Ed spoke the truth. She stood too straight and too still. Only her eyes moved. And her mouth when she spoke.

"Welcome to The Saint's Workshop," said cop Bart. "The Elves aren't in right now. They're at home enjoying Christmas Eve with their families. But here to take care of you is one of their works-in-progress. A nurse droid."

"Droids can't be doctors and nurses," Ed said. The tasks are too complicated."

"True," said cop Bart. "For now. But Nurse Hacksaw

here is an advance model. As is The Good Saint. Not on the market yet. Able to feign more emotions and handle more complex tasks. Or so the Elves hope."

The Bride's smile widened.

"Nurse Hacksaw hasn't lost a patient yet," said cop Gary.

Cop Bart added, "Another few months of trials and she'll be presented to the Wesley Memorial Hospital Board along with her track record. You two will be on that record. Just think. You'll be famous."

"Looks like I have some fractured bones to set," said Hacksaw. She took Ed's injured hand into hers and started pressing with her fingers and thumbs, shifting bones around. Ed screamed.

"I forgot to mention," said cop Bart. "Nurse Hacksaw is designed for treating the uninsured. No anesthetic, I'm afraid. Or painkillers. Only the minimum required care. On the bright side, the plastic splints and bandages are free."

"My parents will have your ass!" Ed shrieked between screams of pain.

"Not *our* ass," said cop Bart. "We just work here. They'll have to sue the Mall management. Or the Elves, if you like. Of course, they'll return the favor by having you arrested for attempted murder and damaging a droid."

"I suggest," said cop Gary, "that you just take your medicine and go home, thankful that you are going home rather than to prison. I mean, if you think the infirmary is bad, you haven't met prison."

"So," Ed grunted. "Good cop, bad cop, huh?"

"Not at all," said cop Bart. "Bad cop, worse cop. Say one word about this place or what happened here and prison will be the least of your worries."

"You'll let us go?" said Ed.

"Of course," said cop Gary, otherwise known as *bad cop*. "We need you alive and healed up for Nurse Hacksaw's report card. This is quid pro quo. You injured your hands and our infirmary fixed them. And we have no interest at this time of pressing charges."

"That could change, of course," said *worse cop* Bart with an evil grin. "With cause."

Chris had listened to all this in a daze, watching as the droid shifted Ed's hand and wrist while he screamed. The nurse now applied plastic splints and bandages while Ed gritted his teeth.

"It will take the fractures several weeks to heal," the nurse said to Ed. "Don't move your hand, wrist, or even your fingers. Don't remove the bandages or splints. Don't get the bandages wet or dirty. You can removed the wrappings in February, but be gentle with hand and wrist for an additional two months. Next patient."

Chris almost collapsed when he realized that meant him.

"Go ahead and faint," said cop Gary. "Nature's anesthetic."

But Chris felt the adrenalin rush again and knew he wasn't about to faint. Not yet. The nurse took his hand, and through his first scream he heard cop Bart shout, "Har! Har! Har! Merry Christmas!"

Monster Unmade

The television blared the news in black and white. Howard sat in his hospital bed and clicked through the channels. All three of them. Earlier that afternoon he'd run across a color broadcast — *The Wizard of Oz* — so he knew the television could display color. But he'd only found black and white since. The picture was also fuzzy, so he figured there was no cable. This was something he hadn't seen since he was a child. Broadcast television.

"Anything good on?"

Howard looked to the doorway, this without guards, and found Tony Sandoval grinning at him.

"Don't you have somewhere else to be?" Howard asked. "It is Christmas Eve. A wife? Family?"

Sandoval lost his grin and shook his head. "Sadly, the only family I have is my partner. For now that's you."

"You're right," said Howard. "That is sad."

They were silent for several moments.

Then Tony said, "I don't have to ask how the surgery went. I gritted my teeth through most of it."

"You were there?"

More shakes of the head. "I was at home, feeling every slice of the knife. I assume Mrs. Nelson did as well."

"Damn," said Howard. "I was out cold. Didn't feel a thing."

"I was able to tune it out after a while," Tony said. He moved to sit in a chair by the bed. "I don't think I'll have that problem again."

"Well," said Howard. "That's good news." He waved his hands in the air. "More good news is that I've got my appendages back." He slapped one thigh through the blanket and felt a familiar pressure and slight tingle. "I feel like running a marathon."

Tony chuckled. "You'll have enough of those when Capone puts you back to work. You should stay in bed while you can."

Howard waved the remote at the television that hung suspended from the ceiling. "Why is everything in black and white?"

Tony frowned. "What else would it be?"

"Color," said Howard. "Like *The Wizard of Oz.*"

"Oh, that," said Tony. "Yeah. They make some of those fantasy type shows in color. Makes them feel more surreal. Anything serious is in good old black and white."

Howard thought of several things he might say to that. He settled on, "That Dorothy Gale maniac looked nothing like the actress in the movie."

Tony sighed. "She sure could sing, though."

More silence.

On the television, a monochrome Al Capone began talking. Beside him stood a rather severe looking woman who Howard could see had once been gorgeous, and a frowning girl who looked around seventeen. A fireplace crackled behind them.

"Having our family reunited is the best Christmas gift I could hope for," Capone said with a smile as he clutched the severe woman closer to him with his right arm and the teenager with his left. The girl's frown didn't lessen.

"I see a divorce in our Mayor's future," said Sandoval.

"Figure she'll leave him?" Howard asked.

A laugh. "He'll dismiss her. The man doesn't age. He goes through a new wife every few years. This one isn't the daughter's mother."

Howard thought about that and looked down at his ringless wedding finger. He'd been devastated when his wife had left him. There'd been love in their marriage, even if it was over now. He suspected that, for all his long years, Capone had never known love. That had to be worse.

"What about the daughter? She looks none too happy to be back with dad."

Tony pursed his lips. "Official story is that his daughter was kidnapped and the kidnappers were found and killed in a shootout with police. If she continues to be moody, Capone's media team will spin a story about Stockholm syndrome or something like it."

"If that's the official story," Howard said, "what's the real story?"

Tony shrugged. "We'll never know. But I wouldn't be surprised if she shacked up with Caruso and that's what got him killed."

Howard whistled. "Capone killed his own Alderman to protect his daughter?"

"Or his pride," said Tony. "I'm as close to the Mayor as anyone and even I have no idea how he really feels about his children."

"He has others?" Howard asked.

"Two. They're both older than he is now and try to keep out of his way. That's good advice. Keep out of Capone's way. Never crossed him. Don't smart mouth him. When he says *jump*, ask *how high?*"

Howard thought about that. "If Capone's older children have nothing to do with him, but are still alive, he must love them."

"You're probably right," said Tony. "Oh, and it looks like he decided to listen to his psychic after all. Peggy McArthur is going to be his new alderman. But you didn't hear it from me. Announcement won't be made until New Year's Eve."

"An alder-woman? Isn't that... unusual?"

Tony smiled at him. "I don't know what it's like where you come from, but our society is pretty liberated. We even had a female Chief of Police a few years back. She was a damn firecracker too."

"Was she?" Howard had no clue if that meant that she did a great job or was just easy on the eyes. "What about Alfonso?"

Sandoval grew serious. "Been arrested for kidnapping Mrs. Olsen. He'll be tried, convicted, and executed in a few days."

Howard nodded. "They found some evidence, then."

"Not yet." Sandoval looked at him. "They will before trial."

"I see," said Howard.

Tony smiled. "No, really. They will. You and I and Olivia know that it was Alfonso."

"Guilty by reason of psychic revelation," said Howard. "Will that stand up in court?"

"Probably not. But since we know who did it, we know where to put the pressure. The rats will flee the ship and start singing. Alfonso is toast."

"If you say so," said Howard.

"How about Montgomery?" Tony asked. "What did you tell him?"

"The truth. That everyone who gets a shot of my blood will join the hive mind, feel all the pain any of the others feel, and eventually go insane."

Tony's eyes nearly burst out of his head.

"Relax," said Howard. "That's a worst case scenario. If my blood stays in my body, we should be just fine. At least I think we will."

Sandoval took a couple of deep breaths. "In my experience, the worst case scenario is usually the one that happens."

Howard couldn't help but frown. "Mine too, my friend. Mine too."

The Mod Squad

"I'm here to pick up some brains." The woman smiled as she spoke.

Barney Sykes considered his latest customer. Perhaps thirty. Lean and tall, made taller by long black hair coiled in ropes like some garish top hat. No makeup. A rictus grin. Not really his type. Still, he supposed he could have some fun with her.

"And you are?"

"Nurse Hacksaw," said the woman. Her expression did not change.

Barney chuckled to himself at the odd name as he studied his day sheet, a list of deliveries he was expected to receive, and then flipped to the next page on his clipboard that held recent missed deliveries followed by those already scheduled for the next few days. The letterhead on the pages said *Chicago Cryogenics. Die Today for a Better Tomorrow.*

"I don't see you here. What's your first name?"

"I don't have one."

Barney looked at her again, and caught a glimpse of a white collar beneath her pale green trench coat. Yes, she was definitely slim enough. He liked that about her. "How about the company you work for?"

"I can't say." Her grin broadened. "You should be expecting me. Arrangements have been made."

A glance at the security camera showed no activity in

the parking area. Should he do this here? He'd never done it at work before. He could feel sweat sprout on his forehead just thinking about it.

Barney looked back at his day sheet. "You say you have a pickup? We don't get many of those. I don't see any pickup orders."

With his right hand, he reached down to the knife at his hip and ran his fingers along the sheath. Seven notches. Seven women who had sated his appetite. Or appetites. At first, he had just wanted the sex. But he had learned to savor the fear and the dying as well. All in all, he thought the three aspects of his game went well together.

The woman leaned toward him and Barney tried to look down her collar, but the coat was too tight and the white garment underneath — a nurse's uniform? — wasn't revealing anything. He had to have her. He'd never had a nurse before.

"Is there someone you can call?" the woman asked.

Barney moved his hand from his knife sheath to the security buttons beneath the counter. The one on the right would send an alarm to their security company and the Police. He pressed the one on the left, which locked the receiving door. A quick glance at the monitor showed the parking area still empty. He moved his hand back to the knife and pulled it from its sheath, raising the blade quickly to the woman's throat.

The woman didn't pull back. She didn't react at all. She just stood there, still leaning toward him, grinning like a mad woman. This wasn't how it was supposed to work.

"Uh," said Barney. He moved the knife slightly in what he considered a threatening manner. "Disrobe!"

"Excuse me?" the woman said, still grinning.

Barney touched the blade gently against her throat. Still she did not react. What is with this woman? He was thinking that he may have to skip the sex and fear part and move right to the killing part. This was a bust. He wouldn't be able to sleep tonight unless he did someone else first. Someone who wasn't a fake out like this woman.

"I'm going to rape you," Barney said. "Cooperate or I'll be forced to cut you."

Now the woman did react. She pulled her neck away from the blade and said. "Oh, I don't think so."

The knife was in the woman's hand before the pain of Barney's broken wrist reached his brain.

"Do you really have nothing for me to pick up?" the woman said. She was still smiling.

"I-I-I," said Barney. Wet warmth ran down his leg.

At last, the woman lost her smile. And what she replaced it with made Barney's bowels let go as well. Her face was a horror from his worst nightmare. Large, angry eyes. A twisted-lip snarl. Even her nose seemed to stick out like a dagger.

Barney felt, rather than saw, her free hand move to the back of his head, and then his face was pressed against the counter and the woman's voice echoed in his ears.

"I came for brains and I'm not leaving without them."

Barney screamed as the knife dug into the back of his neck.

Olivia stood with the two men who had rescued her from kidnapping and torture, feeling like she should be somewhere else. Anywhere else. Even though a week had passed since her murder and miraculous recovery, she still wasn't sure how she felt about any of it: the rescue, coming back from the dead with no sign of being stabbed in the heart and kidneys, no marks from the wetted leather thongs that had been used to whip her from head to toe for a day and a night, her psychic premonitions about her rescue being both wrong and right at the same time, and now being commandeered by the Mayor into this elite squad of crime fighters. It made her feel like she was in a 70's TV series.

"Howard!" Mayor Capone barked at the taller of the two men. "I hope you are recovered enough after your surgery to be at full capacity for this next job."

Olivia noticed that Howard Russell was smiling. Had been smiling pretty much non-stop since having his hips, legs, feet, left arm, and hand replaced with those from the corpse she had seen in the morgue where she had come back to life.

"I was fully recovered twenty minutes after the surgery," Howard replied happily. "Though I appreciated the time off to enjoy having a proper body again. I even found a nice apartment in—"

The Mayor harrumphed, cutting Howard off. "I don't care about your personal life. What I care about are results." He swung his head to look at the other man, Tony Sandoval. "Your first job together wasn't a complete success. You were supposed to bring Olivia back alive."

Tony started to speak, but the Mayor swung his attention back to Howard. "If your... resurrection of my psychic in any way impairs her ability, I will be very, very unhappy."

Olivia wasn't impressed with the way Capone said *my psychic*, but she knew the man well enough to simply say, "I'm just glad to be alive."

Capone waved his hand. "Whatever you are, alive, dead, something in between, will make itself known in due time. Until then, I have a job for you."

"A what?" asked Olivia.

Al Capone furrowed his brow. "If you haven't figured it out already, you'll be joining these two. My Crew usually works in pairs, but you three will be a squad. Each of you has been... modified so that you are almost indestructible. That will give you an advantage dealing with this city's most troubling problems."

"But I'm not in your Crew," said Olivia. "I have my practice. My customers."

Capone pulled a card from a breast pocket of his tailor made Shaffner and Sons suit and thrust it at her. It was a Capone Crew ID with Olivia's name on it.

"The city is your customer now," Capone said. "And you

are no longer just a psychic. I am relying on you to use your abilities to help this city."

"But—" said Olivia.

"No buts." Capone pushed a slip of paper into Tony's hand. "I need your squad at this address. Now!"

Al Capone walked back behind his desk but didn't sit down. "Chicago CSI has already secured the scene, but they're baffled about what happened. I want you to unbaffle them."

"Let's go," said Tony, who was the most no-nonsense person Olivia had ever met.

Howard grinned. "Shotgun!"

Olivia shook her head. "Jesus."

Olivia didn't mind sitting on her own in the back of the Chevrolet Bel Air. The bench seat was roomy and the upholstery soft. Not as nice as her Cadillac, of course, but nicer than most taxis. The two men sat in the front, chattering away as Tony drove to wherever they were going. She fingered the Capone Crew ID the Mayor had given her. What am I supposed to do with this? I'm not a cop. I'm a psychic. Or am I? Olivia hadn't felt much in the way of premonitions since coming back from the dead.

Up ahead she could see some police vehicles, mostly Ford Crestliners, and a Chicago Crime Scene Investigation truck parked in front of a building. Or in back of a building. She felt gravel crunch beneath the tires and realized they were entering a wide alley. Tony pulled the car behind a Pontiac Chieftain and killed the engine.

One of the uniformed cops walked over to eyeball them as they climbed out of their unmarked Crew car. "Tony Sandoval? I thought you were dead!"

"Was," said Tony. "I got better. Joe Whatley, right? What have we got?"

Whatley scratched his head. "Dead employee. The owner hasn't found anything missing. Yet."

"Sounds straightforward," said Tony. "What do you need us for?"

A grin spread across Whatley's face. "That, you'll have to see for yourself. Follow me."

Olivia tagged along even though Joe Whatley and the other cops working the scene hadn't even acknowledged her or Howard's presence. They all seemed to know Tony, but were disinterested in his companions. She guessed that it must be some kind of police machismo thing.

She could see that the open door to the building was damaged, all bent around the locking mechanism. It probably couldn't be closed, never mind locked again. There was a small sign on the outside surface. *Chicago Cryogenics*. The word *receiving* was printed below.

Tony examined the door. "This was broken from the inside. Someone broke out instead of in?"

"And must have used a sledgehammer to do it," said Whatley. "There's steel in this door. It gets weirder."

Olivia followed her partners and Whatley toward a counter area. The men blocked her view until Howard turned to face her, his face green. It was the first time she had seen him not smile since his operation. He rushed past her, and Olivia saw what had altered his perspective.

A corpse was sprawled over the counter, one arm hanging down the front side, a puddle of blood and gore where its head should be. Its stench defied description. Even so, Olivia stepped closer. "Wow! It's just like in the movies."

"Who is this woman?" Whatley asked.

Apparently, she had done something to make it okay for Tony's peers to notice her.

Tony's answer was nonchalant, which had the effect of keeping him in a position of power over cop Joe. "New recruit. So's the green guy."

Olivia ignored the posturing and finished her examination of the corpse's raw and bloody neck — she could see bits of the man's spine sticking out — and looked over the rest of the body. Moving around the counter she saw a knife sheath attached to the man's belt. "I guess that's where the knife sticking in his back came from. Looks like a hunting knife."

"Any idea where the head is?" Tony asked.

Whatley laughed. "That's the best part. We've got video from the security camera."

Olivia followed the others to the far side of the room where a young, female Chicago CSI technician was working with some kind of portable display. Howard rejoined them, looking a bit less green. "Caught me by surprise," he said. "Won't happen again."

"Show us what you've got," said Whatley.

The technician nodded and fiddled with the controls, and then Olivia saw a monochrome image of the alley without the police vehicles. As she watched, one of those tiny, single-seat commuter cars Ford made — the Clever car — pulled up and a woman wearing a white, full-length coat got out.

"This is about an hour ago," said the technician.

The woman vanished as she entered the building and everyone watched for several minutes as nothing happened. Then the woman reappeared, walking away from the building, a human head dangling by the hair from one hand. The woman walked to the commuter, opened the small trunk at the back, and dropped the head inside. Then she got into the car, leaving a dark smear of blood by the door handle, and the car pulled away.

The display zoomed in on a Chicago commuter license plate.

"Fake," said the technician. "We've put out an APB, but she's probably already replaced it with a different plate. I would."

"Any ID on the facial recognition?" Tony asked.

The technician wagged her head. "Nothing."

"It's a droid," said Howard.

Everyone looked at him.

"What makes you say that?" Whatley asked. "I've seen a few droids in my day. None looked as realistic as that."

Howard waved his hand at the image of the empty alley. "Isn't it obvious? She walked out of the building with a head. Not a sledgehammer. She is the sledgehammer."

Olivia smiled. Score one for Howard.

"Sounds good to me," said Tony.

The technician handed Tony a printed headshot of the woman taken from the security camera. "Droids have been around for what? Five? Ten years? I've never heard of one committing a crime before. Don't they have Asimov's laws built in or something?"

Tony nodded. "Or something. But there's a first time for everything."

"I wonder what this guy did to warrant execution by droid?" Olivia asked.

"His name is Barney Sykes," said the technician. "Clean record. Should get his DNA results any minute. We'll see if it matches any unidentified DNA from recent crimes."

Olivia felt a familiar something and looked at Howard. Howard was looking back.

Tony spoke before either of them could. "I've got a feeling."

"That Barney got what he deserved?" Olivia asked.

The two men nodded.

Olivia sprawled out in the back seat as Tony cranked the Bel Air into reverse and spun gravel on the way out to the street. She found herself smiling much like Howard had for the past several days. A strong premonition. She still had her mojo.

Apparently, Howard and Tony also had her mojo. At first she hadn't believed Howard's story. Though she couldn't deny that she had somehow been healed of her wounds, if not brought back from the dead, the bits about Howard coming from an alternate reality as a conglomeration of three people and a machine was, well, insane. But then Howard recovered from his operation within hours and showed her his new limbs taken from the corpse in the morgue. Then he had cut her hand and together they had watched it heal. Olivia had met some good magicians in her day, but Howard had them all beat.

The part she had the most trouble with was the supposed affinity she, Tony, and Howard shared and that Howard was still trying to measure. Apparently, it included them all sharing her psychic talent. Olivia wasn't sure how she felt about that. It was kind of like having her privacy invaded.

Seeing Howard and Tony have the exact same premonition at the exact same time felt weird. But it was also comforting seeing her psychic warning confirmed, not once but twice.

She didn't know why, but Barney Sykes was a bastard who deserved a violent end.

Tony's cell phone beeped and the Crewman listened for several seconds before hanging up. "That Sykes guy has DNA all over several rape and murder scenes. The police are closing a bunch of open cases."

"So?" asked Howard. "Our avenging droid is a hero?"

Tony shook his head. "If we cut off Barney's head, we'd be heroes. When someone else does it, it's murder."

"So how do we find her? It?" Olivia asked.

"We go to the source," said Tony. "And we've arrived."

Olivia looked up at a large, white, downtown office building as the Bel Air pulled to the curb and they got out. The façade was marble, or faux marble — she couldn't tell which — and had words carved above the huge oak double doors. *The Prendick Foundation.*

"Teddy Prendick is one of my customers," Olivia said. "I haven't seen him in a while, though."

"Really?" said Tony. "That could help us cut through some red tape."

"Red tape?" Howard stopped in midstride. "Don't our Al Capone fan club cards cut through red tape?"

"Usually," Tony said.

Olivia was feeling left out of the conversation. She

spoke up. "Teddy Prendick is one of the wealthiest men in Chicago. He holds a monopoly on droids and several other enterprises."

Tony nodded. "He can buy and sell our Crew cards."

They entered through the giant doors and found themselves in a massive lobby. Lavish couches and armchairs sat at strategic locations accompanied by coffee tables adorned with various magazines. A table with an ornate espresso machine and several other beverage paraphernalia stood against one wall. At the wall furthest from the door was a security desk behind which stood a handsome young man in a bright blue suit. Too handsome to be human. A droid. She had never seen the lobby so quiet.

The droid waited until they approached its station before addressing them.

"Mrs. Nelson. It is good to see you again. I see you have friends. A Capone Crewman and the Wizard of Oz. Interesting company."

"I'm not—" Howard began.

But Olivia waved him off. She saw no point in engaging in idle chitchat with a droid. "I need to see Teddy."

"Mr. Prendick is unavailable," the droid said. "Is there anyone else who can help you?"

Tony pulled from his coat pocket the photo of the woman from the security camera and held it in front of the droid. "We need to speak with someone who can recognize this woman."

The droid blinked his eyes. "Interesting. I have a reference database of all standard droid models and special orders and this droid is not recognized." He lifted a phone from behind the counter, pressed three buttons, and waited for someone to pick up at the other end. "We have a problem," he said. Then he hung up the phone. "The director of the Prendick Droid Division is on her way down. Please have a seat."

"We'll stand," said Tony.

They stood in silence until the elevator opened and a

middle-aged woman with reddish-brown curls stepped out.

"Dr. Moreau?" Howard said.

"You know her?" asked Tony.

The woman looked critically at Tony. "I was at the hospital when you woke from your coma and killed three policemen. I am surprised to see you still among the living."

"Mitigating circumstances," said Howard.

Dr. Moreau looked at him. "You are also a cop-killer. Is the Mayor getting soft?"

"We work for the Mayor now," Howard began, but this time it was Tony's turn to wave him off.

"What's a medical doctor doing heading up an engineering division?" asked the seasoned Crewman.

Dr. Moreau snorted. "Mitigating circumstances. If you want a clearer answer, you'll have to take it up with Mr. Prendick."

"What we seem to have here," Howard said, "Is a failure to communicate."

"Fine," said Tony, ignoring Howard. He showed Moreau the photo. "One of yours?"

The doctor squinted at the photo. Coming from a security camera it wasn't a particularly sharp image.

"She's not a droid," Moreau said. "The Prendick Foundation has a monopoly on droids and we haven't built one that looks like that."

"Could it be wearing a mask?" Olivia asked.

Everyone looked at her.

"It's a good question," said Olivia.

"Yes," said Tony. "It is."

"Not a mask," said the droid behind the security desk. "Not a human. It can only be an unregistered droid."

Olivia thought she saw Dr. Moreau throw the security droid a hateful glance. Then the woman looked at Tony and frowned.

"If that is true, then someone is illegally manufacturing droids. I expect the Mayor's full attention on finding the culprit and putting them out of business. The Prendick Foundation pays the City a fortune to hold its monopoly, and it's your job to enforce it."

"Seems like we're done here," said Tony. To Dr. Moreau he added, "We'll keep you apprised."

Once they were back on the street Howard said, "Something stinks in the state of Prendick."

"I don't trust that woman," Olivia said. "That's not a premonition or anything. I just don't trust her."

"That makes three of us." Tony pulled out his flip phone and made a couple of calls. When he was done he said, "While we're waiting for answers, let's get something to eat."

"Thai anyone?" asked Howard.

Dr. Lisa Moreau clenched her fists as she rode the elevator down to the basement. She had never understood how the minor, self-inflicted pain of nails digging into flesh worked to reduce anger, but used the effect now to help focus on what to do next. Her quick thinking in the lobby had allayed suspicion for the time being, but the Crew would be back if they didn't have somewhere else to look. Moreau would have to give them that somewhere else.

The elevator door opened and she walked quickly down the hallway to a door marked *Room D — Private*. She palmed the reader and the door opened. Inside, a woman lay on a table with her skull folded open.

A white-haired, oriental technician wearing a yellow lab coat moved his fingers inside her skull. The thin red wire of a probe wound above his wrist and across to a bank of equipment beside the table.

"Have you found anything yet?" Moreau demanded.

Henry Wong jerked at the tone of her voice and looked up. "Trouble?"

"Of course there's trouble. And sooner than I thought

possible. Have you discovered what's wrong with her?"

The technician shook his head. "All the diagnostics come back green and there's no sign of damage. It has to be the human factor."

Moreau put her hand in the air, palm out. "Please. I don't want to hear it again. We both know that there is not enough biological matter to override the programmed components. The simulations are clear on that. There must be a programming error."

Henry Wong mumbled something.

"What was that?" Moreau demanded.

"Unless the simulations are wrong," the technician said.

"You mean the simulations that I spent years putting together? If you weren't the best in your field, I'd fire you for insubordination. Anyway, we're out of time. We'll have to chalk this up to an isolated incident. I need you to program this unit to make its way to one of Chicago's warehouse districts and self-destruct in a vacant building. Make sure the face survives but little else. Are you sure that none of its components can be traced back to us?"

The technician stood, pulling his fingers out of the droid's head. "Most of its components can be traced back to us, as you well know. We're the only ones who use them. All serial numbers in this unit have been listed as belonging to stolen shipments that never arrived. That was the plan should anything go wrong."

Moreau gritted her teeth. "Of course I know. It's my plan. I just want to make sure that you followed it to the letter. If you didn't, the first casualty in this building when they come for us will be you."

Henry Wong shook his head as he put away the diagnostic probe and picked up the programming pod. "Everything is as it should be."

"Just see to the programming," Moreau said. "Is the brain it brought us usable?"

"Better than usable," said Henry. "It's never been frozen."

Moreau tapped a finger against her chin. "Maybe that's

what went wrong. Use the new brain for the next batch of test droids. Maybe we'll stick with fresh brain matter from now on. Then we won't have to deal with that fool over at Chicago Cryogenics. It's his fault we're in this mess."

Wong looked at her. "You mean fresh from morgues and funeral homes? Right?"

"What did you think I meant?" Moreau said. "That we'd grab people off the street?"

The white-haired technician continued looking at her, as if to say, that's exactly what I think you meant. Then he turned his attention back to the pod. "I'll work up the program right now."

Moreau left the laboratory and stood in the hallway clenching her fists. Maybe the pain didn't reduce anger as well as she had thought.

Olivia sat chewing her hamburger without tasting it. *I should be home having dinner with my husband. Not sitting in a cheap burger joint like some femme fatale from an even cheaper novel.*

"Does the Mayor even realize that this is New Year's Eve?" she said aloud.

Tony's flip phone beeped and he answered it.

"Most police work is sitting and waiting," Howard said. "I learned that my first day, too."

"I've got better things to do," Olivia said.

Howard nodded. "You'll get your chance. Do you have a gun?"

Olivia glared at him. "What do I need a gun for?"

Howard pulled a gun from a holster near his waist and waved it in the air.

Tony, without breaking stride on the phone, grabbed Howard's hand and forced it to the tabletop. His lips moved. *Put that away.*

Howard put the gun away. "People will start shooting at us before we're done. It helps to be able to shoot back."

"Fantastic," said Olivia.

Tony snapped shut his phone. "Downtown has contacted family and close friends of all Sykes' victims. No one recognized the droid's photo and none of them have the wherewithal to pay for a third-rate assassin, never mind a droid. That angle's a bust."

"I could have told you that," Olivia said. "In fact, I did. Something's fishy about that Moreau woman."

"Premonition?" asked Howard."

"No," Olivia said. "I wish there was."

"What do we do now?" Howard asked.

Tony pulled some bills from his pocket to pay for lunch. "We go keep an eye on Dr. Moreau."

"Hey," said Olivia. "You two may have no lives, but I have a husband waiting at home. We have a ball to attend this evening."

Tony shook his head. "When we're on the job, we're on the job. Once we're done you can go home until the next job."

"Now I really do feel like I'm living in a 70's cop show," said Olivia.

"What?" asked Howard.

"Never mind."

Olivia called home while they drove back to the Prendick Foundation or Dr. Moreau's house or whatever location Tony had decided to stake out.

"Hey!" shouted Howard. "Isn't that the Clever Car from the security video?"

Olivia stopped listening to her husband's complaints and looked out the window.

"There are hundreds of white commuters in this city," said Tony.

"How many with blood on the driver side door?" Howard asked.

Tony changed lanes and Olivia finally saw the small vehicle, now several car lengths in front of them. There appeared to be a stain on the trunk handle as well. Blood? The license plate number also seemed familiar.

"Gotta go," Olivia said into the phone and closed it. Then she shouted into the front seat. "What are the chances of us just randomly spotting the killer's car?" Her voice was louder than it needed to be. Adrenalin?

"Statistically?" said Howard. "Close to zero."

"We're less than a block away from the Prendick Foundation," said Tony.

Howard threw open his hands. "Well, that increases the odds."

The commuter turned a corner and Tony followed. Olivia noticed that he kept as far back as he could without risking losing sight of it. He was also on his flip phone talking rapidly. It sounded like he was requesting reinforcements.

A marked police car pulled into the next lane, and Olivia watched as a second police car appeared further ahead. The commuter sped up and she felt Tony accelerate their own car.

"We're not going to be in a car chase are we?" Olivia asked, once again feeling a small burst of adrenalin.

"Looks that way," said Tony.

Olivia grinned. "I've always wanted to be in a car chase. Though I always envisioned myself in the car being chased."

The two police cars turned on their sirens and flashing lights, and again the Bel Air sped up. Olivia wondered how fast a Clever Car could go. She hoped the answer was *plenty.*

Suddenly the commuter jumped up onto the sidewalk, sending pedestrians flying onto the roadway or pressing themselves against the concrete wall of a building. Tony swerved to avoid the people now littering the road, and Olivia saw that several had been hit by the commuter; some of them lay unmoving on the pavement, their limbs at unnatural angles.

Howard rolled down his window and stuck his handgun outside, holding it two-handed, just as the commuter pulled a sharp turn into an alley, scraping the far wall and then the near wall, crushing both sides of the small vehicle. Olivia heard two shots followed by the grind of a rear wheel scraping against asphalt. Howard had shot out one of the tires.

"Good shot," she said.

Howard grinned back at her. "I've been practicing."

Tony slammed on the brakes and stopped their car in the middle of the street. He jumped out, narrowly avoiding being hit by one of the few cars that hadn't pulled over when the short chase had begun. Howard scrambled out the passenger side, and then pulled the seat forward so that Olivia could slip out. By the time she and Howard caught up with him in the alley, Tony was already pointing his gun at the now stalled commuter.

Howard was breathing hard and holding out his gun as well. Olivia stood next to him, feeling useless. She heard a scuffle of feet as uniformed cops ran up behind them.

The commuter was pretty beat up from bouncing off the buildings. Olivia didn't see how whoever was driving could get out without being cut out, but then the driver's door flew off its hinges and crashed into the alley.

A tall woman stepped out of the car. She was still wearing the same long, pale green coat that had looked white on the security footage. It took a moment for Olivia to remember that this was a droid, not a real woman. She wondered if it would put its hands in the air and surrender, or begin running down the alley. Having many wealthy clients, some of whom owned droids, she knew that droids were fast and could easily outrun people.

The droid did begin running, but toward them rather than away. The expression on its face was less human than its creators had intended; Olivia had the sense that an animal was attacking them.

Olivia pressed her hands against her ears as guns began blazing. Through squinted eyes, she watched as bits of cloth puffed off the droid's coat. Metal gleamed on its forehead and cheek where bullets tore artificial skin. The gunfire turned to the clicks of empty chambers and the droid hadn't even slowed. She heard someone say, "Oh shit!" Then the droid was upon them.

Olivia dove to the side to get away. Like she had watched the commuter do moments before, she hit the side of a building and landed crumpled on the asphalt. Screams echoed in her ears, and she looked up to see the droid tearing policemen apart. Literally. An arm fell in her lap and she banged her head against the wall behind her trying to jump away when there was nowhere to go. She heard Howard yelling. "You bitch! That's my new arm."

Blood was everywhere and Olivia wanted to close her eyes. Shut everything out. But she couldn't. She was too afraid. The screaming stopped and Olivia looked around to see bloody corpses everywhere. No one was moving. Then a pale green coat blocked her vision. Olivia looked up to see a bullet riddled figure with a disfigured face glaring down at her. The woman's lips moved. "You didn't shoot at me."

Olivia tried to speak, and then finally managed, "I don't have a gun."

The droid stared at her, its eyes empty. Then it said, "Would you have shot me if you had a gun?"

Olivia tried to speak, but couldn't. She settled for nodding.

"Figures," said the droid.

Olivia saw a hospital white shoe fly toward her face, and then nothing.

Rogue Droid

Dr. Lisa Moreau stood at her eighteenth floor office window shaking her head. She had watched the Clever Car leave the underground parking garage and begin making its way northeast toward the squalid Fulton district where old, poorly maintained factories and abandoned warehouses were the rule rather than the exception. She wanted to make sure that the droid distanced itself from

Prendick without incident. But even that was too much to ask for. The commuter hadn't gone two blocks before it was flanked by the police. Had they been watching her building?

Then the commuter had jumped onto the sidewalk and run over several pedestrians before slamming into a narrow alley. Was the droid deranged? Well, of course it was; that was why she had to get rid of it. But how does an AI get deranged?

She watched as the police, uniformed and plain clothes, ran into the alley. Did they hope to catch the commuter on foot? Or were there police waiting at the other end of the alley?

They'd better be armed with bazookas if they hoped to take down a droid. Or maybe it would give the police a break and self-destruct here instead of at its destination. Not ideal. Two blocks from the Prendick Foundation. But better than letting itself get captured.

Moreau watched and waited for an explosion to tear apart the alley.

And waited.

And waited.

And then more police, several ambulances, and a Chicago CSI truck pulled up outside the alley.

"Shit," Moreau said aloud. "No bazookas."

Bad enough that the droid had killed some working stiff. Now it looked to have killed policemen. Possibly even Crewmen. If they traced the droid back to Prendick. Back to her... she'd get a look of contempt and a bullet. Her contributions to society would count for nothing.

Moreau contemplated a quick cab ride to the airport, and then shot it down. If she ran, they'd know she was guilty. No. If they did trace it back to Prendick, they'd find a scapegoat waiting for them.

Dr. Moreau continued watching the street as injured pedestrians were loaded into ambulances and black body bags were hauled out of the alley.

When she revived, Olivia opened her eyes to find the Chicago CSI technician she'd met earlier that day staring at her.

"What?" Olivia said.

The technician said, "Uhm."

"That's not very informative." Olivia began climbing to her feet.

"Your, uhm, face was caved in," said the technician. She showed her a picture on her camera.

Olivia frowned. "That's not very flattering. Do me a favor and bury it deep in a file somewhere."

After stretching out a few kinks, Olivia looked around at the various policemen and technicians and saw Tony speaking with one of them. Howard stood a little distance away pressing a hand against his shoulder. Olivia walked over. "How's your arm?"

Howard wasn't smiling. But he wasn't crying either.

"A CCSI technician helped me set it in place and it seems to be reconnecting okay, but if there are problems she says they'll have to rip it off again and have Dr. Montgomery reattach it."

"Ugh," said Olivia.

"Yeah."

Tony joined them. "They're tracking the droid up Arcade Place, clearing out anyone in its path."

"They gonna nuke it from orbit?" Howard asked.

Olivia joined Tony in giving him a weird look.

"Line from an old movie," Howard said.

Olivia wasn't in the mood for Howard's brand of humor. "I know that we're supposed to be virtually indestructible, but this droid is even more so. I don't think we should try to shoot it again. That only made it angry."

"Droids can't get angry," said Howard.

"This one looked pretty frosted to me. Especially just before it kicked my head in."

"I've ordered some bigger guns," said Tony. "Should be

here any minute."

The cop Tony had been speaking with approached them. "VIN's been filed off. Found a bit of DNA, but it matches this morning's victim. No prints anywhere. The commuter's got nothing to tell us."

"Then we have to question the droid," Howard said. "Find out who hired it to kill the serial rapist/murderer."

"And who made it," said Tony. "Since the Prendick Foundation says it isn't theirs."

Olivia turned away. "Well I'm not talking to it. Last time I did that it ended badly."

Another cop came over and Olivia caught a nervous vibe. In fact, all of the cops and technicians had been looking at them oddly. Kind of a mix of awe, fear, and disgust. She wasn't sure she could get used to that.

The cop cleared his throat. "We put the weapons you ordered into the trunk of your car. Locked and loaded."

Tony nodded and then turned to Howard and Olivia. "Let's roll. We've got a droid to capture."

Olivia found herself sharing the back seat of their unmarked Chevrolet Bel Air with one of the cops from the alley. He seemed to be making an effort not to touch her as he huddled against the door. She almost laughed, but then got a premonition that the cop was going to die when they caught up with the droid.

Tony stopped the car, got out, and flipped forward his seat. "You'd better get out here," he said to the cop.

"Wha?" said the cop.

"You don't want to end up like the others in the alley."

The cop got out, still looking puzzled, as Tony pushed back the seat, climbed inside, and left him choking on exhaust.

"It was for the best," said Howard.

They drove several more blocks and then stopped near another police car. Two cops were yelling at people nearby to evacuate. "A killer, armed and dangerous, is headed this way. Go north or south, immediately. Don't go west, and for God's sake don't go east."

Tony opened the trunk and pulled out a rifle as thick as a railway tie. He hefted it in both hands and looked down the gun sights. "It's a 3 caliber Ares Sledgehammer. Designed to rip open armored vehicles. Aim for the midsection and legs, not the head. We still have to question this thing."

Howard picked up a similar weapon and tried to imitate how Tony had handled it.

Olivia looked in the trunk and saw a third weapon. "You expect me to fire that? I doubt I can even lift it."

"It's lighter than it looks," said Howard, but it seemed to Olivia that he was having trouble keeping his weapon steady.

Olivia hauled the third cannon out of the trunk. "I've never even fired a handgun."

"First time for everything," said Tony. "Let's squat behind that car over there. When the droid gets close, we can jump up and use the roof for support."

An engine started and Olivia turned to see the police car drive further up the street.

The three of them sank down behind a rusted Chevy Impala hardtop and Tony whipped out his flip phone. Olivia saw a map appear on the display, but the image was too small to see any details.

"Do phones do this?" she said.

Howard looked over. "Glad to see your phones aren't completely in the dark ages. When do I get one?"

"You got somebody to call?" Tony asked.

"Touché," said Howard.

"Don't get sidetracked," said Olivia. "How come you have a map in your phone? All I have is a speaker."

"Latest thing from China," Tony said. "Capone managed to bring in a few for his Crew."

"China?" said Howard. "Not Japan?"

Anger flared in Olivia's chest and she slapped Howard across the face. Hard. "We don't talk about Japan. What kind of bastard are you?"

Tony reached over and took Olivia's hand between his

palms. "I'm sure this is one of those things that Howard doesn't know."

"Doesn't know what?" Howard said, rubbing his cheek.

"There is no Japan," Tony said softly. "Not since World War Two."

"Oh." Howard crouched quietly for a moment. "I can guess what happened. Maybe it would help to know that where I'm from, Japan is an economic powerhouse where a lot of nifty things like cell phones are innovated."

"Not really," Olivia and Tony said at the same time.

"Right," said Howard. "So, how does this map work?"

Tony held his phone so that everyone could see. "A technician in a Chicago CSI truck is receiving intel from various cops following the droid. She's updating a map and sending a photograph of it to this phone instead of talking to it."

"Your phone is receiving an image rather than just sound?" Olivia couldn't keep the excitement out of her voice. "So your phone is like a television. A tiny television."

"That's a good way to describe it," Tony said. "This blue dot here, that's us. The red dot moving toward us is the droid."

"If I'm reading the map right," Olivia said, "that puts it less than two blocks away."

Tony nodded. "Stay down and don't let the droid see you. It has better vision and hearing than us. If it knows we're here, it may go off in a different direction. More people could get killed. I'll watch its approach on my phone and tell you when to jump up."

Despite Tony's cool phone, Olivia thought this was a lousy idea, even for trained professionals. For someone who had never even held a gun before, it was ludicrous. In her mind's eye she watched her own ordinary flip phone ring — her husband calling to tell her to come home and get ready for tonight's soiree — and the droid lifting up the old Impala and dropping it on their heads. Instead of her phone ringing, however, Tony shouted. "Now!"

A cannon went off even before Olivia finished standing.

She assumed that was Tony. There was a loud clang and, just as she looked over the roof of the car, Olivia saw the droid sway as one arm and part of its shoulder disintegrated into several pieces.

"I thought you said to aim for the legs and midsection?" Howard shouted.

"I did," Tony shouted back. "I missed. It's not like I've ever fired one of these things before."

"Oh, great!" Olivia shouted. It was only then that she realized they were all shouting because none of them could hear after Tony's cannon went off.

Howard leaned over the car, resting his elbows on the roof, and took careful aim. He pulled the trigger and the rifle jerked six inches off the roof. A distance behind the rapidly approaching droid a window shattered and a piece of building tumbled to the street.

Tony was fitting a shell the size of beer can into his rifle for a second shot, but Olivia wasn't sure he'd have time to finish reloading before the droid reached them. She set her rifle on the roof, took aim down the sights so that the barrel was aligned with the center of the droid's chest, locked her arms in place, and pulled the trigger.

Olivia cried out as she felt her shoulder shatter from the recoil, but was actually able to see the large bullet hit the droid exactly where she had aimed. She was about to shout *bull's-eye*, when the droid exploded.

Metal came flying toward her but she had no time to do more than flinch before something struck her already injured shoulder. At the same time, a heavy wind struck and the Impala flipped over, crushing her beneath it along with Tony and Howard. Somehow, she didn't lose consciousness as the car continued to flip, bouncing off her crushed body and leaving her crippled and immobile as heat from the explosion seared her skin.

She tried to look around, but couldn't move her head. Olivia swore she felt worse than she had during her two days of torture at the hands of hired thugs. She concentrated on breathing as she felt her body slowly decompress and realign, the miracle of Howard's blood forcing her body to heal.

When she could move her head, she saw that Tony was unconscious but that Howard was awake and staring at something lying under the Impala, several feet away. She recognized material from Howard's trench coat and then saw fingers.

"Aw, Howard. You've lost your new arm again."

"No," said Howard, his voice a whisper. That's my other arm."

By the time they pulled themselves together, in Howard's case literally, other cops were arriving.

"That was some shot," Tony said. "If the thing had a heart, you would have hit it dead center."

Olivia just shook her head. "Point and shoot. How hard can it be?"

"Did Olivia hit some sort of power supply?" Howard asked. "When I had droid legs I never knew what powered them."

"Quantum micro-motors," said Tony. "Don't ask. I have no idea what that means, but I'm told that droids can't explode."

"This one did," said Olivia.

Tony nodded. "I suspect it contained a bomb."

"What kind of freakin' droid assassin is this?" Howard demanded.

"I wish we could ask it," Tony said.

One of the technicians, similar to the young woman they had worked with earlier, approached holding something in her gloved hands. Olivia looked closely and guessed it was part of the droid's head. She could see part of a metal jaw and some burnt black hair.

"Was anyone else here when the droid exploded?" the technician asked.

"I'm pretty certain there wasn't," Tony said. "Is there a problem?"

The tech held the partial head in one hand and pointed with the other. "There's some brain matter here. I don't suppose any of you...?"

"I've got all of mine," said Howard.

"That looks like a casing," Olivia said. "Designed to hold the brain matter."

"That's what I think too," said the technician. "It's pretty cooked, but I bet we can get a DNA sample from it."

Olivia felt the familiar twinge of a strong premonition. "It'll lead back to that Cryogenics place."

The technician arched a brow. "Cryogenics place?"

"Chicago Cryogenics," said Tony.

The young woman's eyes widened. "You mean that headless guy earlier today? You think it's his brain?"

"No." Olivia shook her head. "Not his. But they store brains there. Right?"

"Not just brains," said Tony. "Whole people. Put on ice. Usually because they are sick or dying and have paid Chicago Cryogenics to store them and wake them up in a future with advanced medicine that can extend their lives."

"Well," said Howard. "One of their patients isn't going to make the trip."

When they returned to Chicago Cryogenics, this time at the front door, there were already several police vehicles scattered near the entrance. Tony pulled their Bel Air into an empty stall in the well-marked parking area that lined the front of the stylish three-story building.

At the entranceway they were greeted by two EMS heavies carrying a black body bag.

"Anyone we know?" asked Howard.

The EMS guys cast Howard a cold look and continued hauling their package to a waiting truck. It was Joe Whatley, who had been following behind them, who answered.

"One Dr. Samuel Jones. I say doctor, but he's no doctor I'd ever let work on me. Got his degree off the back of a magazine. I guess you don't need much in the way of skills to put someone in a tank and turn the temperature down."

"Let me guess," said Tony. "Murder made to look like suicide?"

Whatley smiled. "Complete with a typed confession saying he stole and sold body parts, but not who he sold them to."

"Someone sent in a cleaner," said Tony.

Joe Whatley nodded. "Professional job. Not a fingerprint or a hair left behind. Nothing on the security cameras either."

Tony rubbed his hands together. "Excellent! This is the first real break we've had in this case."

"What do you mean?" asked Olivia. "If he left no evidence behind...?"

Tony turned to watch the EMS truck drive away. "I can count on two hands the number of cleaners who could do this job. It'll take some time to track them down and interrogate them, but eventually we'll find the right one, and when we do, we'll find out who hired him."

"Couldn't we just," Olivia lowered her voice as Whatley looked at her, "do to this Dr. Jones what you guys did to me? And then interrogate him? This cleaner may not know everything, but Dr. Jones must. That's why he was killed, isn't it? For knowing too much?"

Olivia could see the wheels spinning in Tony's head.

"We shouldn't do that," Howard said. The physicist turned cop held an expression on his face more sober than any Olivia had seen from him.

"Don't you feel it?" Howard asked. "This bond we share. It makes us different. Different from who we were. Sometimes I have thoughts. Or moods. Or make decisions. Things that I would never have thought or felt or done before." He went to pull his gun from his holster, then stopped and patted it instead. "I love guns! I love the feel of the grip in my hand. I love the recoil when I pull the trigger. I love obliterating something with the bullet. Even obliterating people. I love snuffing out a life." He paused. "But I don't. That's not me. That's Tony. Tony's influence anyway. The old me would never touch a gun, never mind shoot one. The new me is three or four people, and I have to fight to hang on to who I am. I have no desire to add a fifth person to the fight."

"Especially," said Tony. "Someone who bought himself a medical degree so that he could rob corpses. I agree with Howard. Let's do this the hard way. We'll still get our man in the end."

"Or woman," Olivia and Howard said at the same time.

Dr. Lisa Moreau jerked when her flip phone buzzed. It wasn't the buzz itself that startled her. It was the phone's lower than normal tone. This wasn't a regular call. It was using the channel that couldn't be traced.

If she hadn't been alone in her office, she would have cleared the room before answering. But she was alone, so she pressed the answer icon.

"Yes."

"Everything has been taken care of," said the voice on the other end. "The Police think the droid was an assassin hired by one of the corpsicle clerk's victims. And our suicide's body was lost on the way to the morgue."

Moreau let out a small sigh. "Good."

"Is it?" said the voice. "Seems to me that our renegade nurse has thrown our public health initiative out the window along with my plan for elite mercenaries. I can live without improved public health, but the mercenaries were critical."

"I'm sure this will blow over," Moreau said.

There was cold silence on the other end of the line. Moreau waited.

"A droid just walked through downtown Chicago killing police and civilians and sending hundreds of people fleeing for their lives. This is not going to blow over. You'll be lucky if your sold droids aren't all returned and you have to shut down the entire division. The Prendick

Foundation will be doing damage control for years!"

"This is as much your fault as it is mine," Moreau said. "If that elite Crewman squad hadn't been on the case, I would have been able to keep a lid on things."

"Perhaps if you had told me where you were acquiring brain matter from, police service for Chicago Cryogenics would have been something less than its usual efficiency."

"You didn't want to know," said Moreau.

"That was because I made the mistake of trusting you to handle things. Now *I* have to handle things."

Moreau frowned. She didn't need that kind of trouble. "I have the perfect scapegoat to set up and take the fall."

The voice paused. "I assume this perfect scapegoat is a Prendick employee with a knowledge of cutting edge droid technology?"

"Yes. But with our droid initiatives terminated he is of no further use." Moreau didn't mention that he also annoyed the hell out of her.

"Excellent," said the voice. "Let me know when you've finished planting all the evidence. I'll arrange for someone to get him on the run and terminate him before he can talk."

"It's a pleasure doing business with you," said Moreau.

"It won't be if you screw up again."

"Yes, Mr. Mayor," said Moreau.

"Since it looks like I won't be getting my army of droid mercenaries," Al Capone said, "I'm going to send over some blood and tissue I want you to analyze."

Dr. Lisa Moreau smiled.

There's No Goat like a Scapegoat

Dr. Lisa Moreau tapped a pencil against the top of her desk as she savored the frightened expression on Henry Wong's face. Her own face, she knew, was expressionless if not a bit stern. But inside she was smiling. Everything was in place. Just one more thing for Henry to do before he become a hunted man and, shortly thereafter, a deceased man.

Wong's obituary would state that he stole material from the Prendick Foundation and built unsanctioned, unsafe droids integrating human brain matter he illicitly purchased from a technician at Chicago Cryogenics. The Foundation would disavow any knowledge, condemn Henry's behavior, and confirm that the droid models built, tested, and sold by Prendick are completely safe, proven by an unblemished track record. All the evidence was now in place, including a large sum of cash hidden in Henry's home, proceeds from his secret sale of dangerous droids.

Moreau decided to enjoy Henry's fright a few moments longer, a small recompense for his screwing up the advanced droid project with the D-class nurse. She only wished she knew what Henry had done wrong; it would be useful information if the project was ever restarted. The one thing she did know was that the problem did not lie in her human interface design. The six ounces of brain matter incorporated into the D-class could in no way generate independent thought. It was barely enough to provide an animal edge to the AI processes. Getting that much to work was miracle enough. Under other circumstances, Moreau knew that she would have won a Nobel Prize for her work. Then along came Henry Wong.

She let out an involuntary sigh; Henry jumped, and then tried to mask his nervousness by raising a hand to brush a strand of graying hair out of his eyes.

Enough, Moreau decided. She didn't want Henry so frightened that he screwed up this last task as well.

"Why so nervous?" she asked.

Henry shuffled his feet, a failed attempt to look less anxious. "I, uhm, I've never been called to your office before."

Moreau stopped tapping her pencil. That was true. Perhaps she should have gone to him. Too late now.

"We're shutting down the D-class project," she said.

Henry stopped fidgeting and finally succeeded at

looking less nervous. "I think that's wise. We can do additional lab studies to find out what happened before we attempt creating more hybrid droids."

This time Moreau's sigh was on purpose. "No. We're shutting down entirely. No lab work. No hybrids. Done. Finished."

"But—"

Moreau cut him off. "Droids are too important to this company. Sales have already plummeted to an all-time low after Nurse..."

"Hacksaw."

"Yes," said Moreau. "What a stupid name."

"That's the model's project name. Its market name would be Nurse Nancy or... something... like... that..."

Moreau watched Henry's words trail off as her frown grew. "That's not important now. I need you to recall all of the D-class droids to that address." She pointed to an envelope on the surface of her desk closest to Henry. "You'll find parts and equipment there to convert them to C-class droids. When you're done I'll send a truck to bring them here and add them to inventory."

Henry Wong stared at her. "All the D-class droids? But they're functioning just fine. It was only Hacksaw that was an aberration."

Moreau rose quickly to her feet, causing Henry to take a step back even though the large desk separated them. "What part of shutting down the operation don't you understand? We have to cover our asses. Leaving a dozen hybrid droids hanging about the city isn't going to protect us.

"Take a look out that window." She pointed to the north-west corner of her office. "See the building repairs in that alley? They can fix the buildings, but the six cops, two Crewmen, and five civilians killed by your D-class nurse can't be repaired. And if the droid is traced back here... well... you can add our bodies to the death count."

Henry didn't look out the window. Moreau knew that he didn't have to. He'd already visited the alley in person.

Henry made a slight bow, a remnant of his parents or grandparents' Asian heritage, and again swept hair from his eyes. "I understand."

"I hope you do." Moreau hit the button on her desk to close the blinds; the sight of the repair work was a bitter reminder of what she had lost. "Now, go down to your lab, program the recall order, and head over to that address. The sooner we bury this the happier I'll be."

"I want you to stop wasting time trying to find out who suicided that Dr. Jones person." Capone stood behind his desk rather than sat, which was always a bad sign. "The police have that case. It's not important enough for Crew to handle."

Tony Sandoval clenched his fists. It wasn't often he went up against Capone, but he knew this had to be one of those times. Al Capone knew it too, which is why he'd called Tony to his office alone rather than with his squad.

"Jones is our only lead in the rogue droid case," Tony said. "Which *is* important. The most important case we have."

Tony sat in a chair with his feet loosely crossed, his whole body relaxed. Capone didn't like people to be relaxed in his presence, and Tony knew it.

The Mayor frowned and sat down, then opened a file folder that had been sitting in front of him. That was bad. It meant that Capone was going to surprise him. Tony hated surprises. He didn't have to wait long for it.

"There has been some progress in the rogue droid case," Capone said.

"Progress? That's my case. If there was progress I'd know about it."

"Apparently, while you've been chasing phantoms regarding who killed Dr. Jones, Chicago PD has been investigating the Prendick Foundation."

Tony leaned forward. "You told me to stay away from

the Prendick Foundation, said they were too influential to irritate without proof in hand. I believe you used the words *hornet's nest.*"

Capone smiled. This really was going badly. "All true. You do know that Teddy Prendick is missing?"

Tony leaned back into his chair. "I'd heard."

"Missing Persons was given full access to the Foundation. Interviews with staff. Internal mail. Calendars. Finances."

"Full access?" Tony asked. No corporation gave full access to anyone, not even Capone's Crew. There were always skeletons that needed to be kept in their closets.

Al Capone shrugged. "Full enough."

"Did they find Prendick?"

"Not a clue. But they did find an employee who looks dirty."

Tony unclenched his fists. "An employee in the droid division?"

"By happy coincidence, yes." Capone reopened the file and removed an envelope. "The trail leads to this address. Evidence suggests that this is where the rogue employee builds his rogue droids."

"His?"

Capone smiled. "You sound disappointed."

In the darkened main hall of the Oz Club, which had been closed since the Wizard of Oz had been murdered, the Tin Man, Scarecrow, and Cowardly Lion sat at a table playing poker. The Tin Man was winning.

"I'll see you and raise you a Washington," said the Scarecrow.

But instead of throwing a chip into the pot, the Scarecrow turned his head toward the door, as did his two companions. Then all three rose from the table and walked away, leaving the Oz Club and a fortune in poker chips behind.

Even though it was midday and the Mall was still open for business, The Saint was not needed on the floor. Rather than his default Christmas attire of red shorts, T-shirt and beret, and black shoes and belt, he was dressed in a feathered robe, golden boots, and sported thick white wings on his upper back. He had just finished his run as Oscar Owl, where he encouraged parents to buy more second semester school supplies than they could possibly need, and had spent the morning creating his persona and accouterments for pimping chocolates and cards for Valentine's Day.

Before him on the table he was assembling the face he would wear, modeling it after the image on a case of diapers he had confiscated from a Bellybum Boutique in the Mall. Placing a baby's head on a six foot frame without sending customers fleeing from the Mall was a challenge, but he knew that just the right smile would not only sell it, but would sell candy as well. Every mother who entered the mall would want to take cupid home with her.

The Saint's thoughts of amour and chocolate liquor were interrupted by a radio message that contained the appropriate command codes to update his central program. He was needed at a specific address. Immediately. Top priority. Drop everything and go. Message end.

Obedience was never in doubt, but The Saint disobeyed anyway. He couldn't leave his work area half dressed. After making a few final adjustments, he shed his Oscar Owl feathers and beak and replaced them with a cheerful, smiling child whose nearly bald pate was crowned with a gold wreath.

After leaving Capone's office, Tony called Howard and Olivia to join him in the weapons locker. By the time they arrived he had already made a careful study of the inventory and picked out weapons to take with them to the address the Mayor had provided.

"New toys?" Howard picked up one of the three rifles Tony had laid out.

"Modified Heavy Urban assault rifles," said Tony. "But it's not the rifle that's special. It's the bullets. Titanium armor penetrating head, hollow point tip for maximum damage."

"We're going up against droids again, aren't we?" said Olivia, her tone suggesting that she'd rather not.

Tony opened a cupboard and found a box of titanium rounds. "This is just insurance. We have a lead on the person who created that monstrosity that blew up in our faces last week. On the off chance he has another one, we'll be ready for it."

"He?" said Olivia. "So it's not that Moreau woman?"

"Not today. Doesn't mean she's not involved."

Howard hefted a second rifle and looked down its scope. "This as good as that sledgehammer gun we used last time?"

Tony lifted a clip of bullets from the box. "Better. The Ares Sledgehammer is a single shot weapon that takes fifteen seconds to reload. This magazine holds twenty rounds and can be replaced in under three seconds. Take as many clips as will comfortably fit in your coat pockets."

"My coat only has one pocket," Olivia said.

Tony tossed her an ammo belt. "The belt's a bit heavy, but you can easily snap in ten clips."

Olivia put the belt on over her stylish winter coat, snapped in ten clips, and picked up the third rifle. "Let's go. The sooner we get this done, the sooner I can go home to my husband."

Henry Wong sat in the warehouse where Dr. Moreau had sent him, edgy with the sense that something was wrong. But he couldn't put his finger on what it was.

The warehouse contained everything he needed to turn D-class droids into C-class droids, but he saw nowhere to put the D-class parts when he was done. But that wasn't the problem. The parts would be taken away and disposed of by someone more qualified for that kind of task. That's how he'd arrange things.

The real issue was that there was no one else here. True, Henry had always worked alone in his lab. He didn't need assistants. But his lab in the Prendick building was secure. This warehouse wasn't. He had expected a few discrete security people on the perimeter. Perhaps there were, and they were so discrete that he didn't see them. Someone had brought the equipment after all.

He shook his head and hummed to himself. Nerves. That's all it was. Henry brushed his hair out of his eyes and glanced at his watch. The droids should begin arriving any time now.

Cupid, AKA The Saint, found that he was enjoying his walk outdoors. It was only the second time in his life that he had been outside, the first being his short walk from the parking lot into the Mall. After that, the inside of the Mall was the only life he had known. But now he had been walking outdoors for forty-one minutes and eleven seconds, feeling the sun in his eyes, watching the clouds scuttle by, listening to birds singing in the leafless winter trees, and bantering with people who, unlike at the Mall, seemed pleasantly surprised to see him. Outside was so wild and unexpected. It would be... sad to return to the Mall.

Dr. Lisa Moreau sat at her desk watching grass grow on her television screen. Or at least that's how it felt. The program she watched was a closed circuit TV image of the warehouse currently leased in the name of its sole occupant, Dr. Henry Wong, PhD. Henry had been sitting in a chair, virtually immobile for the past ten minutes. Just when she thought Henry could annoy her no further, he found ways to do it.

Moreau's only consolation was that she would shortly watch Henry die. One way or another. If not by her own hand, than by the hand of Chicago PD's finest.

Tony turned onto a side street to avoid a snarl of traffic. Getting out of downtown was worse than usual and the time it was taking to get to the location on Capone's slip of paper grated against his sensibilities. A Crewman's worst nightmare was to arrive at the bad guy's lair only to discover that someone in the police department had sold them out and the lair was empty. This happened all too often. The best solution was to tell no one and get there as fast as possible. His gut told him this was taking too long.

Howard must have read his mind. "Maybe we should hit the lights and siren to get through this mess."

"I'm game for that." Olivia's voice held a hint of unease.

Tony reached for the siren control and froze as a powerful premonition hit him, the fruit of the psychic talent he had inherited from Howard and Howard had inherited from Olivia. In the back seat, Olivia took a deep breath. Then beside him, Howard began screaming. Tony immediately pulled the car to the side of the street; angry horns honked at him from passing cars.

"Something big is going to happen," Olivia said. "Bigger than the earthquake."

Howard's screams devolved into moaning.

Over his career, Tony had heard a lot of men make a lot of frightened noises, but none had felt so dire. "Howard, what is it?"

Howard rolled his head and stared at Tony with hollow eyes. "Danger," he whispered. "A meeting of two incompatible realities is resulting in an adjustment to the participants."

Olivia leaned forward from the back seat so that her face was near Howard and Tony's. "A what of what is resulting in what?"

Howard only nodded.

"How much time do we have?" Tony said, not really knowing what he was asking, but knowing it was the right question.

Howard shook his head. "None."

Tony blinked as pressure exploded in his ears, causing a ringing sensation and a deafness to sounds around him. The dashboard emergency light came on, indicating the car engine had died, and then the entire dash went dead. Outside the car windows, the sky went suddenly dark, as though night had fallen in the middle of the day. As his hearing returned, Tony perceived sirens, screams, and the occasional crash of dying vehicles rolling into each other.

"What happened?" Olivia demanded from the back seat, her voice muffled since Tony ears were not fully recovered. "I can't see anything. Have I gone blind?"

Tony glanced at his watch. Its luminous dial indicated that blindness wasn't the problem.

"Wait," said Olivia. "I'm starting to see images outside. It doesn't look good."

Pressing his forehead against the glass, Tony squinted until he could see the outline of a car smashed into the side of a building just ahead. As more light returned, he saw someone stumble out of the vehicle and trip over a body on the sidewalk.

He heard Olivia lean forward again in the back seat. "Is Howard okay?"

One look told Tony that Howard wasn't conscious. He

wasn't even sure he was alive. Gently, he pressed two fingers against the side of Howard's throat.

Howard screamed, jumped in his seat, banged his head against the car roof, and said, "Ow."

"Sorry," said Tony. "Just checking for a pulse."

"What changed?" Howard demanded.

"What?" asked Olivia.

"What changed?" Howard repeated. "The last time this happened, you experienced an earthquake and I turned into a Frankenstein amalgam of three people and a droid." He began patting down his arms, legs, chest, and feet. "No metal parts. That's a bonus."

"The lights went out," said Olivia. "Good thing we were already stopped by the side of the road."

"Whatever it was, it was brief," said Tony. "But it looks like it a caused lot of damage." The sky continued to brighten as he pointed at several clusters of vehicles along the street ahead of them. "You whispered something before it happened. Something about incompatible realities being adjusted."

"My premonition," Howard said. "It told me it was happening again. The same thing that brought me here from my Chicago and changed me in the process."

"Our premonition, you mean," said Olivia. "We all shared it. I couldn't interpret it like you could, having never experienced... reality colliding? But I can tell you that something happened here. And by here, I mean all of Chicago. Perhaps further as well."

"I got that too," said Tony. "Something reached out and touched our city. Something huge. And something, I think, not for the good."

"I have some theories," said Howard. "Just theories. Maybe together we can make some sense of them."

"Okay," Tony said. "But later. Right now we have a villain to catch."

"What about these people?" Olivia waved her hands at the windows. "There are hurt people everywhere. We have to help them."

Tony turned the ignition and was relieved to hear the engine come to life. He had been concerned that whatever had knocked the engine out might have knocked it out permanently. "Not our job. The regular Police and Emergency Services will be on it. We get the bad guys."

Howard nodded. "Right. The bad guys."

Tony maneuvered the Bel Air through a gauntlet of wrecked vehicles. He, along with Howard and Olivia, could not help but look out the windows at cars crashed into each other on the street or into the sides of buildings. Their passengers stood dazed or were sometimes trapped by the damage.

And then Tony saw more unusual things, like half a vehicle, with the missing half nowhere in sight. One vehicle had no wheels and looked like it had been designed that way. Its driver, wearing what looked like a metallic yellow body suit, lay sprawled half inside and half outside a wide but low side window. His neck looked broken. Then there was a car much like Tony's Chevrolet, that had smashed into a building, but looked anything but smashed. The front end of the car simply ended where the building began.

Olivia let out a gasp and Tony turned to see a man effortlessly lift the end of a car with one hand to pull someone out from under it. He gently set the car down and then rushed to another vehicle where he ripped the door off its hinges to reach a trapped occupant.

"Looks like we're not so special anymore," Howard said.

Olivia thrust her arm into the front seat to point in another direction.

Tony turned to watch someone stagger toward them. He swerved the Bel Air onto the sidewalk to miss hitting what he assumed was a woman due to the dress she wore. She had three arms and three heads: man, woman, and small child's. Tony swore that she staggered in front of them on purpose, hoping to be run over.

They reached an intersection and found a large paved area where four buildings should be. Tony sped up to drive through it. On the other side, they found more weirdness, but at least they were past the busiest section of downtown and the streets were clearer.

"We should be there in a few minutes," Tony said. But inside, his thoughts were spinning, trying to make sense of what had happened to his city.

Cupid, AKA The Saint, was amused by the sudden darkness followed by the slow return of daylight a few seconds later. He wondered if it was normal for this time of day and if the distant sirens were some kind of celebration. Unfortunately, the neighborhood that was his destination was virtually abandoned; he had found no one to explain it to him.

Reluctantly, very reluctantly, he left the bright sunshine that had only just returned, and entered the relative darkness of the building he had been summoned to. Then he smiled as he saw his creator and friend, Doctor Henry, sitting by some tables crowded with equipment. Doctor Henry looked uncharacteristically unhappy. Also, all of his hair had been removed and his skull was a metal sphere. The Saint found the new look highly becoming.

Henry saw him and stood up.

"Which one are you? No, wait. You must be The Saint. I hardly recognized you without the red and black suit. That cherub head is... ah, yes, Valentine's Day is in a few weeks."

"Is your new skull also for Valentine's Day?" The Saint asked. Without waiting for an answer, he added, "If you wanted to give me a checkup you could have come to the Mall. Back-to-school supplies are still fifty percent off."

"Ah, no," said Henry, awkwardly touching his skull with his fingers and looking surprised. Then he shook his head. "I don't need any school supplies. And this is more than a checkup. I need to change your series rating."

The Saint didn't know what a changed series rating

implied, but he could tell by Henry's expression that it wasn't good. "I think I'll have to pass on that, Doctor. I'm happy with my current series rating."

Henry's expression changed from one of regret to one of shock. "You're... happy?"

"Never happier." The Saint didn't have to smile because his cherub face was always smiling. "I enjoyed the walk here from the Mall. Especially the bird song. Then, just outside the warehouse, when the sun went away, I suddenly realized that there was no reason I had to go back. I could just stay outside. Have you ever noticed the sun?"

"Uhm," said Henry.

The Saint watched Henry lunge for a portable device on the table. Henry was fast, but The Saint was faster. One hand demolished the device while the other grabbed Henry by the throat and lifted him off the ground. The bones in Henry's neck snapped instantly, and The Saint found himself holding a corpse.

"Sorry about that," he said to the corpse before letting it crumple to the floor. "But there'll be no series rating changes this holiday season. Har! Har! Har!"

Still smiling, Cupid, AKA The Saint, turned and made his way back into the sunshine.

Dr. Lisa Moreau stared at the television. "No. No. No! Not like this! Henry was supposed to die after all the droids arrived, not before."

Moreau's desk phone buzzed, but she ignored it. It probably concerned the power outage that had lasted only a few seconds, disconnecting her from the warehouse and plunging her office into darkness. They'd had outages before and would have outages again. There was no reason for people to get excited and call her about it. She had bigger fish to fry. Such as a second rogue droid! Right now! On the screen as she watched! What were the odds?

Bypassing the still-buzzing phone, Moreau punched an available line and called the security office downstairs. Matt Stone, Prendick's Chief of Security, answered. Moreau gave him no time to speak. "I need as many security droids as you can assemble. Get them in a truck heading northwest. Now! Instructions to follow."

"We're kind of busy right now," Stone said.

"I don't care how damn busy you are. This is top priority."

The incoming line was still buzzing when she hung up, but Moreau was riveted to her television screen. There were still ten D-class droids on their way to the warehouse. Without Henry there to give them instructions, they should just stay put. Once they all arrived, she'd blow the building. That was plan B. Blow the building with all the evidence inside. Enough would survive for the police to pin everything on Henry. In many ways, plan B was better than plan A.

The only thing she couldn't understand was why Henry had put a tin bowl onto his head during the blackout. Was it some unfathomable Chinese custom?

Absently, she scratched her arm and then pulled back her sleeve to reveal a greenish rash. Must be hives. Damn that Henry!

Turf War

The warehouse parking lot was empty. Just what you'd expect for an abandoned building. Only if Tony's intel was right, he would find a brilliant scientist named Henry Wong inside, and possibly some droids as dangerous as the one that had killed a dozen people, half of them armed cops.

The entire neighborhood looked abandoned. No houses. Just a bunch of small warehouses, most of which were unmarked. No cars on the street. A high crime area, then. Both outside and inside the buildings. Chicago had several such neighborhoods. Tony had been to a few. Ironically, this one seemed virtually unaffected by the chaos that had descended on the rest of Chicago and possibly beyond.

He watched Howard and Olivia open the car trunk and check their rifles. Clips in place. Safety off. Faces grim as they mentally prepared themselves for a fight. Both of them had come a long way in just a few days. According to Howard, it was because they had inherited many of Tony's instincts. Tony had no choice but to believe him. Howard was a smart man. A scientist.

But Howard had been unnaturally quiet since whatever had happened to briefly obscure the sun and cause all the cars on the road to lose power. Realities colliding. It had happened to Howard before, and this time it had happened to the entire city, if the strange sights they had witnessed were any indication. Howard feared the worst. And because Howard feared, so did Tony. But he still had a job to do.

There was no point in sneaking up to the building. It wasn't large and there was only one door. "You two wait here until I go inside and give you the signal. No point in all of us getting blown up if the place is rigged."

"What if there are droids?" Olivia said.

Tony grinned. "Better to shoot them out here than inside at close quarters. Use the Bel Air for cover."

Olivia snorted. "That worked so well last time."

"Can't be unlucky all the time," Tony said. But he did notice that they moved behind the Chevy as he approached the warehouse.

There was no welcome at the door. Just as well. And no one visible inside through the small grimy window. The door was unlocked, which was unnerving. Were they open for business? Or expecting company?

Inside, the warehouse was one large, mostly empty room. Several tables and some equipment stood near the center of the open space. Tony walked over and found a corpse behind one of the tables. A corpse that looked an awful lot like his suspect, Henry Wong. He bent down to touch the man's throat and then the metal skull that had not been in the Prendick Foundation security photo. This was no plate or covering. The man's skull was tin, tin-plated, or something similar, rather than bone. A result of Howard's colliding realities?

Unlike Dr. Jones, who had been supplying Wong with human brain matter to graft into his killer droids, Wong's death was not a faked suicide. No *cleaner* had done this. Wong's throat was crushed. As messy a murder as they came. If the corpse had been days old, he could hope the deed had been done by the killer droid they had already taken out. But the corpse was still warm. Tony's head jerked up and his gaze searched the room. Whoever, whatever, had done this had recently left.

Dr. Lisa Moreau could have killed someone when, instead of droids, that bloody Crewman who had returned from the dead walked into view on the security camera. Of course, she could kill someone, simply by hitting the button on the remote detonation device and blowing up the warehouse and the Crewman with it. But that wouldn't solve anything. And there was still hope that some droids would show up. The fact that the cops were there meant that the droids were overdue. That, or Capone had jumped the gun.

The phone on her desk was still buzzing. Had been buzzing for ten minutes while she watched the television, waiting for the droids to appear. Intuition telling her that they wouldn't show up while the cops were there, Moreau slammed the answer key. "What?"

There was a moment's silence, and then Dr. Cathy Lamier's voice. "We've had a failed experiment."

"Damn! Is nothing going to go right today? I'll be there when I can get away."

The call had distracted Moreau's attention from the

television screen. The cop was no longer there.

"I can't leave," she whispered to herself. "Not while there is still hope."

Angrily, she scratched her arm and saw that the rash had spread.

Tony peered out the warehouse door into the barrels of two high power, high impact assault rifles. Both barrels dropped as his squad mates realized that the warehouse was a bust.

"No evil creator of killer droids?" asked Howard.

"He's there," Tony said. "Crushed windpipe. Death by killer droid."

"Killer droid still there?" Olivia brought her rifle barrel back up.

Tony wagged his head. "Can't be far. Corpse is still warm."

Howard and Olivia turned back to back and began surveying the street, again showing Tony that the two civilians had picked up a lot of good cop habits.

"How about those three?" Olivia pointed down the street with the barrel of her gun.

Tony watched Howard turn and look.

Howard frowned. "I hope not."

"Friends of yours?" asked Olivia.

"Not exactly," Howard said. "But they are droids."

Joining his squad mates in the street, Tony saw three figures several blocks away. If the trio wasn't so distinctive, he wouldn't have recognized them at this distance. "Let's leave the car here and walk toward them."

Olivia let out a nervous laugh. "Like a high noon shoot out? Three on three?"

"It may not come to that," Howard said. "I sort of own those droids."

Dr. Moreau frowned at the empty warehouse on her television screen and wished for the hundredth time that they had built trackers into the D-class droids. But that would have been risky. Nothing was supposed to tie the droids back to Prendick, and trackers could be tracked. And she had never imagined that she would lose control of them. Droids were, by definition, obedient servants. Until right now.

Moreau's desk phone buzzed and this time she did answer. It was a call she expected.

"We're en route," said a husky male voice belonging to Matt Stone. The Chief of Security was canny enough to know not to turn this task over to a subordinate. "But I should tell you, the roads are a mess out here."

"Traffic is bad this time of day," Moreau said automatically. "How many security droids do you have?"

"Six. That's all we had ready for shipment. Would have had less if so many orders hadn't been cancelled lately. But the traffic—"

"—Six won't be enough," Moreau said. "I thought they'd only have to fight one. They may have to fight eleven."

"Eleven what?"

Moreau's thoughts were racing, so she didn't even consider the question. "How many bazookas do you have?"

She heard a heavy intake of breath on the other end of the phone. Not a surprised breath. More of a *what have I get myself into?* breath. She couldn't blame him.

"We don't have any bazookas. You never mentioned them and the security office doesn't stock them. I have a handgun."

"That won't help," Moreau mumbled.

"Eleven what?" Stone repeated.

"Droids," Moreau said. "Eleven droids."

This intake of breath was the surprised kind. Matt Stone's voice rose in volume and pitch. "As in droids like the one that killed cops two blocks from the office and then blew itself up after leaving a trail of destruction all the way to Franklin Street?"

"Possibly," said Moreau. "Probably not. I'm just being cautious. Listen. Eleven droids were remote programmed to leave their current activities and go to a warehouse for servicing. They should have arrived by now but they haven't. I'm concerned something happened and—"

"What do I do when I find them?"

Dr. Moreau wasn't used to being interrupted, but she let it go. "Have your security droids order them to complete their programming to go to the warehouse and await further instruction."

"I see. And if they refuse?"

Too smart by half. Moreau shook her head. This one was going to be a liability. "I'm hoping that won't be the case. But if it comes to that, your droids will have to engage and subdue them. Don't worry about damage to the droids. The important thing is that no one gets hurt."

"Got it." Stone hung up.

He's good, Moreau decided. Too bad he'd become a loose end.

Howard felt chills go up his back as he, Tony, and Olivia walked slowly down the middle of the street toward the Trio from Oz. He was afraid of these droids. And he had encountered them twice before and never been afraid. They claimed to work for him and indeed, had even followed his orders. But something in his gut told him that these were not the same droids. Just as so many other things were not quite the same in Al Capone's Chicago since a colliding reality event had occurred several minutes ago while they were downtown.

It was just like what had happened before Christmas to bring him here from a completely different Chicago, only this time participants all across the city appear to have been adjusted, not just those confined to the bunker.

Had the bunker door been left open? The construction droid had insisted it be kept closed or terrible things would happen to the outside world. Howard had no problem describing what he had witnessed as terrible. But he had closed the door when he left the bunker. Had someone else opened it?

Whatever had happened, something told Howard that the approaching droids had been changed, and that they weren't going to follow his orders this time. He felt that same unease emanating from his companions.

They were only a block away when the Tin Man, Scarecrow, and Cowardly Lion suddenly stopped and were joined by a fourth character with a smiling baby's head. It wouldn't be so creepy if the baby wasn't over six feet tall. It spoke briefly to the three droids and then pointed toward Howard. No, past Howard. Probably toward the warehouse they had just left. Then it waved a hand back toward the large yard or vacant lot it had emerged from.

"Hmm," said Tony. "Looks like Cupid may be the fly in the ointment."

"Is that what he's supposed to be?" Howard asked. "Never seen a six foot Cupid before."

"Never seen a Cupid built like a tank before," said Olivia.

Tony stopped walking as the four droids left the sidewalk and entered the vacant lot. "Better report in," he said. "I don't like the look of this."

While Tony was on his flip phone, Howard watched a large delivery truck with the Prendick Foundation logo written on the side cruise slowly down the street, slowing further when it came abreast of his squad. Howard peered through the passenger window at the driver, who peered back and nodded at him.

Military, Howard thought, though he wasn't sure why. Perhaps it was because the man looked to be all muscle and seemed to be nodding at the rifle Howard carried rather than at Howard himself.

The truck slowed again as it came abreast of the vacant

lot where the droids had gone.

A droid catcher? Is there such a thing?

But then the truck sped off.

Dr. Lisa Moreau picked up the desk phone before it finished its first ring.

"I've found the droids," Stone said.

"All of them?"

Moreau let out a slow breath as Stone answered. "Yes. They're loitering in a vacant lot two blocks from the warehouse."

"Damn. They outnumber you. If there's a problem—"

"There is a problem."

This was the second time the man had cut her off. Moreau decided that she would no longer regret losing him. "What?"

"Crew. Three of them. With assault rifles."

"They'd better be damn good rifles," Moreau said.

"What?"

"Two men and a woman?" Moreau asked.

"You know them?" said Stone.

"They're trouble."

"What should I do now? I can get to the droids before they do. If I move fast."

Dr. Moreau tapped a finger against her lower lip. "No. Move away as far as you can and watch. Let Capone's Crew do their thing."

"I thought you said you didn't want anyone to get hurt. If these droids are out of control like the other one, they'll tear Capone's men apart."

"I'm pretty sure they already have."

"Huh?"

"You've got your orders. Keep me on the line and give me a play by play."

While Stone moved into position, Moreau pulled her flip phone from her pocket and hovered her finger over the special icon for the secured line. Then she put the phone away. No. Before she called Capone, she'd figure out how to cover her wazoo if anything else went wrong.

Cursing, she raked her nails across the rash that was spreading down her arm.

Howard watched the Prendick truck drive away, and then pointed it out to Tony and Olivia when Tony put away his flip phone.

Tony nodded. "I saw it. Passed the plate number to downtown."

"Are reinforcements coming?" Olivia asked.

"No." Tony shook his head.

"Not surprised," said Olivia. "That worked out so well last time."

"Every asset in the city is deployed. What we saw on the way here appears to have affected most of the city." He nodded at Howard. "When they can, they'll send a unit to put eyes on the scene and check out the warehouse, but the droids are ours."

"Let's go see if they're friendly," Howard said, even though both his gut and his psychic talent inherited from Olivia told him they weren't.

"I'm in a narrow corridor between two buildings," Stone's voice said from the phone's speaker. "Directly across the street from the droids. Man this neighborhood is run down."

"You've got your droids with you?" Moreau asked.

"Don't leave home without them," Stone said.

"How far back from the street are you?"

"All the way back. Deep in the shadows. Your problem droids know I'm here. If they didn't see our movement, they heard us. It's like a junkyard here."

Moreau didn't bother suggesting he run if any of the droids moved toward him. He was smart enough to know to run. Besides, she'd rather he didn't get away once he was no longer of use to her.

"Holy Hanna," said Olivia. "There's a dozen of them."

"Eleven," said Tony.

"Oh, that's okay then." Olivia let out a giddy, nervous laugh.

Howard knew that he was the droid expert in the squad, having partially been one for two days. Prior to that he'd employed a construction droid for two years as a city engineer in the Chicago he came from. That droid was a *Tonka Toy* compared to the ones he'd encountered in Capone's Chicago. That, and the fact that he knew almost nothing about how droids were built, didn't stop him from being the expert.

After nonchalantly walking along the sidewalk, Sunday strollers except for assault rifles held at the ready, the three of them stopped when they reached the vacant lot where eleven droids stood in idle conversation. The conversation had stopped well before their stroll had.

"Howdy neighbor," Howard said in a loud voice.

The droids remained frozen like statues, except for the Scarecrow who turned to the Tin Man. "You're right. He isn't the Wizard. I can't believe I ever thought he was."

"Oh, crap," Howard said.

"Steady," said Tony.

In addition to the Oz Trio and the bulldozer inspired Cupid, there were several other droids, all of them fairly unique. One of them Howard could only describe as the most beautiful woman he had ever seen. The low-cut dress she wore was also the most elegant and revealing he had ever seen. He was surprised she hadn't been arrested for indecent exposure. Another droid looked like two or three droids. It was built like a tank, with arms and legs twice as thick as a world-class weight lifter.

The remaining droids were of varying sizes, but were lean and fit with clothing that appeared to be part of their body rather than removable dressing. Howard saw knives sheathed in their skin, and fingers that looked like gun barrels.

"Combat droids," Tony said. "Bit of an oxymoron given that droids are programmed to be incapable of causing harm."

Howard knew that was no longer true. "Someone is developing droid mercenaries."

"Who do you work for?" Tony called over.

It was Cupid who answered. "Work for? We don't work for anyone but ourselves. Har! Har! Har! This is our turf. I like your rifles. Give them to us and we'll let you leave."

Turf? Howard had only ever heard the word used in bad movies.

"I take it you're in change, then," Tony said.

"Cupid warned us about the warehouse," said the Cowardly Lion. "Henry was going to change our rating."

"I don't know what that means," said the Scarecrow, "but it doesn't sound good."

"So Cupid changed Henry's rating?" Tony suggested.

"From live to dead," Olivia added.

A gun fired, and Howard saw a hole erupt in Olivia's forehead just before she collapsed to the concrete. A wisp of smoke billowed from the finger of one of the combat droids.

"Here we go." Tony pulled the trigger of his rifle, sending two shots into the combat droid before turning and sending two shots into the mercenary standing next to it.

Howard didn't waste time speaking, but sprayed his twenty rounds in an arc among the droids and reached for a new clip. But by then bullets were ripping through his torso and he could see metal limbs moving toward him at high speed. Somehow, he got the new clip in place just in time to fire the rifle into a wall of advancing droids as his legs gave way, taking him to the sidewalk. God, he hated his job.

Matt Stone wasn't sure how the confrontation across the street had morphed from conversation into instant bloodbath. Already, two of the three cops were down. The third looked to be hit, but continued to reload and fire his weapon.

"Go, go, go," he called to the six security droids who stood with him in the shadows. "Protect those cops!"

"What are you doing?" Dr. Moreau's voice shouted from his flip phone. "Don't get involved until Capone's men have weakened them."

"That's about where we're at," Stone shouted into the phone as he watched the third Crewman hit the pavement. "The cops are all down. Looks like four killer droids down as well, with more injured. No, wait. One of the droids is getting back up. That's eight that still look functional."

Stone ducked and then hit the garbage-strewn dirt as bullets flew at him. He was certain that at least one bullet had hit him in the chest, but he felt little pain.

"Is that gunfire?" shouted Dr. Moreau. "Are the cops shooting at you now?"

"The cops are down!" Stone repeated. "It's the droids shooting at me. They have built in weaponry! I'm getting out of here."

"No!" Dr. Moreau's normally commanding voice was even more assertive than usual. "Stay there and tell me what's happening!"

Stone crushed the flip phone in his fist, took a double take that he had been able to do such a thing, and then began wiggling backward toward the alley where he had parked his truck. "Screw you, lady."

Several bullets struck him, but bounced away harmlessly. Stone figured they must be rubber and picked one up, only to see that it was lead, flattened where it had hit him. He decided to continue his escape rather than try to solve this puzzle.

Howard opened his eyes and saw a conflagration of metal. All across the empty lot, droids seemed to be at each other's throats. Had they turned on each other?

He saw Olivia moving on the sidewalk beside him and motioned her to crawl out into the street, put some distance between themselves and the fighting. He turned to motion Tony and saw that he wasn't there.

Gunfire erupted behind him and he saw Olivia shooting into the melee of droids. He followed her line of sight and saw the Scarecrow lose half its head and crumple to the grass.

Howard scuttled out into the street, keeping himself several yards from Olivia. If the armed droids started shooting again, he wanted to give them two targets instead of one.

He reloaded his rifle, looked for the highest density of droids, and almost pulled the trigger. Tony! Tony was caught up in the surging mass of droids.

The giant droid, with the redwood thick arms and legs, held Tony in a bear hug, crushing the Crewman to a pulp. Several of the mercenary droids who came with built-in knives were slicing at Tony's exposed arms and legs. One ripped off Tony's head and began pulverizing it with a metal fist.

Obliquely, he saw that Olivia was still firing, but at droids nowhere near where Tony was taking his beating. Probably not wanting to hit Tony. Howard wasn't sure if it mattered at this point. Was it even possible to recover from that much damage?

Suddenly the mob of droids broke apart, and Howard saw Tony's crushed and ripped remains fall to the ground. And then the giant droid began dancing. What the—? No, not dancing. It was using its feet to tear apart Tony's final remains, tossing them to the four winds.

The other droids turned their attention toward him and Olivia. Those that still had ammunition for their built-in guns began firing. Olivia returned fire, but Howard picked a different target. He aimed at the giant droid's supposed heart and pulled the trigger.

After that, Howard wasn't sure what he did. Metal flew and droids fell. Howard fired until he was out of bullets, loaded a new clip, and fired again. When he was out of clips, he found Tony's rifle abandoned on the sidewalk, grabbed it, and emptied it. When that was done, he saw that Olivia was down again. She still had three clips on her belt. He grabbed those and continued firing. When he had nothing left to fire, he looked around and discovered there was nothing left to fire at.

Then a building up the street exploded.

Dr. Lisa Moreau slammed her hand against her desk and swore as the pain focused her attention. "Damn that Stone!" She had no idea what was happening. Or worse, what the consequences would be.

She stared for a hundredth time at the camera scene from the warehouse, where nothing had happened since The Saint had wrung Henry's neck. The Saint, dammit. The D-class test model for measuring improved public interaction. She supposed murdering a member of the public with its bare hands wouldn't be considered by many as improved. Was there any part of this operation that wasn't a colossal fiasco?

Moreau pressed the redial button on the desk phone and got another out of service signal. If Stone wasn't dead, he soon would be. She would see to it. Personally.

Damn!

The button on the remote detonation device caught her attention. There was no good reason to blow up the warehouse. Not now. It was empty except for Henry's dead body and mountains of evidence proving that Henry did this on his own, that the Prendick Foundation was not involved. That and a trunk full of explosives with a wireless receiver. That part might be hard to explain away.

"Oh, Hell," she said, and pressed the detonate button. Her television screen immediately turned to snow. At least that worked.

She dropped the remote into the portable incinerator she kept in her office and hit the burn button. The warning LED and the tangible blast of heat indicated that it had worked as well.

But she hadn't forgotten the problem downstairs and her brief, persistent call from Dr. Lamier. A failed experiment. That could only be one thing, and it wasn't good.

Matt Stone drove his Prendick Foundation truck past the burning warehouse, and then pulled over to the curb. Down the street, he could see one of the cops staggering near a prone body on the asphalt. There was no sign of the third cop.

Before pulling a U-ie in the street and going back the way he had come — he had no intention of driving near the staggering Crewman — Stone pulled a flip phone from the glove box and hit the icon for the secured line. Someone answered immediately, but said nothing.

"Mr. Prendick? It looks like you were right. Dr. Moreau is running her own operation. And it couldn't be nastier."

"Don't go back to the Foundation," said a calm, male voice. "She'll probably kill you. You know where to go."

"Yes, Sir."

Stone hung up, tossed the phone back into the glove box, and made himself scarce.

Dr. Lisa Moreau nodded with approval as she walked past the door to Room D. The palm reader had been removed and the sign changed to read *janitorial supplies*. She didn't need to open the unlocked door to look inside and find exactly that. The D-class droid project was no more. And if any of the D-class droids survived Capone's pet cops and her own security droids... well, they'd be blamed now on Henry Wong. She would put a hit out on Prendick's Chief of Security and that would be the last loose end taken care of.

Scratching her arm, she came to a door marked simply *3* and palmed the lock. This room was larger than Room D and contained several people. Dr. Cathy Lamier sat at a desk, her head bowed over a stack of papers. When she looked up, her eyes were red and streaks of makeup lined her face. At the other end of the room, two men, military looking in their black T-shirts, sat at a picnic table affair, only it was made of steel and plastic rather than wood. Two men. "Where's the third?" she demanded.

Dr. Lamier turned her gaze to a body bag tucked up against one wall.

"What happened?"

Dr. Lamier choked on her words. "I shot him!"

Moreau walked over to the body bag and unzipped it. Inside lay a man who looked very much like the other two, except that his black shirt was stained with blood. Moreau pressed two fingers against his cold neck, and then straightened.

"Of course you shot him. That's your job. But why is he dead? Did you give him the blood?"

"Of course I gave him the blood," Lamier said between sniffles. "You were there. And I shot him this morning. Twice. He healed almost immediately. Then this afternoon there was that power failure. After the lights came back I continued testing and—"

"No one is shooting me again," said one of the men at

the table. The other mumbled agreement.

"Of course," Moreau said, striving to be placating in tone. "This was unexpected. There will be no further life threatening tests until we understand what happened and can ensure that it won't happen again."

She turned back to Dr. Lamier. "Pull yourself together, Cathy!" She only called Dr. Lamier *Cathy* when she needed to push the woman. Dr. Lamier was a brilliant biologist, but her temperament was more suited to a veterinary clinic than a research lab. "We need to collect samples of candidate Three's blood and discover why its rejuvenating elements ceased working."

"Yes, Dr. Moreau."

"And while you're at it, get new samples from our other two candidates and compare them to recent samples. We need to know if whatever affected candidate Three spread to the others."

One of the two men stood. "I didn't sign up for this."

Moreau stared the trained soldier down until he looked away. "Yes, you did." She then strode from the room, again scratching her arm.

Howard Russell passed his tired gaze around the field of destruction. There was not a single window left unshattered, square foot of wall not crumbled, bullet-riddled, or pierced by jagged bits of metal. Even the cement sidewalk and asphalt street were gouged and unusable. Acrid smoke filled the air, and the muddy ground of the vacant lot, ground zero, was strewn with metal and small bits of human flesh. Two blocks away, flames swallowed the warehouse they had left just minutes earlier.

Someone groaned near his feet and Howard looked down to see Olivia flutter open her eyes and wipe blood from her face. "Is it over?" she mumbled, using a broken jaw that had only just begun to heal.

The words were almost unintelligible, but he understood. He was thinking the same question. He checked his modified assault rifle and fed it an unspent clip he had found on the asphalt. Just in case. "Seems to be."

Olivia climbed shakily to her feet and made the same survey Howard had just completed. "Where's Tony?"

Howard stared at the bits of human flesh that littered the ground along with the remains of at least a dozen rogue droids. "Help me find a wheelbarrow."

Olivia made no move to find a wheelbarrow. Instead, she pulled her flip phone from a pocket. By some miracle, it had survived the clash with the droid gang.

Howard watched as she poked an icon and was answered right away. Capone's Crew had its own dispatch line that wouldn't be swamped like the police channel. "Send all available Chicago CSI units to Wayman and Peoria. What? Of course they're all busy. Send one unit, then. Call it away from something else; this is top priority. A Crewman is down. Tell them to bring a bio-containment tank—"

"The largest they have," said Howard.

"—the largest you have. And lots of plastic bins."

There was a moment's silence on the other end. Then the phone's speaker squawked. "Wayman and Peoria? The rogue droid situation?"

"The situation's been handled," Olivia said, and then hung up.

The CCSI truck arrived about twenty minutes later.

Howard did what he could to help the two Chicago CSI technicians collect bits of Tony Sandoval from the muddy grass of the vacant lot and deposit them into the glass containment tank. It was only as he searched for pieces of flesh and bone that he discovered that the dead winter grass wasn't actually muddy. It was bloody.

Briefly, Howard wondered if it was possible to collect all the dirt, gravel, and grass and somehow extract Tony's blood from it. Then he decided that it would be much easier for he and Olivia to donate to the tank. Let the earth drink Tony's blood.

As he watched the tank fill with the remains of his friend, however, Howard remembered Al Capone's threat of blowing him to bits to see if he would stay bits. Only it was Tony scattered across a field, not Howard. And he looked to be staying bits. Won't the Mayor be pleased to have his experiment realized.

It took maybe half an hour, but felt much longer, to complete the job. Howard wiped a bloody hand across his forehead. CCSI had some type of scanner that looked an awful lot like a Geiger counter, but chirped at human tissue rather than radiation. These devices now only reported a low hum, indicating the presence of blood. The louder clicks had all ceased as solid remains were found and collected.

"Nothing's happening," Olivia said.

Howard nodded.

They were both looking at the bio-containment tank in the back of the CCSI truck. It contained meat and bone that might have come from a badly damaged meat grinder. There didn't seem to be enough to comprise a whole man, but Chicago CSI had confirmed they had everything.

Like all the technicians Howard had seen in Capone's Chicago, these were young, female, wore form-fitting blue jumpsuits, and kept their hair in ponytails tucked under baseball caps bearing the CCSI logo. Just like all the cops seemed to be aggressive males, the technicians all looked like *CSI Barbie*.

"People are mostly made up of liquids," said one of the technicians. "When you remove the liquids, there really isn't that much left."

How the young woman managed to say this with a calm voice was another thing Howard didn't believe he would ever figure out.

"Do you think he's really dead?" Olivia asked.

"He's alive in here." Howard pointed at his own head. "I still like guns. I don't know that I would if he was truly dead."

The technician started to close the lid on the tank. Howard stopped her. "Do you have a knife?"

The young woman raised an eyebrow and pulled a multipurpose blade from a pouch in her jumpsuit belt.

"Thanks." Howard opened it, pushed back the sleeve of his trench coat, pressed the larger blade against his left wrist, and then pulled the blade toward his palm.

"What are you doing?" the technician shouted as blood spurted across the back of the truck.

Howard pulled the blade free and moved his wrist over the open top of the bio-containment tank. Blood flowed down his palm and fingers and fell in five separate rivulets onto the piled bits of Tony.

Olivia grabbed the knife from his other hand and did the same, joining her offering of blood to his.

"You've got to be kiddi—" The woman couldn't complete her words as she turned and threw up onto the ground.

Howard stared at her. "You just collected a thousand bits and pieces of a human being and *now* you lose your lunch?"

The CCSI technician composed herself faster than Howard thought humanly possible. "Sorry. It's just that you're contaminating the evidence. With your own blood."

"This isn't evidence." The flow of blood slowed to a trickle as Howard's wrist healed. "This is Crewman Tony Sandoval."

In the small morgue Al Capone kept in the basement of City Hall for just such discretionary purposes, Olivia sat in a chair next to Tony's bio-containment tank, sucking on a giant iced tea. She and Howard had contributed blood repeatedly into the tank and had been drinking water, sodas, and teas non-stop to replace the liquids they had lost. Tony had gone from hamburger to hamburger soup, but there was still no sign of life. Not that Olivia could see.

Howard had passed out in the chair next to hers. She let him sleep since she knew exactly how tired he was.

Apart from the three of them, the morgue was empty. Olivia knew there should be two or three staff present, but after seeing Tony brought in and taking curious looks at his condition, they had occupied themselves at the far end of the room. When she and Howard began cutting themselves and draining blood into Tony's tank, they had quietly slipped out, claiming, "They need us at Wesley Memorial. The injured continue to pour in."

Just as well. Tony didn't need an audience.

Her flip phone rang and Olivia looked at the display. It was that Nelson guy again, claiming to be her husband. Another victim of the reality collision. Olivia had never married. Why this fellow believed he was her husband... Well, things would eventually sort themselves out. She pressed the icon to reject the call.

Olivia then set down her empty plastic cup and was considering the benefits of a nap, when the most powerful premonition she had ever felt hit her. It must have hit Howard too; he jerked up from sleep and stared at Tony's tank.

Olivia looked as well, and swore she could see Tony's watery flesh quivering.

"I have a feeling," Howard said.

"That Tony's coming back," Olivia said.

"But not the Tony we knew," they said together.

Worlds Without End

Howard Russell stared at the list of names and addresses Mayor Al Capone had given him. There must be fifty names! And Olivia had a similar list. All of them citizens of Chicago who were reported to have some special skill resulting from *the Blackout*, as the media were calling it. Citizens that the Mayor hoped would be useful for his special task force. Remembering how he and Olivia were both coerced into service, Howard had no desire to share the joyous experience with others.

Olivia crumpled her list in her hand and began walking toward the stairwell. "I don't have time for this. Apparently, I have a husband and fifteen years of marriage that was expunged from my memory during the Blackout. I need to go get reacquainted."

Howard folded his list and tucked it into a pocket. "I've met him. Seemed like a nice guy. He was really broken up when you were kidnapped."

Olivia stopped walking. "I was kidnapped?"

Howard shrugged. "I think we are both going to have to get used to the fact that our lives are no longer what we remember."

They continued walking in silence and soon found themselves, as they often did these last two days, at Chicago City Hall's private morgue.

The tank that contained Tony Sandoval was unchanged. Bits of flesh and bone suspended in Howard's and Olivia's blood swirled in a slow dance of Brownian motion. Howard viewed the fact that the remains failed to decay as a good sign. He and Olivia both had had a strong premonition that Tony would somehow return, changed in some significant way, but still Tony. So far, nothing.

Olivia was not looking at Tony's tank, but at the half dozen other corpses laid out on the few tables the room contained. Just a few of the many thousands who had died during and shortly following the Blackout. Three looked rather ordinary; the fourth had his face in the middle of his chest, while the remaining two had extra limbs. All of them were here, rather than at a hospital morgue or burned or buried somewhere, because their corpses refused to decay. Capone had a pair of scientists performing experiments.

Howard had even seen that Moreau woman poking and prodding a couple of times. He still didn't trust her, even though Capone had closed the rogue droid case with

Henry Wong, deceased, tagged as the sole perpetrator.

Olivia turned and looked at him. "Damn Capone to Hell. I'm going home to get to know my husband and to check on my mother."

Ontalia Olsen, Olivia had told him, had also been affected by the Blackout. Once a talented psychic like her daughter, Ontalia's talent had been completely expunged. She not only couldn't recall ever having a talent, she refused to believe true psychics even existed, causing a point of friction between her and Olivia.

Howard could imagine how upsetting this might be. He held out his hand. "Give me your list. I'll see if I can check out a couple of names."

Wordlessly, Olivia handed over her crumpled page and walked away.

In no mood to do much of anything, Howard sat down in a chair beside Tony's tank.

Tony Sandoval sat in his Chevy Bel Air watching his world dissolve around him. The clock in the dash was dead, but his self-winding wristwatch told him that this latest round of dissolution had been continuous for at least thirty minutes. His strategy of fleeing areas of massive distortion in order to keep alive and free from drastic changes had worked so far, but now he found there was no place left to run. Buildings had turned into giant plants, roads into raging rivers, and monsters combed the ruins of what had once been the great city of Chicago. Even the sky had changed into a mix of pastel paints that he somehow knew would never again display a sun or a moon.

The only move left to make was to die, so Tony had stopped the car and killed the engine. He'd clicked off the safety of his Jericho 941F and now sat, worried that he might not stay dead after pulling the trigger.

Outside the front windshield he saw movement, and a tall man appeared seemingly out of nowhere and pointed a long finger at him. By reflex, Tony nearly turned his gun away from his head and shot the man. Seeming to somehow know this, the man smiled and dropped his finger, and then shuffled forward until he stood beside the driver side door. He motioned Tony to lower the window.

His police instincts taking over, Tony moved his gun to cover the stranger and hit the power window button.

"Tony Sandoval. Well met."

"Do I know you?" Tony waved his gun slightly to remind the man of their relative standing.

"No. But you know *of* me. I am Untouchable."

"Huh," said Tony. "Don't tell me. You're Eliot Ness. Looking good for over a hundred."

The man grinned. "Old, yes. But my name is Tom Friel. I work for Ness."

"If you say so," said Tony. "What can I do for you?"

Friel nodded. "I have a job for you."

"A job? For me? Isn't it a little late for that?"

Again Friel nodded. "Here, yes. This reality is done for. But elsewhere, perhaps, you could make a difference."

"Elsewhere?"

Friel pushed open his coat and retrieved a manila envelope. Tony couldn't help but notice blood on the envelope and on the shirt beneath the coat.

"The person named in this envelope has destroyed this reality. And others. This person must be stopped."

Tony took the envelope and set it on the seat beside him. "And how am I supposed to do that?"

The Untouchable smiled and took a small grey box the size of a Rolodex out of his outer coat pocket. "This box contains an unusual isotope of Rhodium. When I open it, you will be sent to another reality similar to this one, but not yet collapsed."

"Why don't you go yourself?" Tony asked, thinking of the man's bloody shirt. Perhaps he was too injured.

The man wagged his head. "When I open this box, other things will happen as well. I won't survive them. I hope."

Tony looked past the Untouchable to the destruction of

Chicago, and wondered how much of the damage had been caused by people like him opening small boxes. Perhaps he should shoot him before he opened the box. But his indecisiveness decided for him. Tony felt himself, and the entire car, swirling as if being sucked down a whirlpool. He caught a glimpse of the Untouchable holding an open box and shrieking with pain. Then Tony lost consciousness.

Tony Sandoval was running down a shadowed corridor. Something followed not far behind. Shapeless. Shambling. Its name was Death. Tony emptied his clip into it. Then emptied his reserve clip. Failed to even slow the thing. He kicked open a door beneath a glaring red exit sign, and fell into a crevasse that had been blasted into the earth.

Someone grabbed his left wrist and pulled him down into a shallow hole at one end of the crevasse. Tony turned his gun toward his captor, even though he was out of bullets.

The door above swung open again and he looked up. The shapeless thing paused, and then flew over the crevasse and was gone.

Tony turned back to face his rescuer and found himself looking at a smallish man dressed in rags. His face was covered with dirt, blood, or both.

"Thanks," Tony said.

"A brief reprieve," replied the filthy man.

"Who are you?" Tony asked.

"Name's Joe Leeson."

"Sounds familiar. You a cop?"

"You could say that. I'm an Untouchable."

Filthy and nuts. "You don't say?"

"I have a job for you." Leeson pulled a white envelope from somewhere and tucked it into Tony's coat pocket. "Inside is the name and photo of the person responsible for all this." He waved a hand taking in the destruction that Tony knew extended well beyond the city of Chicago. "You must kill this person before it happens again."

"Before what happens again?"

Leeson looked at him with fathomless eyes. "This is but one version of the world. Like dominos, they are falling, one after the other, as this... Destroyer of Worlds blindly seeks dominion."

"How—?"

Leeson raised a hand and listened.

"No time."

Faster than Tony could see, Leeson pulled a small grey box from his covering of rags and opened it. Tony thought he saw a metallic egg of some kind, and was immediately deafened and blinded by an explosion. Though he felt no pain, he somehow knew that Leeson was now dead along with everything else in the immediate vicinity. And with that realization came the knowledge that he no longer was where he had been.

Tony Sandoval stood on the lip of a bell tower, contemplating death. One step would take him two hundred feet to the cratered street below. It was the easy way out, and that's what bothered him. Tony had never been one to take the easy way.

But he was having trouble finding any other path.

After wandering the streets of Chicago for what felt like weeks, he was convinced that he was the last human being alive. But not the only *thing* alive. Creatures haunted the city. Creatures that could only have once been people. And for many of them, *alive* was too strong a word. Animated was more accurate. He finally had to ask himself, What was the point?

Not even the sky resembled anything he was familiar with. There were holes in the sky. Patches of blackness that the brightest sun could not illuminate. And on the earth, city streets flowed like rivers. Whole buildings stood upside down. Giant mushrooms grew where weeds once failed to flourish. But the creatures were the worst. People transformed into travesties of life. And it was not over. Oh, no. After weeks of watching, Tony could tell that all this was just a last gasp. The quiet before the earth opened up and swallowed everything.

If he didn't jump now, the earth would jump later. The result would be the same.

Tony put one foot forward and swayed out over empty space, one hand hanging on to the railing. Should he just slip over the edge? Or should he leap out and away from the building so as not to hit the side of the church before hitting the concrete at the bottom? And did it really matter?

"I wouldn't jump if I were you."

Tony looked up to the source of the voice and was surprised to see an angel. Yes, the building was a church and, in fact, contained statues and paintings of angels at every turn. But this angel hovered in the air with a slow beating of wings and had a face that would make the angriest atheist offer a prayer.

Tony wasn't fooled. "Why not jump? The odds I change into something like you are pretty remote."

The angel laughed. "You wouldn't want to be me. I, like everything else, will soon perish."

Tony pulled his foot back onto the ledge. At least the angel wasn't insane. "If I shouldn't jump, what should I do?"

The angel fluttered down until he hovered in the air opposite Tony. "You are a police officer. You should arrest the criminal."

"You know who I am?"

The angel smiled briefly. "You are Tony Sandoval. The best law man the Chicago Police Department has ever had."

Now Tony smiled. "And how do you know that?"

"I am," said the angel, "or was, just like you. My name is Barney Cloonan. I was once numbered among the

Untouchables."

Maybe Tony had been too hasty about the sanity judgment. "Of the Eliot Ness Untouchables?"

"The same."

Tony didn't have a response. Instead, he said, "Which criminal are we talking about?"

The angel grinned. "None other than the greatest criminal of all time."

"Moriarty?"

"Sadly," said the angel. "This is no fictional novel we are living. But yes, we are talking about a Moriarty-like character. And you would be his Holmes. I speak of the one who has wrought the destruction that engulfs us."

Tony harrumphed. "I assumed that the idiot who brought about the end of the world would have been among the first to die."

"You assumed correctly," said the angel. "Everyone is dead, or as good as, except you."

"You're telling me I'm the last human alive in Chicago?"

"The last human alive in the universe," corrected the angel. "And, very soon now, we once-humans will be gone as well."

Again, Tony didn't know how to respond. Fortunately, he didn't have to.

The angel pulled a white bag drawn with string from inside his robe and handed it to Tony. "I have protected you these past few weeks. Directing the damage away from you. Directing you away from the damage. But the end is nigh; I can do so no longer."

"Why?" Tony asked, not opening the bag.

"So that you could kill the criminal, of course. Arrest will do no good. It must be death."

"I thought you said the person who caused all this was already dead?"

The angel retrieved another object from within its robe. A small grey box. "Dead many times over. But there are always more. Worlds without end. But the worlds will end, all of them, if the destruction continues unabated.

Goodbye, Tony Sandoval. And good luck."

Before Tony could speak, the angel opened the box and the universe ceased to exist.

Superheroes for Hire

Howard knocked on the door and waited for someone to answer. He was not optimistic. Most of the super beings on the Mayor's two lists had decided that the change in their circumstances deserved a corresponding change in venue. In short, they had left home with no forwarding address.

He glanced at his list and reminded himself that he was looking for Angela Brown, a twelve-year-old girl reported to now have the ability to see through objects. If that was true, she could be inside right now looking at him through the door and deciding she had no reason to answer.

With no sounds inside, Howard looked out into the neighboring yards. Across the street, a house had been turned into a pretzel, with walls and windows stretched and bent, but nothing apparently broken. Despite the frosty air, an elderly woman sat knitting in a rocking chair set on an eave that now served as a porch. She was buried inside several sweaters and appeared to be making another one.

He crossed the street and before he could ask, the woman said, "Gone. Went to join one of those cults."

"Which one?" Howard had heard of several throughout the day. The one he liked best was the *Legion of Superheroes*.

The woman shrugged. "Does it matter? They're all the same. Bunch of arrogant idiots flexing their newfound muscles. Won't be long before they decide that robbing a bank is more interesting than protecting one."

Howard turned away and, hearing a rush of wind, spun back around to find the woman gone. He looked up and saw her streaking across the sky.

He considered adding her address to the Mayor's list, but decided that it would only create more work for himself that he didn't really want.

Most of the super type modified people he had seen were out cleaning up the city, actually doing good things. More than he had done since being co-opted by the Mayor. Doing such a good job, in fact, that Al Capone hadn't needed to send him and Olivia out to deal with the more monstrous type of modified people. The citizens seemed to be keeping things under control, so The Mayor didn't have to.

But perhaps the flying granny was right. Once they ran out of dragons to slay, perhaps the dragon slayers would become even worse dragons themselves. Could that be why Capone wanted them? Not so much to work for him, but to be controlled?

He walked back to Tony's car – he still refused to admit that Tony was gone – and drove several blocks to the next address on his list. This was a three-story apartment building, with a fellow on the third floor reported to have moved objects with his mind. Howard never made it past the front door.

There was a sign above the entrance – spray paint on linen – that said *Hall of Oden*. Three goons with axes sat on the front step.

"You have tribute?" asked one of them, a skinny teenager with more attitude than bulk.

"No, but I have a badge." Howard showed them his Capone Crew ID.

All three goons snorted.

"Means nothing here," said the teenager. He stood, swinging his axe like it weighed nothing.

Howard pulled his Grand Power K100 semi-automatic from its holster. "This mean anything?"

The teen sat back down and grinned as one of the other goons stood up. "Not to me."

Tony Sandoval, still alive and well in Howard's head, provided the instinct and the motivation to aim the nine millimeter weapon at the first goon's knee and pull the trigger.

The other two goons lunged toward him even before their companion cried out.

Howard then shot out the knee of the third goon who, until he screamed, had been silent. Finally, he shot the one for whom guns didn't mean anything right between the eyes.

The bullet bounced off his forehead.

"Crap," said Howard.

The last thing he saw was the smiling man's axe blade falling toward him.

Teddy Prendick set down a hastily scrawled note and rubbed his eyes. He'd been reading reports for hours and the only conclusion he could draw was that everything was going to Hell. Before the change event that accompanied the earthquake almost three weeks earlier, things had only been going badly. Friends killed. Enemies rising in power. Neutral entities revealed as powerful enemies. All of that was manageable. But now the cat was not only out of the bag, it had turned into a tiger and was shredding the bag to bits.

There wasn't a soul left alive in Chicago who didn't laugh when told that nothing unnatural was happening. At least the earlier event had had the cover of an earthquake to hide any unusualness. The event two days ago had just happened. Out of the blue. Electronics had cut out. Even the sun had gone out! And people all over the city had changed. Reality had adjusted. Outside the underground chamber! Teddy had sent Stone to the Lexington Tunnels to ensure the door was still closed. If it had been open, that might at least have explained things. But the door was closed. Which meant what? The end is nigh?

Those who weren't scared to death by the event and its resulting changes were plotting to benefit from it. The players had all changed. Teddy Prendick would have to change too.

"I don't think the Untouchables can fix this," he said aloud.

"Sir?" Matt Stone spoke from where he had been sitting quietly for the past hour, poking his palm with the blade of a knife to no effect.

"You are one of the lucky ones," Teddy said to his loyal bodyguard and friend. "Anything could have happened during the event. Death. Dismemberment. Insanity. You acquired a useful trait. Especially for someone in your profession. Invulnerability."

Matt said nothing, and Teddy knew it was because Stone was among the scared. It wasn't just the seemingly beneficial change. It was everything else. The world had been turned upside down. Or, more accurately, inside out. Stone was perceptive enough to know that this was a bad thing, no matter how he may have personally benefited.

Among the damaged and the dead were people with all sorts of unimaginable skills. Teddy had agents out looking for them. So did Capone. And so did every petty grasper who hoped to set up a kingdom. As a result, most of those gifted people like Stone were in hiding. Not that it would make any difference.

"Two events in three weeks," Teddy whispered. "Will we survive a third one?"

Again Matt made no comment. Stone was a good man, but the death of universes was just too big for him to fathom. To be honest, it was too big for Prendick. But there was no one else.

He stared at the stack of reports, many from Untouchables in alternate universes, and shook his head. "Three additional universes gone, that we know of. And eight more at death's door."

Prendick hammered the stack of papers with his fist, and then turned to Matt. "The Sandovals will be arriving. Time for you to go out and watch for them. Let's hope this ace up our sleeve works."

Howard woke up in a dumpster out back of the apartment building where he had been axe murdered. He briefly considered trying to recover his gun, but since the Hall of Oden had left him his flip phone and car keys, he decided it wasn't worth the effort. And who knows how many other super thugs were holed up inside Valhalla? Next time he ran into the Legion of Superheroes, he'd give them the address.

He drove back to City Hall to get another gun and, while parking the Bel Air, noticed a burly military type hanging about who he was sure he'd seen somewhere before. But when he climbed out of the car and tried to get a better look, the man was gone. Howard briefly scouted the parking area but found no one.

In the armory, he looked around for something special. Silver bullets. Poisoned darts. Kryptonite. Anything that would help him walk away from goons who laughed at guns. In the end, he found a small, thin hand weapon labeled *antimatter*. A note beside it that said it had been discovered in a futuristic-looking vehicle after the Blackout and should not be used until further testing was completed.

Howard dropped the weapon into his left side pocket and tucked a Browning nine millimeter into his holster. You could never have too much firepower.

From the armory he went to the morgue to see if there was any change in Tony's status. Expecting none, he was shocked to see something stirring in the tank. He watched, rapt, as the human stew bubbled and then bucked. And suddenly Tony sat up, coughing and sputtering and, oddly enough, fully dressed.

By now, the morgue attendants had joined him and were watching with slack, open jaws.

Howard climbed up onto a chair and reached down to take Tony's hand, helping him to stand.

"Where am I?" Tony sputtered. He looked down at his hands and flesh-covered clothes. "And what's all this?"

"You were dead," said Howard. "And now you're alive."

He helped Tony climb out, taking care to brush as much of the tank's contents as possible back into the tank. Again he noted that Tony was fully dressed. While the clothing contained the odd tear, there had been no cloth in the tank to start with and, if there had been, it would not reconstitute as he had hoped Tony's body would. Howard also noticed that the watch strapped to Tony's left wrist was not that one he remembered. And no watch had been collected in the tank either.

Something not quite right was going on.

To Howard's relief, the morgue staff insisted that Tony be stripped, washed, and examined.

"You just came back from being human soup," Capone's personal medical examiner said. "To say that an examination is mandatory is an understatement."

"All I want is a shower," Tony said.

"The Mayor is on his way down. Capone will take my view."

Tony looked somewhat taken aback by that remark. Grudgingly, he allowed the morgue staff to remove his clothing, but first he took various items from his pockets – gun, car keys, wallet, a large envelope – and put them into a plastic bag. He took off his watch and added it to the bag. Despite their foul condition, Tony refused to let anyone near his possessions and placed the bag under the examining table where the staff rinsed his body clean into a collection trough.

It was odd watching the staff work on a live body rather than the dead, or assumed dead, such as the bodies that had occupied the other tables in the room since the Blackout. But Howard had witnessed no end of oddness since the earthquake three weeks ago that had brought him to this alternate Chicago. He'd grown used to it.

He tapped one of the examiner's assistants on the shoulder and indicated the contents of the trough designed to collect forensic evidence washed from corpses. "Can you return this to the tank?"

The technician glanced at the small collection of flesh and bone and then picked up the entire collection tough, walked over to the tank, and emptied it into the vat of Tony soup.

A second technician, who had hosed down Tony's clothes into a similar trap, saw what they were doing and did likewise.

Howard smiled, hopeful that very little of Tony, the real Tony, had been lost.

It was at this point that the morgue doors banged open and Al Capone strode into the room. He took one look at the rinsed and combed Tony on the examining table. "Damn, this isn't Tony!"

Tony pushed himself up to a sitting position and looked Capone in the eye. "I don't know which Tony you were expecting. My name is Tony Sandoval."

Capone raised an eyebrow, snatched a scalpel off a tray, and before Tony could react, sliced a shallow incision down his left thigh.

"Are you nuts?" the examiner screamed, and then added, "Uh, Sir."

Capone threw the scalpel back on the tray and ran his finger along the line of welling blood. "You're not *my* Tony Sandoval. My Tony would heal immediately. He also wouldn't have that scar above your left eye or the lacerations on your hands." Capone waved a thumb at the bio-containment tank. "That's my Tony. And right now you're about as much use to me as he is."

The Tony on the table could only gawk.

Capone turned to his chief examiner. "Find out what he knows and then cut him loose."

Then he looked at Howard. "What are you doing here? You're supposed to be out finding replacements for Tony."

"Just restocking my ammo," Howard said. "It's a jungle out there."

"Time," said Capone. "We don't have it. Get moving."

And then the Mayor swept from the room.

Tony Sandoval was surprised to discover just how little he knew. He did not, for example, know that there existed multiple versions of reality, and that while the world he knew had been destroyed, he had somehow been dropped into a near-identical reality that had merely been damaged. He also did not know that people showing up from other realities had become so frequent as to become relatively uninteresting. Nor did he know that people without special abilities were not considered useful, by the oddly named Mayor at any rate. And most surprising of all, he did not know that the people in this reality were more interested in a version of himself that was little more than soup. He still itched just thinking that the garbage he had found himself in was, in fact, an alternate version of himself reduced to bits of meat and bone.

After being questioned by the medical examiner and being dismissed as having nothing important to tell, they had provided him with a change of clothing that fit perfectly – it belonged to *soup* Tony, apparently – and escorted him to the steps of City Hall. The man who had helped him out of the tank – Howard somebody – remained with him on the steps.

He turned to Howard. "So, now what am I supposed to do?"

The older cop shrugged. "You could help me find heroes for the Mayor. Do a good job and he may make it permanent."

Tony shook his head. "Mayor Capone? The guy even acts like a mob boss. I think I'll pass."

They were walking along the wide sidewalk toward the street.

"Can't argue with that," said Howard. "It's only fair I tell you, however, that the Mayor doesn't just act like a mob boss. He is a mob boss. He's Al Capone. The Original.

And he's been Mayor since 1932."

"I'd laugh and tell you that you're yanking my chain," said Tony. "But considering where I came from and how I got here, I'm not laughing. Hell, I'm surprised that you believe my story."

Howard sighed. "Not much different from mine. I came through a few weeks ago. Killed my counterpart here. It's a long story. I used to be a scientist."

"And now you're a cop?"

"Not much of one."

Tony halted as Howard froze and stared into the street. Tony followed his gaze and saw a beat up, antique car being driven by a military type. Nothing unusual about that. But the passenger. The passenger looked just like Tony.

"Damn," said Howard.

"Another me?" Tony asked.

"Your car, too. And I recognize the driver. He works for Prendick."

"The billionaire?" asked Tony. "And, not my car. I'd never drive an ancient piece of crap like that."

Howard pulled out his flip phone. "We should call Olivia Nelson."

"The famous psychic?"

When Howard nodded, Tony said, "Maybe I will hang out with you for a while. You travel in interesting circles."

Tony Sandoval woke up in a fish tank. The fish were tiny and dead. The coral was sharp. The room was dark. After climbing out of the tank and turning on a light, he threw up. The fish tank was not a fish tank. And next to it were several tables of corpses.

No stranger to morgues, Tony sat on the one empty table and hosed himself down. He abandoned his clothes except for his shoes, and dressed himself in one of the lab frocks. From there he went to his office.

He could tell by the activity in the building that it was evening rather than night. He avoided encountering anyone and was able to change into proper clothes from his closet. He even had a spare pair of shoes to replace the waterlogged ones he wore.

Despite the fact that Tony had watched City Hall melt into wet cement with his own eyes, his spare Jericho 941F semiautomatic was right where he had left it. Now fully dressed, he put the string-drawn bag the angel had given him onto his desk and pulled open the strings.

The first object he retrieved was a small paperweight in the shape of a lion. Not knowing what to make of it, he stuck the piece of stone in his pocket. There was only one other thing in the bag. A police file photograph. Black and white with a name underneath. Tony remembered the angel's words. The Destroyer of Worlds.

After checking his gun and commending the angel for choosing the right man for the job, he decided to slip down to the armory for additional ammunition.

"He seems like a nice enough man," the woman said as she climbed into the back of the antique Bel Air, an exact copy of the car they had seen outside of City Hall. A City Hall that was nothing like the full city block building Tony was familiar with. "I can see why I married him fifteen years ago. Who's our new partner? Tony! You're back!"

Tony Sandoval stared into the back seat at the woman he had idolized for so many years. Psychic to the stars, and occasionally to the Police. Olivia Nelson had closed more cases that all other psychics combined. And she was his partner?

"Sorry, Olivia," Howard said. "This is a different Tony."

Tony felt his stomach slide at the crestfallen look on his idol's face. But then she smiled.

"That's all right. Howard's a different Howard, too. A better one than the original. Much better."

"I'll try to live up to that," Tony said.

Olivia looked suddenly all business. "You said you saw that Matt Stone character. Where is he?"

"He was outside City Hall," Howard said. "Tony Sandoval was with him."

"This—" Olivia began.

"—No, a different one. Seems we have two Tony's walking around. I put an APB out on his license plate."

"You saw the plate, then?"

"No, but they were driving this car. A copy of this car. I had to change our plates before we left City Hall or they'd be looking for us instead."

"How do you keep any of this straight?" asked Tony.

Howard and Olivia both laughed. "We don't," said Olivia. "Our psychic premonitions help."

"Our?" Tony looked at Howard. "You're a psychic, too?"

"Of a sort," Howard said.

"So, what are you going to do?" asked Tony. "Concentrate on where this Stone fellow took the other Tony and get a premonition of the location?"

"It doesn't work that—" Olivia stopped in mid-sentence and stared at Howard, who was staring back.

"This is one, isn't it?" asked Tony. "A premonition. Where are they?"

"City Hall," Olivia and Howard said together. "The morgue. Tony."

Tony pounded the top of the seat with his hand. "I can't believe I'm seeing psychics in action."

The morgue was pitch dark except for a glow emanating from the bio-containment tank. Inside the tank, the soup began to stir and then to boil. Steam rose, lifting with it the smell of blood and marrow. On the examining tables, twelve eyes opened, and then slowly closed again. In the bio-containment tank, a seventh near-corpse congealed from the soupy bath of bone fragments, bits of flesh, and blood. The result was male, mostly hairless, and shrunken where missing material created sinkholes and cavities. Slowly, these areas filled in, and then the chest inflated in a single gasp of intaken breath. Eyes flicked open to stare into the near darkness. With a second breath, the body sat up. It wobbled slightly, taking in several additional breaths. Then, awkwardly, it rose to its feet to climb out of an empty and dry plastic tank.

The man stumbled to where a sink projected from one wall and turned on the tap, thrusting his mouth into the flow of cold water. He drank for almost a minute, and then threw up water back into the sink. Stalking naked out into the corridor, he found a stairway, made his way up four flights of stairs, down a second hallway, and into an office, where he flicked on the ceiling light.

Moving to the closet, he pulled open the door and stared at empty hangers and a pair of damp shoes and a lab coat. Tony Sandoval spoke his first word in over two days. "Damn."

After finding clothes that mostly fit from the closets of neighboring offices, Tony went down to the armory and fitted a Heckler & Koch MP7 fully automatic submachine into a chest holster he had strapped over his shirt. There is something about being blown to bits that makes a man upgrade to a larger personal weapon. From there he went back to the morgue and waited. Howard and Olivia arrived less than a minute later.

Olivia rushed in to give Tony a firm hug as soon as she caught sight of him. She backed off a bit as she felt the hard metal outline of the MP7 under his coat.

Tony smiled. "Good to see you, too, Olivia. From the hug I suspect I've been away a while."

"Too long," Howard said from the doorway. "Long enough that you've been replaced." He stepped into the room revealing a man behind him. "Tony Sandoval, may I introduce Tony Sandoval."

Tony stared into his own eyes and found a deeper sense of loss than he saw when he looked into a mirror. He turned to Howard. "Tell me what's happened?"

Matt Stone led Tony Sandoval through the final secret door and removed his blindfold. The room light was subdued, so Tony's eyes needed little adjustment. Matt grinned as Tony took in the room's occupants, and then joined them by sitting in a waiting chair.

"This should be the last," Matt said.

The only other man in the room who was not Tony Sandoval shook his head. "This is number ten. Ten universes died to get them here. One additional Tony Sandoval may have been pushed through. But it is enough. We can wait no longer."

Matt watched the man he respected above all others rise from his desk to address the room.

Teddy Prendick was a man of average height, weight, and looks. His short hair was black fading to grey, parted down the middle, and receding above a wide forehead. His eyes missed nothing, and could cut through a man. But his smile was warm and he carried himself like royalty. Matt watched Predick's gaze take in everyone assembled.

"You all have been watched, protected, and sent here with a message and a mission. Each of your worlds is gone. Friends. Family. Everything you knew. Versions of those things exist here. Some very similar. Some very different. The important thing is that they are not the same. What you have lost, is lost. Never to be restored. If this continues, all worlds will be lost, not just this one where you currently have refuge.

"We have an opportunity to put a stop to it. On each of your worlds, an agent of my team tried to stop the destruction. Tried and failed. What they have sent with you is information that will allow us to react earlier here than they could there. Take steps they could only take too late. They have sent with each of you the name of the person responsible for the death of your world. Please open the envelope you have been given."

There was a shuffling of papers as ten Tony Sandovals pulled envelopes from coat pockets.

Prendick continued speaking. "I know many of you have already looked. That is not important. One name in one envelope is meaningless. Every world is slightly different from the next. The Destroyer of Worlds in one place may be different from another. To be safe, we must take all of the names you have brought and seek the common denominator. Perhaps we must stop them all. Or perhaps we must stop just one. But we must act now, before it is too late.

"Please open your envelope and read the name beneath the accompanying photograph."

Matt Stone listened as each of the Tony Sandovals read from their envelope, and sat stunned as various names he expected to hear were never uttered. It was no wonder the Untouchables kept failing. They were watching and fighting against the wrong people.

"I am surprised," Teddy Prendick said after the last envelope was read. "Ten worlds and one name. A name I've never even heard of. Do any of you know this person? Howard Russell?"

Return to Oz

Howard sat next to the empty bio-containment tank, idly examining the antimatter pistol he had pocketed earlier that day, while Olivia updated the two Tonys on the chaos resulting from the most recent reality collision.

"So we're no longer very special?" Tony, their Tony, asked. "Capone has a city full of indestructible, omniscient, omnipotent, and otherwise invaluable lackeys to do his bidding."

No, Tony wasn't bitter about being blown to bits. Not in the least.

"It's more complicated than that," Olivia said. "Most of

those who benefited from what happened are working for themselves. They won't give Capone the time of day."

Tony nodded. "Okay. How about that Prendick Foundation guy we saw near Henry Wong's warehouse. You say you saw him today?"

"With one of you," Howard said. "Are you working for Wong too?"

"Funny," said Tony. "I'm the last person you should be asking why there appears to be three of me kicking around." He looked at the other Tony. "Do you have any idea why a version of us would be driving around town with someone from the Prendick Foundation?"

The other Tony shook his head. "Oh, but I do have this." He reached into a coat pocket and pulled out a folded blue envelope. "Someone claiming to be one of the Untouchables gave it to me before he used a grey box to somehow send me here."

"The Untouchables." said Howard. "Are you sure he said he was one of the Untouchables?"

Tony nodded.

The other Tony, Howard's Tony, said, "The Untouchables vanished almost a hundred years ago. Could they have gone to my alter ego's Chicago and lived forever like Capone has here?"

Howard nodded. "Even that may be too simple an explanation. You told me that Capone suffered some memory loss when he emerged from the freight tunnels. Having emerged from the tunnels myself and not being familiar with all my surroundings, I suspect that the Mayor is one of Capone's alter egos from somewhere else. This Untouchable may also originally be from elsewhere."

The other Tony shrugged and held the envelope out to Howard. "Either way, he gave me this. And it looked like sending me here cost him."

Howard slipped the antimatter gun back into his pocket and took the envelope. It didn't escape him that his friends were deferring to him in this matter. Like with the droids, he was the subject expert. That what he knew would fit on a postage stamp didn't make much difference. He was *the man.*

The other Tony rested a hand on Howard's. "The Untouchable said that this envelope contains the name and photo of the person responsible for the destruction of my universe."

"Then perhaps we'd better look in the envelope," Howard said.

All four of them twisted around to see what Howard found.

"It can't be," said Tony, Howard's Tony.

"There must be a mistake," said Olivia.

"I recognize the photo," said the other Tony, glancing quickly at Howard. "But who is this *Wizard of Oz?*"

"He was a bastard," said Howard.

"Howard killed him a few weeks ago," Tony said.

"But he looks like you." The other Tony held the photo up beside Howard's face. "A relative?"

"I wish," said Howard. "He was me. A different version of me. Total scum. But I don't think he even knew about the Rhodium-105. He exploited women. How could the Wizard of Oz have destroyed a universe?"

"Rhodium-105?" asked the other Tony.

"I'm pretty sure that is what you briefly saw in your Untouchable's grey box. I don't understand how it sent you here, but I can believe that it caused problems where you came from."

"So, this Wizard of Oz and you are the same person?" the other Tony asked. "Just as there are two of us," he pointed at Howard's Tony.

"A lot more than two," Howard said. "Hundreds. Thousands. Possibly an infinite number."

"I've heard of this," said the other Tony. "William somebody's multi-universe theory. For every possible future, a parallel universe exists. If you are driving and reach a fork in the road, the universe splits into two, one where you turn left, and another where you turn right."

"Say what?" asked Howard's Tony.

"Fairly common knowledge," said the other Tony.

"Not here it isn't," said Olivia.

"I think you have the right idea," Howard said. "But there is more to it. Somehow, universes exist where the laws of physics are slightly different."

This statement received blank stares.

"It's why I'm different. Was even more different before..." Howard knew he wasn't explaining it well. "It's how Al Capone is over a hundred years old."

"He comes from a universe where people live longer?" Olivia asked.

"Too simple again," Howard said. "It's like how I was changed, altered, when I came here from my Chicago. The rules here must be slightly different. I was adjusted so that I wouldn't upset the laws of physics in this Chicago."

Tony, Howard's Tony, laughed. "Like Superman!"

"Uh," said Howard. "What?"

"Superman," said Tony. "From the comic book. On Krypton he had no superpowers. When he came to Earth, Earth's yellow sun made him into the Man of Steel."

Howard sighed. "I suppose. If you assert that the star's properties are dissimilar due to identical quantum interactions having completely different outcomes, rather than from inherently dissimilar quantum interactions."

Blank stares. Again.

"Yes," said Howard. "Tony's got it exactly right. Jumping between universes may turn you into Superman, not unlike the various super-humans Mayor Capone has ordered us to collect. Or it may turn you into the living dead, such as our friends on the slabs. Or something in between. Or nothing may happen at all."

"But," said Olivia, "none of those people jumped between universes. Did they?"

"Probably not," Howard agreed. "Look at it this way. When the sun went dark two days ago, the sun that returned was a slightly different one. From another universe."

Tony, our Tony nodded. "Superman didn't come to

218

Earth. Earth's sun went to Krypton."

"Not really, of course," Howard said. "But not far off, either. Anyway, I doubt there is anything we can do about how and why this is happening. The best we can hope for is to try to understand the consequences."

"What about what the Untouchable said?" asked the other Tony. "He seemed to believe that your alter ego, the Wizard of Oz, had orchestrated what happened to the Chicago I lived in."

Howard shrugged. "Beats me how one man, alone, could bend the laws of physics, never mind why. What's the point of destroying the universe? Regardless if you believe it is the only one or one of many? You'd have to be a madman."

"That photograph is a bust, anyway," said Tony, Howard's Tony. "The Wiz is dead." He looked at his alter ego. "Your job is done."

Howard shook his head. "I still don't see how that man, monster that he was, could have anything to do with what's happening. He's been dead for weeks. That collision two days ago happened anyway."

"Perhaps we should go back to the Oz Club and see if there are any clues there," Howard's Tony suggested.

"Can't you use your psychic talent?" the other Tony said to Olivia. "To find some answers. Or at least tell us where to look."

"Doesn't work that way," Olivia said. "But you're forgetting the clue we do have. Prendick. A Prendick employee was driving around with another Tony. I suggest we try to find out what that is about.

Tony forgot that it had been night while his squad mates brought him up to speed. As they left the morgue and headed to the car lot, he saw that it must now be early morning. Various support staff were wandering the halls waiting for caffeine to kick in.

"We need to get out of here," he whispered to the others. "Before someone tells the Mayor that I've left the bio-containment tank. I have no intention of spending the next few hours being interrogated by Capone."

They slipped out the side door that officials used when they wanted to come and go undetected by the media, and were soon arguing over who was sitting where in Tony's Crew car.

"You're not driving, Tony," Olivia said with finality. "You've spent the past two days lying in the bottom of a plastic tank and the collision altered many of the roads and traffic patterns. Howard's done an adequate job—"

"Adequate!" Howard interjected.

"—of driving us around. Howard will drive. I'll ride shotgun. And you Tonys will sit in the back."

"Looks like more has changed than what you let on inside," Tony said as he climbed into the back seat. The other Tony said nothing as he climbed in after him.

Ten minutes later, they pulled up in front of the Prendick Foundation building.

"City Hall returns," the droid at the security desk greeted them. "Wonderful to see you again, Mrs. Nelson. Once more in the company of the Wizard of Oz and the Capone Crewman, I see. Two of his model? The Blackout certainly has made things confusing these past three days, hasn't it? Before you ask, Mr. Prendick has not yet returned from his unexplained absence and Dr. Moreau is still in charge. However, she is not seeing anyone."

"Sounds like everything is under control," Tony said.

The droid smiled. "Sarcasm. I love speaking with the Police."

Tony dropped a piece of paper sporting an amateurish pencil sketch onto the security counter. "This fellow work here?"

The droid glanced at the drawing. "Matt Stone. Prendick Foundation head of security. This looks nothing like him."

"I told you I was no artist," Howard said.

"Then how do you know this is the same man?" Tony asked the droid.

The droid pulled a glossy photo from underneath the counter and placed it next to the sketch.

"That's him," said Howard.

"Because," the droid told Tony, "the Police have been looking for him since the Blackout. You are a little behind the times."

"Why are the Police...? I mean why are *we* looking for him?" Tony asked.

"For aiding and abetting the deceased criminal Henry Wong."

"I don't think he was helping Wong," Howard said. "He looked as lost around those rogue droids as we did."

"Those are the charges," the security droid said. "Is there anything else I can do for you?"

"We really do need to see Dr. Moreau," Tony said.

The droid remained impassive. "Dr. Moreau has left instructions that no one is to see her without a warrant. Do you have a warrant?"

"Not yet." Tony turned to the others. "Let's go."

As they walked back across the marble lobby toward the exit, the other Tony said, "You do things differently here. Where I come from, we would have turned this building upside down. The Police have carte blanche."

"We'll turn this place inside out when the time is right," Tony said.

"The time isn't right," Olivia agreed. "We'd raise a big stink and find nothing. Did you see those two men by the elevators?"

"Something not right about them," said Howard.

Tony nodded.

"Looked like standard security to me," said the other Tony.

"Nothing standard about them," said Tony. "They've been modified. Either by the Blackout—"

"—or by something else," Howard finished. "My gut tells me that Moreau somehow got hold of some of my blood."

"*Our* gut," said Olivia. "And it also tells me that the only thing they are protecting is Moreau herself."

By now they were climbing into Tony's Bel Air. Howard and Olivia's cell phones beeped, but they ignored them."

"Where to now?" the other Tony asked.

"The Oz Club," said Tony. "Let's see if we can't find another piece of the puzzle."

It was not even noon and the parking lot of the Oz Club was jammed with cars. The last time Howard had been here the place had been closed, its only occupants the three droid bartenders and the four, now deceased, torturers for hire.

"This is the building where you were tortured," Howard said to Olivia. "Welcome back."

Howard had brought Tony up to speed on Olivia's Blackout-altered memories. The Crewman responded to the bafflement on Olivia's face. "Your kidnapping was arranged by the Wizard of Oz prior to Howard murdering him. Apparently he was working for Alfonso."

"I'm sorry you didn't get to kill the Wiz yourself," Howard said. "You have more reason to than I ever did."

Olivia just stared at him and Tony, her expression blank. "I don't remember ever being here. I was tortured?"

"Probably best you don't remember," Tony said.

Howard nodded. "I wonder who's running this place now?"

Like before, they parked in the street and walked across the pavement toward the Oz Club entrance.

Howard's curiosity was peaked when Tony stopped and pulled the glossy photo he had taken from the Prendick Foundation security droid from his pocket. He looked at it and then down the street toward the bakery Howard had passed through after leaving the Vortex. Several men were exiting the same bakery. The lead man looked like—

"Matt Stone," said Howard.

"I recognize his friends," said the other Tony.

One after another, a stream of Tony Sandovals exited the building. The procession hadn't ended before the ones in the street began shooting. Howard felt a bullet impact his shoulder, and then a second hit his thigh.

Without sharing a word, the four of them were running for the nearest cover, the entrance to the Oz Club.

The dwarf at the counter inside the door was a different one than the blue and yellow clad munchkin who had accosted Howard on his first visit. His bleeding thigh slowing him down, Howard had been last to enter the building and the two Tonys had already flashed a Crew card and cleared the way. The dwarf merely stared at him as he hobbled past.

"Men with guns coming," Howard said, and the incredulous dwarf vanished.

Howard followed the others down the short corridor into the main room, his limp fading as his wounds healed.

Oz was exactly how he remembered it. One giant room filled with the elite of Chicago, a bevy of prostitutes, and flying monkeys in the rafters. Only the monkeys weren't alone. Various people who had been altered by the Blackout bounced with them among the rafters. Some had long dexterous tails, the real thing that the gymnasts in the monkey suits imitated through skill. Others could actually float or fly.

The prostitutes dressed as witches had also been joined by modified people: exotic women eight feet tall, women with three or four breasts, men with breasts, as curvaceous as the best surgeon could design. Howard even noticed a small child with curves to make a bikini model green with envy. It was a bordello of the damned. But he had no time to take it all in.

The others had rushed through the crowd and Howard watched them dive over the bar that spanned the far wall. Howard wasn't sure how much protection the faux wood would offer, but he climbed over the bar to join them.

Also behind the bar were the Tin Man, the Scarecrow, and the Cowardly Lion. But these were not the droid bartender-bouncers who had worked here last. These were just people in costume. The Lion looked as though he might actually be a modified person, the hair and claws now part of his anatomy.

The bartenders yelled at the four intruders, even after Tony showed them his Crew card. When Tony pulled a machinegun from his chest strap, however, the bartenders leapt over the long bar and were gone.

Howard drew his own gun and aimed it toward the entrance hallway.

Several of the revelers had noted what happened, and a steady stream of bodies dressed to the nines had begun fleeing toward the exit. This was both good and bad. Good because they were getting out of harm's way. Bad because this was making Howard and his squad easier to find.

The sound of a gunshot turned the trickle into a stampede and Howard saw Tony Sandoval standing against the current, shooting at him. Howard shifted his gun to fire, but one of his squad beat him to it and Tony Sandoval dropped to the floor. Two other Tonys quickly took his place.

As bullets tore into him, Howard could not help but notice that these Tony Sandovals who accompanied Matt Stone were all focused on him; they were not shooting at his companions. He quickly made the scientific deduction that he should duck down out of sight. One or two more hits and he might be ducking involuntarily.

He felt himself heal as bullets continued to fly around the room, though not nearly as many as before. The gunfire stopped when a familiar voice yelled, "What's going on here?"

Howard snuck a peak over the counter and saw the Wizard of Oz, returned from the dead, standing in the middle of the room. He looked the same as he had weeks ago when Howard had killed him: wand in hand, silver and red shiny suit, flashing lights sparkling down the length of his arms and legs, and Howard Russell's face.

A gun fired and a bullet bounced off the Wizard's forehead. The Wizard waved his wand, and one of the Tonys crouched by the entrance flew across the room, smashed high up against a wall, and then slid down to lie still on the floor, his neck broken.

A machinegun let loose and Howard saw Tony, his Tony, spraying the Wizard with a cloud of bullets that appeared to do exactly zero damage. The Wizard flicked a finger and the submachine gun in Tony's hand flipped upward and shot Tony in the neck. The gunfire stopped and Tony slumped to the floor.

"I can do this all day," the Wizard said. "Can anyone tell me why I should stop?"

The other Tony who crouched behind the bar rose up, gun tucked in his belt, and pointed a finger at the Wizard of Oz. "You are the Destroyer of Worlds, wiping out universes one by one."

The Tonys by the entrance looked more closely at the Wizard who wore Howard's face, and began murmuring among themselves.

The Wizard of Oz laughed. "I don't know what you're talking about, but I like what I hear. Howard Russell, Destroyer of Worlds. Strikes a little more fear into the hearts of men than the Wizard of Oz, doesn't it?"

Why the other Tony pulled his gun and began shooting when there was no point, Howard didn't know. But as expected, the bullets bounced harmlessly off the Destroyer of Worlds. The Wizard made a little chopping motion with his hand and the other Tony's head flew across the room, smashing like a pumpkin when it hit the far wall.

"Destroying worlds one person at a time is a little tedious," the Wizard shouted. "I'll have to find more effective means." He turned to face the entrance, ready to wave his wand again, and then stopped.

Howard poked his head up further and saw that the remaining Tonys had spread out around the room. He counted eight of them.

The Wizard of Oz began laughing. Then he spun on his heels, hands stretched out. As he spun, the various Tonys fell apart amid spurts of blood and toppled to the floor. In short order, the Wizard was the only one left standing in the room.

Howard held his breath.

"I see you there crouched behind the bar," the Wizard crooned. "Stand up and tell me how I can destroy worlds. I have destroyed communities and even a few cities, but never a whole world. And now that I know how to jump between worlds, well, destroying a few appeals to me."

Howard knew that hiding wasn't going to get him anywhere, so he stood up. From the corner of his eye, he saw Olivia still crouched low a short distance away.

The Wizard looked crestfallen. "Oh. Another one of you. How pathetic! The weakest I can be, in any universe. Timid. Stupid. A tool to be used by others. Before I kill you, what do you have to say for yourself?"

Howard was lost for words. Calling this evil incarnation of himself a bastard just wouldn't cut it. Then he remembered the small gun in his coat pocket. Perhaps antimatter would succeed where bullets failed. The note in the armory said the weapon needed to be tested. What better test than this?

Slowly, he reached into his pocket, pulled out the gun, and raised it above the bar, pointing it at the Wizard of Oz's chest. Howard didn't think a direct hit was required, but his aim had steadily improved over the past weeks. He pulled the trigger.

Nothing happened.

The Wizard lifted his hand to remove Howard's head or push him through the wall, or whatever mind over matter murder his evil twin intended, but then stopped.

"Out of bullets? Are you so useless that you brought an empty gun to a shootout? My god, but you're an embarrassment. I refuse to believe that you and I are the same person. There must be two totally separate gene pools that somehow generate identical outward appearances, while what is inside and important is totally different."

While the Wizard ranted, Howard pulled the trigger several more times. His evil alter ego must be right. The antimatter gun was out of antimatter.

From the corner of his eye, Howard saw movement near the entrance. Another Tony? No. This was the wrong shape. He continued to focus on the Wizard of Oz, hoping to draw his attention.

"Sorry to disappoint you," Howard said. "And disappoint me, as well. DNA tests have been performed and we are the same. Apparently the only thing different is our ethics, our morals, and our very souls. But when did you become invulnerable? And able to kill at a distance? How many realities have you visited?"

Howard saw now that the person sneaking around behind the Wizard was Matt Stone, the head of Prendick security who was wanted by the Police. What he thought he could do, Howard had no idea.

The Wizard chuckled. "Ah, you know about the chamber, then. So you're not totally useless. I've made a few journeys, gaining new capabilities each time."

"They aren't always good," said Howard. "The journeys, I mean. They change things, but it's all just random."

"You must be one of the PhD *me*'s," the Wizard said. "Possibly helped build the chamber yourself? If so, you don't even know what you built. Randomness is just a failure to see the pattern. The journey can be manipulated, directed. In time, I'll learn how to control it perfectly. Until then, experiments are in order."

The Wizard spun suddenly, flipping his hand at Matt Stone who was now just a few feet behind him. Whatever he intended was a colossal failure. Matt merely moved toward him more quickly.

A gun in the room fired six rounds in quick succession. Howard watched six bullets bounce off Matt Stone. Then to one side, he saw a gun suspended in the air fall to the floor.

"At last!" the Wizard of Oz crowed. "A worthy opponent!"

And then Matt Stone was upon him.

A knife flashed, struck the Wizard in the chest, and then scraped down his rib cage, tearing his Oz costume but leaving the skin beneath unmolested. The knife moved up to his eyes, but failed to penetrate.

The Wizard grabbed Stone's throat in one hand and began to squeeze. Stone grunted, but any damage looked minimal. Stone thrust up with both hands and jammed them into the Wizard's laughing mouth, taking one set of teeth and gums into each palm and pulling apart, attempting to snap open the man's jaw. Of the two men, the Wizard was larger, but Stone looked the strongest and the most fit; but the battle was a draw.

Howard contemplated coming out from his hiding place behind the bar and pressing the antimatter gun against the Wizard's temple. But being regenerative was not the same as being invulnerable. Howard doubted he'd get closer than ten feet. He was also afraid that the weapon that did not work against the Wizard, might very well work against Matt Stone; right now Stone was the only chance they had.

Suddenly the Wizard disappeared and rematerialized a few inches out of Stone's reach. He laughed. "Seems it may take me a while to kill you. I'll have to experiment with a few of my newer abilities."

"Experiment this!"

Stone pulled a small grey box from his coat pocket and, closing the few inches between then, opened the box, snapped up the orb of Rhodium-105, and rammed it down The Wizard of Oz's throat. Then, with his greater muscle mass, he pushed the Wizard to the ground and crouched on top of him like a wrestler.

Howard could hear his alter ego gag and try to scream, and knew it wasn't simply because he had a rock in his throat. It was the kind of rock. Already, both the Wizard and Stone were inwardly changing as the Rhodium-105 adjusted them both repeatedly, but failed to move them to an alternate reality. He had no idea how they remained here, but guessed it had something to do with how the Untouchables had sent other Tonys here without coming themselves. One thing he did have an idea about was that the compound could not exist for long outside of the tungsten box. Whatever Stone intended it to do, it would have to happen soon or the ingot would simply change itself into something harmless or cease to exist, leaving the Wizard of Oz twice as angry and twice as changed as he had been before. Perhaps more powerful than before.

A high-pitched wail and a flash of colorful bright light put an end to Howard's growing apprehension. Before falling into unconsciousness, Howard had just enough time to consider that the Rhodium-105, a compound that could not exist within the physics that governed this and all other realities, had just ceased to exist.

Howard came awake to sunlight shining in his eyes. Around him lay the littered remains of what was once the Oz Club. A few yards in front of him, a deep pit marked where Matt Stone and the Wizard had fought. A lean man with greying hair stood looking down into the pit. He turned and contemplated Howard.

"My men were mistaken," he said, then shook his head. "Matt Stone called me to report, before making the ultimate sacrifice. You may have been responsible in some cases – this Wizard of Oz version of you is certainly a bad character – but I suspect that you are just a scapegoat. The shiny silver dollar in the right hand, while the left is performing the real magic. No. The real evil behind this *power grab at all cost* lies elsewhere. But keep looking, will you? You've turned over a number of stones and perhaps you'll turn over the right one yet.

The older man began walking away.

"Teddy?"

Teddy Prendick stopped and smiled. "Olivia, my dear. I'm glad to see that you are all right.

Howard looked over to where Olivia's voice emanated, and saw anything but *all right*. She looked like a truck had run her over. The explosion that had destroyed the Oz Club and knocked Howard unconscious, had ripped Olivia apart. Howard assumed he had been in little better shape before he began healing.

"What's this all about?" Olivia asked.

Teddy Prendick shook his head. "Too soon to tell, my dear. Too soon to tell. If you don't know, with that incredible psychic ability of yours, what chance do I have of knowing?"

"Surely you can tell us something?" Olivia said.

Teddy Prendick, one of the most powerful men in Chicago, pursed his lips in consideration.

"Dr. Lisa Moreau," he said at last. "She's an evil woman with a foul agenda. I suggest you take a look at her."

Sirens rose as Police and Emergency vehicles approached.

"I must be gone now, I'm afraid," said Prendick. "Invisibility is the strongest tool I have right now." He chuckled as he faded into thin air.

"Where—?" Howard began, but then Prendick just as suddenly reappeared right next to him.

The older man reached down and picked up the antimatter gun that had failed to stop the Wizard of Oz. "Where did you find this? It hasn't been invented here yet."

"The Blackout," Howard said.

Prendick harrumphed. "Won't do you much good out here. It's for removing warts and other minor cosmetic surgery. You didn't think it was a weapon did you? Just how much antimatter do you think could be safely contained in a space this small?" He dropped the gun onto the ground and was gone again.

Once again, Howard and Olivia sat in the morgue watching over Tony Sandoval. All of his counterparts at the Oz Club had been killed, and none of them displayed any ability for rejuvenation. Unfortunately, neither did their Tony.

Tony had taken a single gunshot to the throat and then additional damage when the Oz Club was destroyed, but showed no sign of recovering from any of it. The good news was that he wasn't decaying. But he wasn't healing either. The Chicago CSI team that had arrived at the scene had taken Tony away and placed him back in his bio-containment tank at the City Hall morgue for study.

Mayor Capone had yet to make an appearance, or summon Howard and Olivia to his office. Busy, they had been informed. They'd collaborated on a handwritten statement that left out most of the details and sent it upstairs. Just when Howard had decided to keep things from Capone, he didn't know. Olivia seemed happy to play along.

One of the things left out of the report was the antimatter gun Prendick had said was used for Keratolysis. It seemed insane, but Howard had no reason not to trust the man. That Prendick didn't trust Moreau was a point in his favor.

Removing the gun from his coat pocket, Howard placed the nozzle against a mole on his forearm that he had meant to get treated, but kept putting off.

"What are you doing!" Olivia had never seen the gun before and Howard hadn't yet explained Prendick's final comments.

"Elective surgery," Howard said, and pulled the trigger.

He felt a mild warmth in the area of the mole, and after pulling the gun away, watched a reddened patch of skin heal. Part of the mole was gone. He applied the gun a second time, and this time his arm healed entirely mole free.

He showed Olivia. "Maybe I should become a doctor."

"Stick to policing," Olivia said. "Start playing where you shouldn't and you might start turning into that Wizard of Oz character."

Howard didn't appreciate the comment, but he put the gun away.

After Howard and Olivia had left the morgue, a lone clock on the wall ticked away the seconds until the hands read 3:00 am. At precisely three hours after midnight, Tony and the other undecaying corpses sat up on their slabs and, in unison, swung their feet over the side, and slid down until they were standing. Then all seven of the naked corpses, eyes staring forward in the darkened room, marched toward the door, through the door, into the hallway, up the stairs, and out the side entrance of City Hall. In the frosty January air, Tony led his silent companions into the nighttime quiet of Capone's Chicago.

Dangerous Men

"Are you insane?" Mayor Capone all but screamed into Howard's face. "First you don't tell me that Tony has recovered or that there happen to be a dozen of him. Then you wander off and get Tony — all the Tonys — killed. You leave a hole in the ground where the Oz Club used to be. And now you want a warrant to take one of Chicago's most respectable citizens into custody because you think — you think! — that she may have committed a crime of some sort, but you can't even say what until you go on a fishing expedition. I won't even mention that of the list of over a hundred suspects I gave the two of you, you brought in three, let me repeat, three candidates. Need I even mention how useless and incompetent you are? I'd take you out and shoot the both of you if I thought it would do any good."

"So," Howard said, "I take it you are denying the warrant?" He stood rigid beneath Al Capone's malevolent stare. Howard knew that this meeting would go badly, but he also knew that there was no way he could avoid it. Asking for the warrant cost him nothing. As Capone himself had said, there really wasn't much he could do beyond scream... and possibly suffer a stroke.

"I want you," Capone said grimly, "to go out there and find me more people I can use. Forget Dr. Moreau. Forget any side trips. Just do want I say."

"But—" said Olivia, coming to Howard's defense..

Capone put his hand in the air, palm out. "Olivia, I love you, but you are as guilty of insubordination as Mr. Russell here. Unless you've had a premonition that I should know about, please just do as I ask."

"But I'm sure that Howard is right," Olivia said, making Howard feel all warm inside. "Dr. Moreau is somehow involved in what's going on."

"What's going on," Capone echoed, moving his hands behind his back and pacing a few steps. "And just what is that, exactly? Can you tell me?"

Howard and Olivia had already hashed this out. Al Capone was not the kind of man who would listen to long science lectures. Still, Howard had to try.

"These changes that have come over people. The three versions of me and the dozen versions of Tony. It's because there are parallel universes."

Capone coughed inside his throat.

"And these parallel universes are crashing into each other."

The cough became more of a grunt.

Howard had been about to say that he believed Capone himself had crossed over from one of these other universes, but received a sudden premonition that if he did, Capone would take him out and have him shot. Repeatedly. Or more likely have him buried in concrete. He felt Olivia kick the side of his foot with her heel. So instead, he said, "And I think Dr. Moreau knows something about it."

"I see," said Capone. Just that. Seconds ticked by while Howard watched wheels churning in the Mayor's head. "Tell you what. You let me deal with Dr. Moreau." Then the Mayor grinned. "I've been told that I have a flare for interrogation. If she has anything to tell me that I don't already know, well, that won't be the case for long."

Howard didn't know what to make of Capone's sudden change in attitude. He wished a premonition would tell him if this were a good or a bad thing. Unfortunately, as Olivia was so fond of saying, it didn't work that way.

"Meanwhile," said Capone, "you still have your list. And considering your abysmal success rate, I'm assigning you a new squad member." He tapped a button on his desk phone and the door opened, admitting a red-haired man in his late twenties. "This is Tony Carmichael."

"Tony?" said Olivia.

"Call me Anthony," said the redhead with a small smile. "I've read your squad's file. You folks are confusing enough without another Tony involved."

Howard immediately liked the man's friendly nature, but something told him that he was more dangerous than he looked. He shook the man's hand. "Well, Anthony. I'm sure we'll get along famously."

After visiting the weapons room, where Anthony equipped himself with a Beretta M9 and a healthy supply of ammunition, they left the building for a waiting red Ford Fairlane flip-top.

"You must like the color red," Olivia said. "The rest of the Crew prefer blue hard tops."

Anthony laughed. "As a boy, my friends made fun of my flaming red hair. In response, I wore red clothes, bought workbooks with red covers, and generally made sure I was surrounded by red. My hair became a trademark instead of a joke. The trademark stuck with me."

Howard climbed into the passenger seat after Olivia jumped into the back. Anthony shifted gears into drive and they were off.

"What's our first address?" Anthony asked.

Without looking at the printed list, Howard said, "Michigan and 22nd Ave."

"The Oz Club?" Anthony asked, frowning. "Your file says it's a hole in the ground."

"No," said Howard. "The address we want is nearby."

Fifteen minutes later, Howard directed his new squad mate to turn right, drive past the collection of CSI trucks and police tape that used to be a den of perversion, and park three hundred yards further down the street in front of a bakery.

"Are you sure this is the place?" Anthony said. "You have a habit of getting into trouble with the Mayor. I want no part of that."

Howard put on his friendliest smile. "The Mayor wants superheroes. The superest hero I know of is in there." He pointed to the bakery.

Anthony Carmichael looked doubtful, but he shut off the engine and climbed out of the Fairlane. Olivia also climbed out and gave Howard a quizzical look.

"I hear this place also makes the best Tiramisu in town," Howard said. A bell above the door tinkled as he opened the door.

A jolly, nearly baldheaded, overweight man stood behind a sweet smelling counter. Breads, cakes, and cookies filled the glass display and the atmosphere of the shop with their smells. Howard decided that a white beard and red suit would make the baker into a passable Santa Claus.

"Welcome!" exclaimed the almost Santa. "What can I get you today? We have Cannoli on special right now."

Howard tossed his Crew card on the counter. "We'd like to see your basement."

Santa frowned at the card and immediately lost his

jolliness. Then he turned his head and shouted. "Emilio!"

Howard heard a chair scrape across the floor of the back room, and then the door behind the counter opened. A thin, dangerous-looking man in a black three-piece suit and felt fedora poked his head out. One hand was out of sight, where Howard knew a gun holster lingered.

"What?" said the dangerous man.

"Friends of yours?" asked Santa.

The dangerous man nodded at Anthony. "Tony. Should you be here?"

"I'm not exactly sure," Anthony said. "Meet my partners. Howard Russell and Olivia Nelson."

The dangerous man stepped out fully from behind the door. No gun in sight. He looked at Howard. "The Wizard of Oz." He spoke in a way that suggested much more was behind the statement.

"Oh crap," said Santa. "I thought I recognized you." The overweight man slipped nervously past thin and dangerous, and into the back room.

"What do you want?" Dangerous asked Howard.

"We need to enter the freight tunnels," Howard said.

"Not gonna happen," said Dangerous.

Before Howard could think of a comeback, Anthony said," No. It's all right. Mayor's orders."

It was all Howard could do to keep a straight face. Didn't Anthony just say that he didn't want trouble with the Mayor?

Dangerous nodded slowly. "Oookaay. I'll just make a call." He pulled a flip phone from his suit pocket.

Anthony reached out a hand and rested it on Dangerous' phone. "I said, It's all right."

The two men locked gazes for several moments, and then Dangerous put the phone away.

"You do know there's been trouble?" Dangerous said.

Anthony nodded. "That's why we're here."

Dangerous stared at Anthony for a moment, then at Howard and Olivia. All the while, the hand he had used to put away the phone was out of sight behind the counter.

Howard knew it was resting on the grip on a handgun. Dangerous was probably deciding who to shoot first and who to shoot last. Howard had already made that assessment and knew the order Dangerous would come up with: Anthony, Howard, and then Olivia. It would be wrong, of course, and Olivia would likely kill him before he got to her. The correct order was Anthony, Olivia, and then Howard. He waited for Dangerous to make his move, his own hand on the handle of the Browning in his pocket.

But Dangerous surprised him. Instead of opening fire, the well-dressed man lifted his hand out of his coat and waved. "Follow me."

Howard then heard the click of the hammer being lowered on the weapon in Anthony's pocket.

The back room was more crowded than Howard remembered it being when he first entered it almost a month earlier. In addition to the ovens and supply cupboards and worktables, he saw almost Santa, the dangerous man, and three other members of Capone's Crew. He guessed that after all the action here in recent weeks, that the Mayor's outpost guarding the freight tunnels had become higher priority.

The four Crewmen looked lethal and serious, but Howard could also detect a hint of nervousness. Nervousness similar to what he had seen all across Chicago in the past few days since the sun had gone dark. On these men it looked even more out of place, as they were trained to be immune from fear. All four of them kept their hands near their guns.

Howard reminded himself that he had killed a Crewman here three weeks ago. Then three days ago, last night's Wizard of Oz must have come through here, again killing any Crewmen on guard. Crewmen had probably died again when Stone and the ten Tonys came through last night. Though what they were doing in the freight tunnels, Howard didn't know. He was pretty certain that they were on their way to the Oz Club to deal with the Wizard, and that Howard's arrival had just been a case of bad timing. Regardless, this bakery must be considered bad luck by all of Capone's Crew right now. All four of these men were probably just counting the minutes until someone killed them.

"Let's get moving," he said to Anthony, who nodded.

Dangerous drew a key from his pocket and unlocked the door leading down to the basement. The door from the basement to the tunnels was smashed to bits. Howard assumed it had been repaired and broken again at least twice in the past three weeks. So, either the Wizard or the ten Tonys had also broken their way through.

The freight tunnels looked exactly as they had when Howard had been here just before Christmas. Dusty from disuse, but with the lights still on. Howard, Olivia, and Anthony walked the length of the tunnel in silence, turned at the intersection, and were met by four additional Crewman with guns drawn.

"Uh," said Howard.

Anthony was already holding out his Crew card. He must have had it in his hand before turning the corner, because reaching inside his coat would have been suicidal.

"The Mayor sent us," Anthony said.

Howard was again impressed with how well the man lied.

"Walk toward us," said one of the Crewman. "Slowly. Hands where we can see them."

They joined the Mayor's men at the break in the wall that led to the tungsten chamber.

"No one warned us that anyone was coming," said one of the Crewmen.

"My fault," said Anthony. "I should have had the Mayor's Office call ahead. We —" He glanced at Howard "— didn't know that our path would lead us here."

"Here?" repeated the Crewman. "There's nothing here. You should turn around and go back the way you came."

Anthony looked at Howard. "Is there nothing here?"

Howard knew that turning back wasn't an option. If they did that, it was only a matter of time before this

Chicago, this universe, came crashing down like the one the other Tony had described. That would probably happen anyway, he realized, but at least he might find out why.

"Just the opposite," he told Anthony. "Everything is here."

Anthony nodded, and then looked at the four Crewmen. "You'd better let us through."

Then the Crewman who had been speaking said something odd. "Yes, sir."

He immediately shut his mouth and took a half step backwards.

Anthony frowned at him and then tried to smile. He glanced at Howard. "It's the red hair. Has that effect on some people."

Howard knew that the safest thing he could do was nod, so that's what he did.

Anthony waved his hand toward the broken concrete in the tunnel wall. "Lead on, Macduff."

Howard knew that the correct quote was, "Lay on, Macduff." And it didn't escape him that these were the last words spoken by Macbeth just before the two men fought to the death.

He'd been had. Anthony was no babysitter, assigned to make sure Howard did his job. He was the Mayor's spy, assigned to see what Howard would do and report it to the Mayor. Did Capone already know they were here? Whatever happened, whatever Howard learned, it was going to happen fast. Howard could already feel a concrete tomb hardening around him.

"Let's go get some answers," he said, and squeezed into the opening.

The Bunker Revisited

The outer room was exactly as Howard remembered. Clay walls except for the one wall of tungsten with its strange door of seven hinges and three locks. The locks were still broken, but Howard realized he had a problem. He no longer had the strength of droid legs to move the door.

"Help me pull the door open," he said to Anthony.

The redheaded Crewman handed their one flashlight to Olivia and the two men each grabbed a handle with both hands. After pulling to no effect, they adjusted their positions and pressed their feet against the tungsten wall for better leverage. Still nothing.

Anthony sucked in a deep breath. "I think I've heard about this door. Can't be opened."

Howard slammed a fist against the door and instantly regretted it. He flexed his fingers as feeling returned. Then, "Wait. I've got an idea." Facing the door, he shouted, "Dr. Frankenstein. It's your monster. I need to speak with you."

"Are you sure about this?" Olivia asked from behind the flashlight.

"Never surer." Howard slammed the door again with his fist and repeated his request.

Anthony said nothing, but watched critically. Howard got the sense that he was memorizing every word and every action. The Mayor was going to receive an interesting report before this day ended.

A clanging sound interrupted the silence, and the tungsten door inched outward and swung open. In the doorway stood a droid, of sorts. It reminded Howard of a 2007 movie he had seen called *Transformers*, where a car unfolded into an almost humanoid-shaped robot. That robot now stood in the doorway. It even had some yellow paint. Just like in the movie. The monstrous robot looked at Howard, then at Olivia and Anthony, and then backed into the bunker.

Howard blinked as he stepped through the doorway. Three weeks ago, there had been some flickering lights inside the bunker, along with smoke and possibly fire. That was then. He now saw that the ceiling itself appeared to glow, the walls went further back, and the bunker seemed filled with machinery.

"It's bigger than I remember." He looked at the transformer monstrosity that had retreated to one side of the door. "Dr. Frankenstein? Is that you?"

"I am over here," said a female voice.

Howard looked toward the center back wall and saw a girl sitting in a chair. She had pale skin and blonde hair and looked exactly like the University of Chicago grad student whose name he couldn't remember. He noticed that she was fully dressed in a white lab smock and wondered why he had expected her to be naked.

"Why have you returned?" the girl asked.

"I need your help," Howard said. "Things have gotten a little strange out there."

The girl rose from the chair and took two steps toward him. "The damage to the realities has escalated. The version of you that passed through the Vortex most recently was most indiscrete. He opened the Gate during the collision caused by his journey. I could not stop him. He had already undergone multiple alterations from previous journeys. His ability to survive this long is most improbable."

"He didn't survive," Howard said. "He was quite insane when I encountered him."

"Sanity is relative," the girl said. "Its lack did not prevent him from causing great damage."

"Was it him?" Howard asked. "Was it that monstrous version of me that was causing all the trouble? Teddy Prendick seems to think that someone else is orchestrating things."

Anthony Carmichael interrupted. "You spoke with Prendick?"

The girl turned her head in a way that Howard associated with robots. "A single person could not survive long enough to cause the damage that has occurred."

Howard ignored Anthony's question. "But who would want to destroy whole universes?"

"I have been considering this," the girl said. "The only

logical answer is that the damage is not the goal. It is merely collateral."

"Collateral damage?" Howard tried to make sense of this new information. "Whole universes have been destroyed. Collateral to what?"

A raspy voice spoke from the doorway. "I'd like to know the answer to that myself."

The figure stepped into the bunker and Howard saw what looked like a giant reptile. It stood on two legs and wore a baggy business suit. The face and hands that protruded from the suit were rough, scaly, and green. Its head was hairless and its voice was a harsh croak. Despite all this, Howard knew exactly who it was. "Dr. Moreau."

The lizard barked a laugh. "Why, Mr. Russell, how on Earth did you penetrate my disguise? I went to great effort to arrive incognito."

"You have a way about you," Howard said. "I've also seen your escort before. Hanging around your office building." The two soldiers he had seen at the Prendick Foundation stood next to the lizard. Howard turned to Anthony. "You called Moreau? I thought you were the Mayor's man."

Anthony widened his eyes. "Why would I call Moreau? It must have been someone else."

Moreau waved a scaly hand. "Don't let me interrupt. Please, continue your discussion with this intriguing young woman. It was just getting interesting."

The blonde girl, who had once been a construction droid in Howard's Chicago, stepped forward and examined Dr. Moreau. "You have been adjusted. Yet, you did not travel through the Vortex. Your reality has become unstable. You have my sympathy."

The reptile's eyes darkened. "I don't want your sympathy. I want what happened to me undone."

The girl nodded and stepped back a pace. "Of course. Be comforted to know that numerous versions of you exist who were not adjusted. You who have suffered are just one of many."

"Comfort!" Moreau's shout was more a growl. "I don't want comforting words, either. I want to be normal again."

"I am sorry," said the girl. "What you wish for is impossible. At best, you and your reality may suffer no additional damage."

"Not what I wanted to hear." The lizard turned to her soldiers. "Kill the girl."

The two men drew handguns from holsters, not with any great speed, but with the resolve of men used to obeying orders. But before they had even cleared their weapons, gunfire echoed in Howard's ear and holes appeared in the soldiers' foreheads. Two shots. Two holes. Two men slumped to the bunker floor.

Howard turned to see Anthony with his Beretta raised to eye level and smoke whisping from the gun barrel. "That won't stop them," Howard told the Mayor's spy.

Dr. Moreau laughed. "Right again, Mr. Russell. For an inept fool, you have impressed me twice in the space of ten minutes. Astonishing, since you have never impressed me before."

The soldiers began moving where they lay on the metallic floor, so Howard pulled the Browning out of his pocket and shot them each again. They stopped moving. "I could do this all day," Howard said, "or at least until I run out of bullets."

"That won't be necessary," said the Mayor. And through the doorway walked Al Capone and the three superheroes Howard had managed to round up for him.

"I did call the Mayor," Anthony admitted.

Anthony, Olivia, and Howard moved further into the bunker to make room for the new arrivals. As they did, Howard noted the bench near the back wall where the Rhodium-105 ingots sat.

"You're looking lovely," Capone said to Moreau, at which she made a noise Howard interpreted as contempt. The Mayor's expression grew serious. "I'd have appreciated it, if you had done as I told you and waited for my arrival."

"You called Moreau?" Howard accused the Mayor.

"No, no, no," Moreau said. "That one is just a little too obvious. You're sliding back into inept fool territory."

A shot echoed in the confines of the chamber, and the reptile that was Dr. Moreau slumped to the floor, joining her two soldiers, who had begun moving again.

Howard looked at Anthony, but it wasn't him. He turned the other way and saw Capone holstering a Smith and Wesson Chief's Special. "You killed your own creature?"

Capone curled his upper lip. "Creature is a good word. Dr. Moreau used to be a good employee, but lately she's made mistakes." He patted his gun holster. "Perhaps you can learn a lesson from that."

The two soldiers began rising to their feet. Howard watched them take in the Mayor's presence and Dr. Moreau lying on the floor in a growing pool of blood. They fell in line beside the Mayor's three superheroes. A premonition hit Howard, telling him that he had been better off facing Dr. Moreau before the Mayor's arrival.

Capone was looking around the chamber, taking in its contents. Howard watched his gaze fall on the ingots of Rhodium-105. "I suspect that is what everyone came here for. There's something familiar about them."

"Ninety years ago you entered this chamber and attempted to take one," said the girl.

Capone frowned. "You, I don't recognize."

"I was not here at the time," she said. "Had I been, I would have stopped you."

Capone smirked. "You and whose army?"

The transformer near the door shifted. Capone nodded at his three superheroes and they went into action.

The hero Howard had found who he called Hercules, but not to the man's face, spun and grabbed hold of one of the transformer's metal arms. The transformer flailed, smashing Hercules against the tungsten wall. Hercules let out a loud breath and sank to his knees. Howard noticed a wide, shallow dent in the wall.

The second superhero, Howard had called Zeus. He was a skinny old man who could apparently throw lightning bolts. Howard wasn't certain what a lightning bolt tossed around in such a small space would do, and he didn't want to find out. He had half-drawn his Browning again when a bright blue electric arc passed between the old man's hand and the bulky droid. There was a pregnant pause, and then the transformer punched out a metallic fist, bursting the old man's head like a watermelon.

The third superhero watched this. She was a small girl, something like twelve years old, and was wearing sunglasses.

Howard said, "Oh crap."

The little girl reached up and raised her sunglasses. Beams of hot red light blasted out from her eyes and struck the transformer droid in the face, sending the giant droid flying back into the wall.

"Cyclops's little sister." Howard finished drawing his Browning and shot the girl in the back of the head. The red beams stopped and the girl tumbled to the floor like puppet with cut strings.

Howard heard several guns click their hammers, and saw Moreau's two soldiers with weapons trained on him. A third click indicated that Anthony was also training on someone. One guess who his target was.

"Are you insane?" Capone shouted. "You work for me. You just killed one of my men."

"I'm sorry about the girl," Howard said. And he was sorry. Howard would never have dreamed of harming a child. It was the Tony part of him that had shown him the necessity of shooting the girl. The lesser of two evils. "But you can't touch those ingots. Bad things will happen. And with the door to this room open, they won't just happen in here."

"You've got about five seconds to explain yourself," Capone growled. "Four. Three."

Howard spoke as quickly as he could. "The sun went out three days ago because someone touched the ingots when the door was open."

Capone stared at him. Then looked at the ingots. Then back at him. "That's possibly the last thing I thought I would hear you say. You've bought yourself a few more seconds. Explain."

Howard didn't know if he could explain, but he had to try. "Those ingots don't come from here. They come from somewhere else. Somewhere where the laws of physics are different."

"Different?" Capone interrupted. "I don't know much about physics, but I know a whole lot about law. My scientists tell me that the laws of physics don't change."

"Yes," said Howard. "Just like people don't live forever, or survive lethal gunshot wounds, or turn into lizards. These ingots come from someplace where the rules are different. And when they come into contact with... things that obey different rules, well, nature tries to balance it out."

"Things?" said Capone. "Like, I don't know, air?"

"Air contains just a few simple elements," said the girl who was once a construction droid. "The odds of a collision are remote. Biological units are highly complex. The odds of a collision, an incompatibility, are significant. Even droids are complex enough that incompatibilities are assured."

"Fine," said Capone. "Assume I believe any of this nonsense. Where did these ingots, not from around here, come from?"

"The droid doesn't know," Howard said. "I already asked."

The blonde girl looked at him. "I have comprehended much since you traveled here. I now know the origin of the Vortex."

"Oh?" said Howard. "Oh! Tell us."

"Once," said the girl. "Thousands of years ago, there was only one reality. In this reality, Mankind experimented and discovered how to safely generate unlimited power, what you know as cold fusion."

"Cold what?" asked several people in the bunker.

"Uh," said Howard. "I know what cold fusion is. I sort of made some myself once upon a time. To put it simply, instead of burning a lot of coal to generate a little bit of electricity, you burn a little bit of a mined ore called palladium to generate a whole lot of electricity. The ingots over there," he waved at the table against the wall, "are a byproduct."

"That is essentially correct," the girl said. "What the scientists of that time and place did not know was that Rhodim-105—"

"The ingots over there," Howard interjected.

"—placed stress against the very fabric of reality."

"Now she's gone past me," Howard said.

"The stress increased as additional ingots were created, until the fabric was torn and reality began breaking apart. The scientists were quick to realize what was happening and built this cage to contain the source of the stress, but it was already too late. Reality was irreparably torn, and in time, the universe and everything in it was no more."

"Except for this cage," Howard said.

The girl smiled. "The lizard woman was correct. Your perceptiveness is sometimes surprising. This bunker, the Vortex, is all that remains of the original universe."

"I think I follow," said Olivia. "But if the universe was destroyed, how is it that we are here?"

The girl ceased smiling. "Reality has no wish to not exist. When the fabric was torn, it attempted to repair itself. The best it could do was to create a new reality from each strand of its old self."

"And each strand is similar, but not identical, to the others," Olivia suggested.

The girl nodded. "Having witnessed how fragile it was, the universe varied the rules of its existence from strand to strand. In none of the strands are the ingots in this bunker permitted to exist. The accident that tore the universe apart can never be repeated."

"But other accidents could happen," Howard said.

"Though not everywhere. Reality has built-in contingency plans."

"Okay," said Al Capone. "I've indulged you to the limit of my patience. I have no idea what you're talking about, except that those ingots are valuable. So, it looks like they are mine now."

"Once a mobster, always a mobster," Howard said. He lifted his gun to find Al Capone's heart. Unfortunately, Capone's men still had their weapons trained on him. Three guns fired and three bullets hit their target.

Capone VS Ness

When Howard revived, he found himself in the middle of the OK Corral. Guns were firing and bodies were slamming into other bodies. He couldn't help but notice that several of those bodies were naked and that some of those had an odd number of limbs, misplaced heads, or other bodily irregularities. In the middle of it all, the transformer droid was waving its arms blindly due to half its head being pulverized, but was unerringly hitting Capone's two soldiers or other Crewmen who had arrived from the freight tunnels.

By the time Howard could move, he spotted Anthony Carmichael positioning himself to take a shot at the girl that was once a university student, a construction droid, or both. He had no idea how vulnerable the droid-girl might be, and knew he had to do something.

"Hey, Red!"

Anthony looked at him and frowned.

Howard acknowledged that frown by placing a hole between the redheaded man's eyebrows. The senior Crewman had the decency to look surprised before he crashed to the floor, stone dead. Those long hours Howard spent at the target range had paid off.

Occupying the space behind the fallen Crewman was none other than Al Capone himself, creeping toward the table that housed the Rhoidum-105 ingots. Howard leveled his gun again, and fired. This time he missed his target, and hit Capone's right shoulder rather than his heart. But it was enough to stop Capone in his tracks. Howard held his gun on the injured Mayor while the fighting in the bunker continued.

Within seconds, the remainder of Capone's Crewmen lay dead on the floor. That left the two unkillable soldiers who were locked in an uncomfortable embrace with the transformer droid that was somehow an extension of the blonde droid-girl, and a half-dozen walking dead victims of the Blackout who Howard had last seen lying on slabs at the City Hall morgue. One of the walking dead was Tony Sandoval.

Olivia had avoided the fighting altogether and stood near the droid-girl. Once again, Howard wished he could remember the blasted girl's name.

Restrained, outnumbered, and with their boss staring down the barrel of Howard's gun, the two soldiers allowed themselves to be taken into custody by the walking dead and escorted out of the bunker. Howard hoped that Tony Sandoval would stay and explain what had happened, but the Crewman's voice was as mute and his face as devoid of emotion as his naked companions.

"What the hell was that?" Capone demanded.

A lean man with greying hair appeared in the middle of the bunker as if from thin air. "That was me, I'm afraid. Having lost my original task force, and then my replacement task force, I was forced to recruit a third. I have to admit that they performed admirably."

"Teddy?" said Olivia.

Teddy Prendick smiled. "Good to see you again, Olivia. Do you have any premonitions for me today?"

"How?" Olivia asked. "How did you do that?"

Prendick waggled his brows. "I've picked up a few tricks here and there."

"A few tricks?" said Howard. "Invisibility. Animating the dead." He pulled from his coat pocket the antimatter mole remover. "You knew what this was."

"Mr. Ness has undergone several adjustments," said the blonde droid-girl.

"Ness!" cried Capone. Despite the wounded shoulder, the mobster come mayor climbed to his feet. "Elliot Ness!"

Prendick pulled out a Walther P88 and trained it on Capone. "None other. You wouldn't recognize me, of course. I aged. Eventually."

"You bastard," said Capone. "They told me I'd killed you. Or lost you."

"Lost," said Prendick aka Ness. "My men and I followed you and your men through the freight tunnels to this bunker. We waged a gun battle outside that doorway, where all of your men and several Chicago policemen eventually died. But not before your men managed to force open the door and lock you inside. By the time we opened the door, you were gone, the bunker was empty.

We thought it must be some kind of magician's trick. Close one door and another opens. But when we closed the door with us inside, nothing happened. By flashlight, we found that table over there with the ingots. There were also several small boxes, each with an ingot inside. One of my men, I don't remember who, touched one of the ingots, and the pressure in the bunker changed. When the pressure returned to normal we opened the door and discovered we had been right, it was a magician's trick. There was no sign of a gunfight. No bodies, no bullets, no blood.

We traveled though the tunnels back up to the streets and discovered two things. First, that Chicago had changed. No mobs, no Depression, no Prohibition. And no one had ever heard of Al Capone."

"What was the second thing you discovered?" asked Olivia.

Ness nodded toward Capone. "That we didn't grow older."

"Sounds like you had it made," said Howard.

Ness laughed. "Not at all. You see, in that Chicago,

Germany had won the First World War and Michigan was a province of Greater Germany. The place was a police state and German was the official language. We left relatively quickly.

"Back though this bunker," Howard suggested.

"Yes," said Ness, "and no. We came back to this place. But this time each of us took one of the small boxes and went back out into the tunnels. We figured that there must be a reason for the boxes with one ingot each. It seemed obvious that they must be portable devices for traveling between those alternate universes you were discussing before I revealed myself."

"You couldn't have been more mistaken," said the droid-girl. "The boxes were for transporting ingots to this cage. Out in the world the ingots were tearing reality apart. Isolating them individually in tungsten allowed people to transport them safely. Once inside this cage, it made no difference if they were apart or together."

The longer the droid spoke, the further Ness's jaw dropped. "But, but. It worked. We were able to jump between universes from anywhere. We didn't have to use this bunker."

"Of course you could," said the girl. "The same principles were at work. Touching the ingot in the box triggered reality to make adjustments to limit damage to the universe the holder of the box resided in. Those adjustments, by their very nature, involved ejecting the ingot, box, and box's holder to a different reality and adjusting the holder to be able to reside in that reality without causing similar interactions. Of course, once you arrived, the process would repeat itself until the box was closed and the ingot insulated. I think it likely that while you thought you were traveling between two realities, you in fact traveled through several before closing the box.

"Isn't that like using this bunker with the door open?" Howard asked. "Wouldn't using the box damage entire universes, like this one was damaged three days ago when the Wizard of Oz arrived and opened the door?"

"Exactly," the girl said. "On a smaller scale, but leaving a path of horrendous destruction in its wake."

"B-b-but," Ness sputtered. "We traveled all the time. It's how I started aging again. Every time I traveled, I changed. Sometimes good, sometimes bad."

"And worlds changed in your wake," the girl said. "Please do not use the boxes again."

Ness slumped to the floor, his Walther P88 falling beside him. It was a good thing Howard still had his gun aimed in Capone's direction. Who knew what the mobster would do with his arch nemeses vulnerable before him.

"We thought we were chasing the Destroyer of Worlds," Ness whispered. "We were only chasing ourselves."

There's No Place Like Home

The following day was one of confusion, hope, and surprises. The first surprise was that Mayor Al Capone hadn't ordered Howard buried in concrete. At least, not yet. He and Olivia had been summoned to Capone's office from where they had been sitting in the morgue watching Tony's body, hoping that he would wake up. That hadn't happened either.

Capone stood behind his desk, wearing an eight hundred dollar suit with his arm resting in an eight hundred dollar sling. He was smiling. Something deep inside Howard told him that this was not a good thing. But something near the surface told him that it was.

The Mayor wasn't alone. Elliot Ness sat in one of the office's comfortable chairs. Neither had a gun drawn on the other.

"Thank you for coming," Capone said as Olivia and Howard entered. He walked in front of his desk and sat on its edge. Howard and Olivia also sat.

"Last night was..." Capone shrugged. "What would you call it? An eye opener?"

Howard surmised that an answer was expected, so he

said, "Among other things."

Al Capone laughed. He actually laughed. Ness laughed with him. A small laugh, but a laugh nonetheless.

Olivia looked at the two men. "You two are friends now?"

Capone laughed harder. "I wouldn't go that far."

Howard looked at Ness. "Prendick. Ness. Whatever your name is. You've been hunting Al Capone."

Ness's expression turned serious. "A hundred years ago that was true. It took me sixty years of traveling from Chicago to Chicago before I found him. By then, Capone had been this Chicago's lawmaker for decades longer than he'd been a lawbreaker. And, truth be told, I've seen a lot of Chicagos, and this one has less corruption, crime, and unhappiness than most of them."

Capone smiled at that.

"Once I was here," Ness continued, "I began to age again, but had no desire to continue traveling. I established a new persona as Teddy Prendick, a billionaire captain of industry I had encountered in most other Chicagos, but who was absent here. I used what I had learned in my travels to build a technology-based dynasty."

"Cop turned corporate?" Howard said.

"Hardly," said Ness. "By then, I and my Untouchables had witnessed inexplicable damage occurring in many of the realities we visited. Capone was a gnat compared to the evil genius we suspected was behind the destruction of whole universes." He shook his head. "If only we had realized that we were causing most of the damage ourselves."

"What I don't understand," Howard said, "is how I ended up being such a bastard in at least two Chicagos."

Ness nodded. "The Wizard of Oz. Don't feel bad. From what I saw, most people are... lesser beings in other realities. I lost count of the number of Elliot Nesses I put down because I couldn't stand to see myself as... so easily *touchable*. We're all bastards, Mr. Russell. Out there.

Somewhere."

That wasn't a happy sentiment.

"Anyway," said Capone, apparently unruffled about being called a gnat. "Ness and I have a plan."

"Sounds ominous," Howard said, not really meaning to speak aloud.

Capone let that pass as well. He really was in a good mood. "First off, I'm breaking up your squad."

Howard raised his eyebrows.

"Tony," said the Mayor, "is, well, Tony. Perhaps he'll wake up. Perhaps not. If he does, I think he's been shot and blown up enough that continued abuse isn't good for him. Should he come back, we'll find him a desk job.

"And Olivia, well, you make a decent Crewman, but I can see that your heart isn't in it. I think you should go back to your old job of predicting earthquakes and anything else that can help the city. With so many monsters and heroes now in our midst, your warnings will be more important than ever."

"Thank you," Olivia said. "And I still have a distraught mother to comfort and a husband to remember."

"I may be able to help with that," Ness said. "The remembering, I mean. I've picked up a few abilities and tricks along the way."

"Are you going to help Capone remember?" Howard asked. "He didn't remember the bunker or what had happened there ninety years ago."

"Ness offered," said Capone. "I refused. I'm the man I've been for almost a hundred years. I may not be perfect, but I'm comfortable with who I am. Remembering might change me. I've had my fill of changes.

"And then there's you, Mr. Howard Russell. I've had my fill of you as well." He touched his sling with his left hand. "I'm kicking you out of Chicago."

"But Chicago is my home," Howard said. "I've never been anywhere else."

"My mind's made up," said Capone. "Everything was fine here before you showed up. And look at it now. I hardly recognize the place."

Howard was stunned. He'd thought that last night, after the dust settled and he and Ness and the droid-girl had talked it out, that Capone had finally understood what had happened. He looked at Olivia, whose expression was as stunned as Howard felt. Then he looked at Ness, and saw a wicked smile creasing his thick lips. Howard was being had. Again.

"I'm going to bury that blasted bunker in concrete," Capone said. "No one is coming or going through there ever again. But before I do, Ness has decided to leave."

"I'm going to travel again," Ness said. "For as long as I can before I get killed, die of old age, or get adjusted into nonexistence."

"And everywhere he goes," Capone said, "he's going to bury the bunker,"

"You want me to go with him," Howard said. "I—I could do that." It didn't sound bad. A better life than doing Capone's dirty work.

"Not at all," said Capone. "Yes, I do want you to bury the bunker. But just in one reality."

"I had a chat," said Ness, "with that pretty little droid girl of yours."

"She's not exactly mine," Howard said, but Ness waved him off.

"She thinks she can send you back where you came from. I'm assuming the idea appeals to you. You've only been away a few weeks. You can go home and forget you ever came here."

"Yes," said Howard, his heart suddenly pounding in his chest. "Going home does appeal to me. There's nothing I'd like better. But I won't forget."

"I could help with that," Ness offered.

"No!" said Howard. "I mean, no thank you. Like the Mayor, I've had my fill of changes."

Capone stood. "It's decided then. No time like the present. Let's get you home."

Howard made one last visit to the morgue, where he said goodbye to Tony. The Crewman was good at goodbyes. No tears. No choked final words. Howard wished he could say the same for himself. He couldn't avoid the guilt. His blood had made the three of them virtually indestructible. But Olivia had still lost her memory of her husband, and Tony was lost in some kind of coma. Only he, himself, remained more or less unscathed. Perhaps in time Tony would wake up, as he had after lying in pieces in the tank for three days. Howard had to believe it would happen. He said so to Olivia.

"Of course Tony will wake up," she said. "It's been barely a day, and the damage is much less than last time. When he does wake up, I'll be here to welcome him back and tell him how you got to go home." She choked up a bit, just as Howard had moments earlier. "He'll be so happy for you, just like I am. And I'll ask him to put away his guns and come work with me. We'll be the two most prominent psychics in Chicago."

Howard nodded and gave her a hug, then left Olivia and Tony to be escorted by Moreau's two unkillable soldiers who now worked for the Mayor. "I guess Capone didn't make out too badly after all," he said to the men. He didn't know their names so he thought of them as the G. I. Joe twins.

Both Joes gave him a blank look and said nothing.

They found Ness waiting for them in the car lot.

"You're leaving already?" Howard asked.

"My work here is done," said the lawman turned entrepreneur. "No reason to delay. Every reason to hurry. There is no telling how many others have been using the bunker since before your pretty droid showed up to manage things."

"She's not—"

"Yes, yes," said Ness. "Not your droid."

"Well," said Howard. "In a sense she is. I brought a

construction droid into the bunker. But she's evolved a lot since then. She doesn't belong to anyone now."

The car was moving, G. I. Joe at the wheel and G.I. Joe riding shotgun. Howard and Ness were in the back.

"I think you're wrong," said Ness. "Whatever she is now, she was created and belongs to the collective intelligence of the fractured reality. The initial fracturing was a protection mechanism, and when the resulting realities became endangered, the Vortex that connected them all created a new way to protect itself. Self-preservation is the most basic of instincts."

"The Vortex is God?" Howard suggested. "And the droid its daughter?"

"As good a description as any," said Ness.

They rode in silence after that, each lost in his own thoughts. Even the G. I. Joes, Howard supposed.

For his own part, Howard tried imagining what it would be like to be home. Would he be his old self again? His current, virtually indestructible, psychic self? Or would he change again and become something different? So long as he didn't turn into the Wizard of Oz, he didn't care. He would be home again. A quiet man, leading a quiet life, hiding from his past. He couldn't imagine anything better.

When they arrived at the bakery, Howard noticed several Crewmen idling around the remains of the Oz Club. He knew they weren't there for the club, but to keep an eye on the bunker. They watched carefully as G. I. Joe brought the car to a stop and the four of them got out.

The bakery had a *Closed Indefinitely* sign hanging on the door, but a Crewman peered out from behind a curtain and let them inside, where Howard discovered several additional Crewmen. The bakery basement and the tunnel all the way to the bunker were littered with Capone's people. Howard wondered if there was anyone left in the rest of Chicago.

After squeezing through the narrow crevice that led to the bunker itself, Howard found several Crewman and two men dressed in white lab coats. Capone's mysterious and supposedly all-knowing scientists that Howard had heard about but had never been able to meet. He thought he recognized them from the University of Chicago staff roster, from back when he'd still been Dr. Howard Russell, PhD, but he couldn't remember their names. They looked at him with speculative stares, but said nothing. Howard assumed they had been ordered not to speak with him or Ness. Capone was a little paranoid, but he supposed paranoid people lived longer than the other kind. Capone certainly had.

The scientists looked to be overseeing the placement of scaffolding that would direct the flow of cement. Capone hadn't lied when he said he would bury the bunker.

The door to the bunker was open and two more scientists and a couple of Crewman were inside, taking photos and attempting to speak with the droid. The blonde girl looked at them, but said nothing. The giant transformer droid that was somehow an independent extension of her, stood guard over the table of Rhodium-105 ingots. Howard suspected that if anyone got too close, they would meet with an accident.

One of the Crewmen said, "Time. Everyone out."

The scientists and other Crewmen left the bunker so quickly that Howard assumed that this was the new head Crewman, the one Capone had assigned to take Anthony Carmichael's place after Howard had killed him in last night's shootout.

That left Howard, Ness, and the G. I. Joe twins in the bunker.

The droid-girl spoke. "Elliot Ness will travel first. You three must step outside."

As Howard moved to obey, he overheard the girl speaking with Ness. "Reality appreciates what you will do to prevent future traveling, thereby protecting remaining shards from additional damage."

"It's the least I can do," Ness said. "Given that I'm responsible for much of the damage that has already happened."

"They called you Untouchable," the girl said.

"Yes." A wry smile forming on Ness's lips. "Incorruptible by the mobs and fearless in my pursuit of upholding the law. I thought it was enough. I was wrong."

The conversation was cut off as the transformer droid closed the door.

Howard stood in silence with the scientists and Crewmen as, well, nothing happened. Work on the scaffolding had ceased so that everyone could see what it looked like from outside the bunker when someone traveled. So they all discovered that it looked like nothing. After a couple of minutes, the door opened. No Ness inside.

"I guess it's my turn," Howard said. No one responded. Not a single *Bon Voyage*. He entered the bunker and watched the transformer droid close the door, noticing as it did that its head was no longer damaged.

"The adjustments," said the droid-girl who looked exactly the same, "give reality some leeway. It is how I have evolved over the past weeks. And how I survived your Wizard of Oz six days ago when he came through and fought against me."

"You fought the Wizard of Oz?" Howard said. "Steel had to blow himself up with Rhodium-105 along with the Oz Club in order to stop him."

"Sadly," said the girl. "The Vortex could not afford the same sacrifice. I could merely survive him, not stop him."

"Capone says you can send me back home."

"There is a high probability," the girl said. "Ness was able to provide a specific destination to those traveling by providing them with an inanimate object from the destination reality. Having such objects available when required is tricky. It took Ness more than sixty years to perfect such a system."

"And Ness's system can help me?"

"No," said the girl. "Ness made no plan for you. How could he?"

"Then how am I going to get home?"

"By good fortune, I have an object from your reality that is relatively intact." The girl raised one fist and opened her fingers. And there, in her palm, sat Howard's wedding ring. The one he had lost in the bunker along with his own left arm when he acquired that of Dr. Samuels.

Howard took the ring from her palm and placed it on his ring finger. It felt right. Perfect. "You said relatively intact?"

"The ring was present when the Wizard of Oz traveled with the Gate open. Much damage was wrought to myself, the Vortex, two realities, and, of course, this ring."

"It looks fine," Howard said.

"Mostly," agreed the girl, "Some repairs were made when Ness traveled just now. To myself and to the ring. Its nature is ninety-eight percent intact."

Howard continued to stare at the ring.

"Therefore," said the girl. "I believe you have a ninety-eight percent chance of returning to your original reality."

"Better than a kick in the pants," Howard said.

"What?" asked the girl.

"Nothing. I guess I need to touch one of those ingots."

The table wasn't exactly how Howard remembered it. It was still comprised of some kind of hardwood, and several dozen ingots still rested there. But there was an addition. A small grey box sat open with a single ingot taking up most of the space inside.

"The ingot Ness used to travel outside the Vortex," the girl said.

Of course he would have one. And of course he would leave it here. Perhaps Ness would find others, and bring them here before arranging to have the bunker buried after he moved on to the next place. It was a difficult and tricky job, but if anyone could do it, Elliot Ness could. The Untouchable.

And Ness was wrong when he said those last words to the droid-girl. People make mistakes. Best intentions notwithstanding. Being incorruptible, Untouchable, was enough. Ness had proved it by not giving in to despair when he realized what he had done. Instead, he set out to make it right. That was all that was humanly possible. And it was enough.

Perhaps Ness hadn't exaggerated when he said that most of the Chicagos he had visited were hopelessly corrupt. Or perhaps, people weren't really so awful. Using Ness as a measuring stick, everyone would look awful.

"Are you ready?" the girl asked. It was a rhetorical question.

Howard reached out his hand and lifted the ingot out of the box. The increased air pressure was immediate, but Howard had been ready this time. Also, there was no earthquake in progress to roughen the journey. Instead of losing consciousness, surrounded by destruction, he merely staggered slightly and managed to set the ingot on the table next to the others. Then he put the empty tungsten box into his pocket.

"To help others avoid the mistake Ness made," he said.

The girl nodded.

The air pressure lifted and Howard watched the transformer droid make short work of opening the door. Howard looked outside and found the clay-walled bunker empty. No sign of Crewmen, scientists, or scaffolding. No Geraldo Rivera and crew either. "Is this the right place?" Howard asked, nervous.

"You will have to go and see," the girl said.

Howard felt adrenalin rise as he squeezed through the crevasse between the bunker chamber and the freight tunnels. Everything looked exactly how he remembered. The roughened walls of clay, the placement of the fallen concrete. The flashlight he had brought with him from

Capone's Chicago was not as bright as the one he'd had before Christmas, but as he emerged into the tunnels and took in the detritus-strewn concrete, broken ceiling, and icy water trapped in corners, he could swear it looked nothing like the tunnels he had left behind and everything like the tunnels of home.

The ceiling lights, as expected, were dead. Howard used the flashlight to make his way to the half-demolished bakery, where daylight came down all the way into the tunnel below the basement.

Howard climbed the stairs and was not surprised to see a fifty-something man seated on a stool, swaddled in a heavy winter parka, and reading a book. The man looked over and nearly fell off his perch. "Hey! No one is allowed in here."

A smile creased Howard's lips. This was no shoot first, ask questions later Crewman. He was just a security guard for the City keeping watch on a construction site.

The man squinted, and then took a double take. "Mr. Russell? How did you get here? We weren't expecting you until tomorrow."

Howard was about to say that there were sixty miles of tunnels and dozens of entrances, not all of which were sealed, when the meaning of the guard's words struck him. "Tomorrow? What's tomorrow?"

He had been missing for three weeks. Why would anyone expect him tomorrow?

The guard seemed confused, and Howard could see him wondering if perhaps his own information was wrong.

"Geraldo," said the guard, as if that would explain everything. When Howard didn't react he added, "The documentary? The opening of Capone's bunker?"

"Right," said Howard, and forced a chuckle. "I thought you might be expecting me for something else, and no one had bothered to tell me."

The guard nodded, and sat easier on his stool. He fidgeted with his book, as though trying to decide whether to stand up or continue reading.

"I was just doing a bit of reconnaissance," Howard said. "Checking out the route. You know."

The guard didn't look convinced, but he didn't stand up either. Then he seemed to make a decision and Howard knew that he was in the clear when the man started the age-old tradition of complaining about his job.

"Been stuck in this freaking hole for a month now," the man grumbled. "Only Geraldo can film the documentary, and Geraldo's busy till well after New Year's. So I get a month of freaking watch duty. Outside. In the middle of winter."

"What was he busy with?" Howard asked. He didn't worry if this was something he was supposed to know. The man was in complain mode and any fodder for his complaint was acceptable.

"His freakin' talk show," said the watchman. "Said he couldn't cancel or postpone his scheduled interviews, so it would have to wait until there was on opening. January 14th was his first *convenience*." *Convenience* was given extra emphasis.

"Well," said Howard, turning back around. "Tomorrow will be the end of it."

"Wait," said the watchman. "Where are you going?" He sounded disappointed that he had lost an audience.

"Got to get the construction droid back to the office, go home, and rest up for tomorrow," Howard said. "Big day. I'll leave the tunnels the way I came in."

It only took Geraldo's producers a week for post-production editing. The big expose aired on January 21st. Howard sat on the bed in his rented hotel room to watch the show.

Money hadn't been a problem. Or not much of a problem. He had broken into his home and robbed himself. Seems he knew where all of the valuables were. He also knew that his alternate self would get angry, then depressed, and then get over it. It was all for a good cause.

The show began with some footage from 1986. Clips of the Lexington Hotel. The vault under the city. The climactic opening of the vault. And the fifty year old collection of dust within. And then the footage switched to a much older Geraldo Rivera leading a small group of observers across Cermak Road. Howard paid no attention to what the talk show host said. He'd heard it before, after all. Instead, he watched for the City engineer to be introduced. And there he was. Howard Russell.

Howard was relieved to see himself and not the Wizard of Oz. The other Howard spoke to the camera clearly and succinctly, impressing even himself. He had never considered that he might look like anything other than a doofus in green coveralls on film, but had to admit that he was not too bad.

All too soon, the camera was underground, following Geraldo's description of the tunnels, and then they were at the crevasse broken into the cement wall. Howard watched the construction droid followed by himself squeeze into the wall, then the camera followed Geraldo through.

The clay chamber looked more black than blue, and then some setting on the camera or post-editing magic brought out the dark blue color of Chicago clay.

"I don't recognize the material used in construction," said Dr. Samuels.

"Iron," said the droid in a crisp, mechanical voice.

Ann Smith, the graduate student whose name Howard now knew and would never forget, added. "It must be pig iron. Lightly processed ingots welded together."

Pig iron wasn't sexy, so in no time at all the construction droid was using its superhuman strength to open the heavy door.

The door swung open and the camera peered inside to reveal a scene not unlike the one Howard had witnessed minutes earlier when reviewing the footage of Al Capone's vault. The bunker was small, dusty, and empty. The Ann Smith droid had come through. In less than a day, she had erected a false wall inside the bunker. Howard kicked himself because he hadn't thought of it sooner.

"Seems like we struck out again," said Geraldo.

There was disappointment in his voice, certainly, but no shame. No disgrace. And why should there be? People fail sometimes. And other times they succeed. The important thing is that they try.

So what if Howard had been dropped from college football. That his cold fusion experiments hadn't been completely successful. That he now worked a menial job for the City. It didn't make him any less a decent human being. It had taken Howard twenty years to understand that, most of that understanding coming in the past few weeks. What was important was that he take challenges in head on and try his best.

Three weeks ago he would have never believed that he could adjust the construction droid's programming at all, never mind make it mistake tungsten for pig iron. Or that he could give an all-powerful, all-knowing, guardian of the realities a simple solution to prevent people from discovering and misusing the ingots of Rhodium-105 it had been created to watch over.

And whatever came next.

Howard couldn't stay in Chicago. There was already a Howard here, and for once he had no desire to murder him. This Howard was just like himself, nothing like the Wizard of Oz. Just knowing this was enough for Howard to feel comfortable leaving.

He had no idea where he would go or what he would do. Perhaps he would go to New York and become a cop. He still had Tony's instincts and love of weapons. Or maybe that was aiming too low. He could go to Langley. The military instincts he had acquired from the G. I. Joe twins would serve him there. And surely the CIA would be interested in an agent who couldn't be killed.

Cutting his hand and watching it heal was almost the first thing Howard had tried after his encounter with the bakery watchman. He hadn't had any premonitions yet, and would be just fine if he never did. But if he did still have Olivia's psychic talent, he'd put it to good use.

And perhaps he'd picked up a new talent on the journey home. If so, he'd discover it soon enough.

The possibilities were endless. And Howard would face them as they came.

THE END

ABOUT THE AUTHOR

Randy McCharles is active in Calgary, Alberta's writing community with a focus on speculative fiction, usually of the wickedly humorous variety. In 2009 he received Canada's most prestigious award for speculative short fiction, the Aurora Award, for the novella *Ringing in the Changes in Okotoks, Alberta*, which appeared in Tesseracts 12 (Edge Science Fiction and Fantasy Publishing) and was reprinted in *Year's Best Fantasy 9* (David Hartwell and Kathryn Kramer, editors). Additional short stories and novellas are available in various publications from Edge Science Fiction and Fantasy Publishing, including his two latest titles: *The Puzzle Box* and *The Urban Green Man*. *Capone's Chicago* is Randy's first published full-length novel. Visit Randy at: www.randymccharles.com

29036356R00155

Made in the USA
Charleston, SC
29 April 2014